best gay erotica 1997

selected and introduced by

Douglas sadownick

edited by

Richard Labonté

CLEIS
PRESS

Published in the United States by Cleis Press Inc., P.O. Box 8933, Pittsburgh, Pennsylvania 15221, and P.O. Box 14684, San Francisco, California 94114.

Printed in the United States.
Cover design: Scott Idleman / Blink
Text design: Frank Wiedemann
Logo art: Juana Alicia
First Edition.
10 9 8 7 6 5 4 3 2 1

"Sex With God" © 1996 by Tommi Avicolli Mecca, excerpted from *Il Disgraziato,* a performance piece presented at Josie's Cabaret & Juice Joint, San Francisco, summer 1996. "Southern Sheriff" © 1995 by Gary Bowen, first appeared in *Power Play 8* and *Hard Kink,* hardkink.hotsex.com, Feb. 1996. "Tricktych" © 1996 by Pansy Bradshaw; "chainsaw fuck" first appeared in *Steam,* vol. 2, no. 2. "Steel Gray" © 1996 by Ken Butler. "The First Branding Journal" © 1996 by Cornelius Conboy, originally appeared as "The Branding Journal" in *Drummer* magazine, issue 191. "Cocksucker's Tango" © 1996 by Justin Chin; excerpts from "Queen" broadcast on the HBO documentary *Sex Bytes,* 1996. "Lance as a Redneck Spiritual Adept" © 1996 by Ferd Eggan. "The Surrogate" © 1996 by Jameson Currier, excerpted from the novel-in-progress *Where the Rainbow Ends.* "Threads" © 1996 by J. Eigo. "Exhibitionist Memoir" © 1996 by Roberto Friedman. "Brideshead of Frankenstein Revisited" © 1996 by Jack Fritscher. "Blue Hawaii" © 1996 by Robert Goldstein. "Heat Wave" © 1996 by Kevin Killian. "The Lady in the Hatbox" © 1996 by R.L. Kitzman. "Griffith Park Elegy" © 1996 by Al Lujan. "Je T'Aime, Batman, Je T'Adore" © 1996 by Kelly McQuain. "Scenes from a Sex Life (Searching for Intimacy)" © 1996 by Douglas Mirk. "Social Relations" © 1996 by Scott O'Hara. "When the Cat's Away..." © 1996 by Lawrence Schimel; first appeared in *Mandate,* Nov. 1996, as "Surrounded," by David Laurents. "Crescendo" © 1996 by Simon Sheppard. "Miserére" © 1996 by Michael Patrick Spillers, excerpted from *Cocks, Chaos & Communion,* a performance piece at Highways Performance Space, summer 1996. "Palladium" © 1996 by D. Scott Travers. "Motherfuckers" © 1996 by Emanuel Xavier.

contents

FOREWORD

On the one hand (or is that with one hand?), you want a story you can throw a boner with in bed. On the other hand (with both?), you want a story worth reading right to the end, not just up to the functional part.

Is it "porn" when the writing's awkward and crude and plotless and faceless but full of cock and cum, and "erotica" when there's seductive character development and a jazzy soulfulness to the writing, along with a modicum of cock and the word is spelled *c-o-m-e?*

Who cares. There's a craft to combining the boner and *"bon mots,"* and the twenty-three stories in this collection do just that, as they range from raging hard-on to wrenching passion.

The late John Preston insisted, more or less, that "erotica" was just a polite and pretty word for "pornography" and that any distinction was, well, crap. Then he went ahead and launched *Flesh and the Word,* those most successful of men's sex anthologies, and darned if most stories in the first three volumes weren't quite good literature, thank you very much. Their success proved for publishers that there was both a pool of good writers and a market for good writing of the porn variety, opening the way for enough new work that what were once just a couple of shelves of Starbooks and Gay Sunshine titles have expanded to several shelves, groaning with the promise of throbbing pleasure within.

So while this second edition of Cleis Press' *Best Gay Erotica* series is proud to be known as erotica—there's surely a stirring of porn in our pants.

What is an editor to expect when he's charged with compiling a "best gay erotica" collection? Endless relievable woodies as he sits at his desk, flipping through hundreds and hundreds of pages of hundreds of thousands of words of panting prose? The editorial "we" wishes. How about incipient repetitive stress syndrome complicated by whacked-out eyes, after flipping through hundreds and hundreds of pages of hundreds of thousands of words of imperiled prose.

Of the submissions received or solicited, there were a gratifying number which tickled my literary fancy, and a good number which tickled my libido, and a healthy number which did both. It was easy to select forty-three, ranging from great to better-than-good, to dispatch to Douglas Sadownick, the judge this year. He was charged with choosing the winners, and there were more than we could fit into this collection: the best of the best. With one exception, his picks appear here.

In keeping with the fact that *Best Gay Erotica* is a judged contest rather than an editor's-fancy anthology, all stories were sent his way with all references to authors deleted (in fact, he picked two stories by Jack Fritscher and two stories by Jameson Currier, not knowing they were by the same writers). It's a system I hope future editors and judges embrace.

The exception to the judging process is R.L. Kitzman's "The Lady in the Hatbox," which was to have been printed in *Wilde* magazine in 1996—and if it had been, I certainly would have considered it for reprinting. Kitzman's tale, a print-noir extravaganza, was winner of the John Preston Erotic Writing Award for men, announced late in 1995 at a Preston Memorial conference in Providence, Rhode Island, with acceptance by *Wilde* as part of the honor. The magazine folded before the story appeared. So, this year, it's included as "Editor's Choice."

What it has in common with several of its companion stories—most notably those of Jack Fritscher ("Brideshead of Frankenstein Revisited"), Pansy Bradshaw ("Tricktych"), Tommi Avicolli Mecca ("Sex with God"), Simon Sheppard's shaggy Top- and Bottom-dog story ("Crescendo"), and especially Kelly McQuain's superhero parody ("Je T'Aime, Batman, Je T'Adore")—is a sense of humor. It's not easy to giggle and ejaculate at the same time, but it sure is fun when it happens.

McQuain's story is one of many which provided the "erotic charge" I asked for when I posted the call for submissions. A lot of what gets us off comes from memory, and for a lot of gay men, earliest sexual memories—the pleasant ones—come from catalog pages, comic books and the flicker of TV and film images...moments we could eroticize without getting caught, memories we could carry until our coming out, a form of imprinting, which often defined our choices or our fancies or our lusts later in life. Some of us chose to choose Batman types, other Robin types: McQuain's deft what-if parody of the superhero duo crafts them into the sort of characters many of us wished they had been.

"With practically no 'out' role models growing up, I had to invent them where I could," McQuain wrote after his story was accepted. "Thus 'Je T'Aime Batman, Je T'Adore' grew out of childhood fantasies involving the dynamic duo. Later, as a student studying in Scotland, I had a poster from the Batman and Robin TV show of the sixties taped to my dormitory wall. Often I would drift off to sleep wondering about the erotic possibilities between the campy Dark Knight and his faithful sidekick. Years later, these thoughts grew into the piece included here, which I consider as much an account of my early dreams as I do a short story."

The erotic charge is more overt in some tales: in the exhibitionism of Roberto Friedman's boy on the beach ("Exhibitionist Memoir"), in Lawrence Schimel's married man on the prowl ("When the Cat's Away..."), in Emanuel Xavier's night of frenzied lust realized ("Motherfuckers"), in the painful almost self-loathing finally releasing sex of Gary Bowen's sheriff ("Southern Sheriff"), in Cornelius Conboy's intense branding ceremony ("The First Branding Journal"), in Robert Goldstein's Hawaiian want-wanderings ("Blue Hawaii"), in Ken Butler's match of a muscled young man to his idealized silver-haired Daddy ("Steel Gray").

In other stories, the charge comes from the language: Justin Chin's take-a-breath-and-read cocksucking meditations ("Cocksuckers' Tango"), J. Eigo's five lyrical sex memories ("Threads"), Al Lujan's encounter with a dangerous need ("Griffith Park Elegy"), and Kevin Killian's universe-askew tearoom tale ("Heat Wave").

And in some—by Jameson Currier ("The Surrogate"), Doug Mirk ["Scenes from a Sex Life (Striving for Intimacy)"], Michael Patrick Spillers ("Miserére"), D. Travers Scott ("Palladium")—that charge is a brew of terrible need and inspirational transgression, a blend of provocative behavior and intellectual raunch.

Possibly the most provocative story is Scott O'Hara's "Social Relations," dropped from inclusion in his own Masquerade/Bad Boy collection in 1996 because it draws on two of the many "taboos" good erotic writing must deal with—the fact that we can find (many of us did) our brother's bodies fetching, and the fact that boys, at a very young age (many of us were), are the sexual men they will grow into being.

There needs to be more thinking like O'Hara's in gay male erotic writing, and outlets like *Best Gay Erotica* can provide them: no, not just incest stories, but stories corkscrewing themselves into that part of our psyche—Sadownick's "genie inside"—and pulling out the ecstatic second that makes sex work, the terrifying truth underlying ultimate satisfaction.

Richard Labonté
October 1996

introduction

In the years following Stonewall and preceding AIDS, many gay men strove to divorce sex from intimacy. Bathhouse emporiums were created for lustful athletics that often depended on an almost militant anonymity. As Charley Shiveley tells us, cocksucking was seen as an act of revolution; the more anonymous the more radical. Gay men, along with many heterosexual people, explored this unbridled sexual experimentation for what now seems like a key historic purpose. Extrovert behavior in the form of sexual freedom offered an effective tool in challenging the conservative and suffocating values of the fifties and sixties. One cannot underestimate how shut down and repressed life felt to people, especially homosexual people, just thirty years ago.

The Eisenhower-Nixon Era threatened mass destruction to the world and soul via the literal weapons of napalm, censorship, racism, sexism and homophobia. Nothing short of a revolution was required to shake up such psychic fascism. Libido fired that social revolution, and homosexual libido was particularly effective. If there were clumsy gestures of desperation characterizing the empowerment of heretofore oppressed people, who is to say that certain emotional mishaps (greed, rejection, superficiality) could have been absolutely avoided? In stripping gay erotic life from heterosexual suburban values, many gay men thought it important to differentiate, and even divorce, sex from love. Now that's quite an ambitious task. You might as well try to split an atom with your bare hands. But the sexual activists of the seventies tried their best to permit men to make love in the quickest and most accessible of manners, even if that meant emotional intimacy became a certain casualty of the times.

Today, many gay men see that such a divorce between heart and cock is not only ill-advised but quite impossible. The stories in this collection all point, in one way or another, to the inseparability of sex and relatedness. In "When the Cat's Away" and "The Surrogate," the authors, Lawrence Schimel and Jameson Currier, have little capacity or interest in speaking about sex outside of romantic obsession. Writes Schimel, "I missed waking up next to him and feeling his early-morning piss boner pressing against my thigh." He also misses walking into the bathroom to find his friend's small messes, like "a string of dental floss floating in the toilet, waiting to be flushed away."

To both Schimel and Currier, the notion of biologic drive, or animal lust, as the only motivating force in gay erotic life is simply rendered ridiculous when one considers that it takes a certain kind of man to do the trick, to turn you on, to send you to outer space, to get you hard, that is, if you're gay.

These stories point us to the world of gay male psychology, of course, to the inner psychic reality of the gay individual road too many gay men have previously frowned on, and often for good reason. Shrouded as professional psychology was in homophobic practices and interpretations, it has had little to offer gay life. But now many gay men, including many of the writers of these stories, refuse to live a life encased in layers of defense against inward feeling. Love and its subjective mystery will not be discounted, despite how we have been taught to prize cold fucking.

Analytic psychology suggests that there is a natural tendency in all people to visualize the creative force of eros—to regard the soul figure as an entity who guides and directs one's erotic libido during life. Straight people experience this soul figure in the form of a feminine entity. Homosexual men engage in an analogous experience with the figure of the masculine double. Generally most gay men experience this "erotic being" in a lover or a crush. This is called "projection." It is a natural and unconscious process that leads us into relatedness with others. Confusing one's lover with one's soul figure, which, in truth, is hard to avoid, has the effect, nonetheless, of erasing the actual identity of the man with whom one has fallen in love. Perhaps this is one reason why gay men have perfected the art of anonymous fucking. Now, due to the heartache and depth of awareness we've experienced because of AIDS, some gay men are gaining the capacity to wrestle their own nasty defenses against painful feeling and to ask questions about recollecting this soul projection—during sex, during romance—for the purpose of developing new consciousness and depth of personality. Now they can project again, but with a new mindfulness and revitalized sexuality.

The truth of the gay psyche is quite mesmerizing and even revolutionary, for it suggests an infinite potential for homosexual love within the unconscious. As Schimel, Fritscher, Mirk and Eggan suggest in their respective stories, every turn-on produces a spontaneous stirring of an object or complex or subpersonality in the gay personality. When in "The First Branding Journal," Cornelius Conboy writes, "The anticipation of the branding is making the boy insatiable. Last night's sex was transcendent, the kind of over-the-top power exchange we fantasize about often and achieve too rarely," he implies this much: we are not the Masters of Our Own House; sex and eros prove that to a "T." Something clicks on inside when we get turned on by a man who corresponds to inner needs and wishes and associations. This is not new information. Ancient gay wisdom traditions have always treated homosexual love as a path to the Glory on High.

The inner view—this awakening of the homosexual life-form inside a gay individual when he relates erotically to another—can no longer be so easily discounted, even when it comes to the quickest j/o. A genie wakes up inside an otherwise mundane person, stirs him, gets him out of his head, his thinking function, his reason. What is that force? A living entity in the unconscious? A personality within, of the greatest magnetic allure, separate from the conscious mind, that awakens each and every time we get turned on? This force, implies Fritscher in "Brideshead of Frankenstein Revisited," is nothing less than God. It is quite homophobic, actually, to suggest that it's merely lust that draws the protagonist of Michael Patrick Spiller's "Miserére" to the man whose "homemade tattoos buckle as he squirms with silent, self-assured machismo." And a great energy system brings the pissee and pisser together in Justin Chin's "Cocksuckers' Tango," while an alien, supernatural magnetism throws the protagonist of "Blue Hawaii" by Robert Goldstein into the "t-room of a cheap hotel," where "tiny bubbles is replaced by pearly shells and I've been lucky to get a booth with a glory hole."

In "Motherfuckers," Emanuel Xavier writes about a Bronx love between Supreme, a Puerto Rican banjee boy, and Mikey X, a man whose attitude screams "fuck-you-all-while-sucking-on-a-lollipop." Despite the focus on class, color and Catholic homeboy culture, the story conjures up the eternal archetype of The Masculine Double most effectively. An ache, nearly incestuous in its intensity, makes Supreme, "the fiercest, most notorious graffiti-artist in New York City," thrust "his wet tongue deep inside Mikey's mouth..." while an ineffable spirit inside Mikey gets him "stunned, yet excited by the violent assault." This homey is named "Supreme" for no small reason. He conjures up the most sovereign of feelings in his sexual mate.

Despite the various geographic sites in which these stories take place—the Hudson River, the streets of East Los Angeles, the Burger King on Kalakaua Avenue—they suggest that gay men are finally beginning to partner their inwardly felt feelings of inferiority and glorious archetypal seizure in the process called "gay individuation."

As Jameson Currier puts it in "The Surrogate," you are attracted to a certain someone who does a certain something in your psyche and that's where the magic comes in: that "certain something" awakens a sleeping figure in one's unconscious—and one's phallus!—and that awakening should be understood as nothing short of the most profound inner spark separate from one's ordinary sense of "I." It also awakens feelings of inferiority, too. Yearning always will. Becoming a more artful player in owning and managing this divine seizure entails that one also learn something about owning and partnering feelings of loss, rejection, and simple loneliness.

Homosexual love becomes the supreme teacher. As Michael Patrick Spillers describes: "If they come to you, like little gods, with all that's beautiful throbbing in their greased palms—you just have to watch them sail by. You can't grab on for too long." Doug Mirk's "Scenes from a Sex Life (Striving for Intimacy)" suggests that to see a hard-on as referencing anything but a glorious and disturbing kind of stirring, to see the seizure of desire as anything but the inward feeling of transpersonal love in the sanctum of one's heart, is to undervalue erotic yearning and longing and reduce the psyche to an amoeba that merely reacts instinctively to stimuli. The man whose ass Mirk's character eats isn't just a comely boyfriend. He is a screen for the projection of a gay soul figure: "I feel the drips of cum between my tits, mingling now with his sweat, his legs clamping tighter around my face, and he falls on top of me, the sight of his beautiful ass still there for me to behold." The partner may provoke the arousal, but the seizure, the turn-on, the possession are one's own. To fail to take the inner view of what happens during a turn-on is to do ourselves the greatest disservice in charting an indigenous homosexual culture and erotica. As a character in J. Eigo's story "Threads" says, "Our beauty...is something even the showerhead weeps to see."

These stories state that simple and sexy inner truth over and over again. To be at all erotic about gay life, to begin to understand something of the energy system called "homosexual eros," one must also become somewhat psychological about oneself. As one writer in this collection has written, "Sex takes place in the mind; if my head is in the right place, my body cooperates." Yes, he likes his cocksucking raw, but he also hungers for relatedness: "I mean, the fact is, I like being manhandled. Face-fucked. Controlled, manipulated, used. But when it becomes mindless brutality, punishment for punishment's sake...my interest fades, the fantasy pops like a soap bubble..." One must begin to take oneself seriously as an inner being. Wishes, needs, impulses, desires: this is what forms the pivot around which men live and fantasize. In the feeling world of gay men, the man of one's dreams is the sun to which all attention is directed. Nothing makes the attraction of the moth to the flame more real than sex.

But can we ask ourselves questions before the fucking begins? Where are our feelings, really, before they get attached to the man who put the "strange smegma" on the sheets, as Jack Fritscher so elegantly puts it in his enticing tale about uncut boys? Can we contain our nuclear emotions before we project them on the "angel skimming the ground"? Even these days, still, despite so much therapy and so much grief, and despite more conversation about gay male sex and intimacy than ever before, most of us tend to focus all our energies on outward effects—the sex act, the sex object, the Circuit Party. But what about the inner homo god object? To ask such a question is to begin to take gay erotica personally and thus to come out inside.

That process to own one's Greatest Potential inwardly cannot take place without a corresponding acceptance and partnering of one's worst self and most *awful* inferiorities. Wholeness, in this psychic world view, necessitates that a person balance his most inferior self with his highest romantic yearning. Thus a great tension within the psyche takes place, a tension that suggests one see the rejections and acceptances of gay life as part of a myth of gay becoming.

Gay erotica then becomes a tool to help us begin a relationship to symbol and myth: the symbol of the masculine double, the myth of homosexual love. This myth, by the way, according to Butler ("Steel Gray"), Spillers ("Miserére"), Xavier ("Motherfuckers") and Chin ("Cocksuckers' Tango") is the greatest story ever told. It's greater than the "gays in the military" story and even a little better than the "gays in the matrimony" saga, because this story has to do with inner ways of being gay, not just extroverted displays of visibility or acceptance. It has to do with the inner value system of the Gay Individual and his own unique path and how sex connects mind, body and spirit in an accelerated way that has virtually nothing to do with fitting in or assimilating.

These stories help us begin our own inner investigation, one that might balance a movement previously quite extroverted and focused almost exclusively on visibility and group participation. None of these writers suggest that we value symbolic truth at the expense of political inequities. That would be impossible and rather reckless. Rather, developing a relationship to inward feelings deepens and matures relationships on the outer social and political levels. One takes ownership for one's feelings, thoughts, memories and associations. One becomes a more loving and thus radical partner—even during the anonymous quickie. This is different from making a lover into a surrogate parent or savior. Or into an extension of your narcissistic needs and rage.

We are just now beginning to withdraw some of our attention from community building and crisis control and Circuit Party tweaking to look more carefully at inner states and inner crises. It is a profound moment in the gay movement. It is also an early one. The discussion of psychological truth in gay life is really at its initial stages. Therefore these stories ask questions more than they provide answers. They suggest how radical it is to direct at least some of one's attention inward, so radical that most gay intellectuals haven't caught up with this new advance in thinking and feeling. Gay academic thinkers, for example, have monopolized intellectual discourse with a valuable but ultimately one-sided observation of class, gender and race and the attendant power discourses that often leave out discussion of how to integrate spirit with matter.

The storytellers in the collection you are about to read ask potent questions about the Gay Self, about the state of inner feelings, even as they rigorously name power inequities, racial injustices, sexist oppression and homophobic slander in the social world. A concern about cultural representation and social inequality need not come at the expense of a discussion of soul—as the stories here demonstrate. One reality actually depends on the other. For that reason, this collection marks a change of attitude that ought to have profound implications for gay letters—and gay sex—in the years to come.

Douglas Sadownick
October 1996

Brideshead of
Frankenstein Revisited

JACK FRITSCHER

Sebastian, that certain summer, I found intolerable, scooping up uncut boys with a net along the Bavarian strand. The young men liked Sebastian's naturally muscular body as much as his decadent blond good looks, and his dollars *americain*. We, Sebastian and I, were in a slow drag becoming undestined as lovers. "It's still the same old story...as time goes by." We were "Skinners." Our foreskins had brought us together, but the handwriting was on the wall. Strange smegma was on the sheets.

For myself, I preferred the company of Anne Rice's Beauty trilogy as well as that of the minister's handsome son, an overheated and underventilated classic blond boy of eighteen who relieved his sexual tension through meditation and intense gymnastics. We had met, Dieter and I, eyes first, across the small tables of an outdoor café. Something in the breeze, perhaps the sweet smell wafting from the cheese inside his blond foreskin, or was it his dazzle in the noon light, caused me to raise my glance from Beauty's frolics.

The sea, wind, and blue sky combined into a sudden explosion of sunburst blondness. His hair raised in the gust of breeze and fell perfectly back in place. Very *Deco!* He smiled and dropped his hand from his sweating glass of Perrier down to his naked thigh. He smiled again. I set my marker in Beauty and smiled back. He knew I was the companion of the infamous Sebastian and that knowledge made him, if not bold, then daring.

Sebastian at last was good for something.

Dieter moved his hand up his thigh, rubbing it across his white nylon athletic shorts, dropping the concave palm of his strong gymnast hands over the big convex cup of his cock and balls, groping himself, adroitly, for just a moment. He pulled the nylon shorts so tight I could see the transparent outline of his cock.

He was uncut.

Even his face was one of a confident uncut male.

I'd spied not just the size of his dick, but a clear outline of his large nipple of foreskin wrinkled, folded, and long as a sausage sleeve tied off with two inches to spare.

My own nine-inch cock hardened. I shivered with uncontrollable pleasure as my cockhead mushroomed out through my tight foreskin that rolled back and down my shaft like an O-ring on a sky-bound shuttle. Tight 'skin. I like it. I got it. I wondered about the minister's son. How tight is the foreskin of a cherub?

I sipped the last of my Bavarian coffee.

Oh God. Ohgodogodogod!

A bead of sweat, bright as a crystal, formed in the cleft of his strong blond chin, caught the sun, glistened and dropped to the top of the channel between his lean hard pecs. The tip of my tongue grew dry and hard. I could tell he appreciated the subtle sensuality as the sweat-bead, slower than slow motion, micrometered down his chest, stopping for an instant in a direct horizontal line between his sweet brown tits, themselves small and sculpted and aching with virgin hunger.

His chest and tensely lean torso were not hairy, yet he was not smooth. His pecs, belly, forearms, and legs were downed with the babiest of blond hair, enough to catch the sun, adding to his physique an aura of gold. He was an angel skimming the ground. He sat motionless. My cock strained hard in my shorts. My foreskin felt tight as a rubber band around my shaft. I sucked in the smell of smegma packed in under the corona of my cock.

I wanted him, with my hands gripped tight in his baby blond hair, to teethe the cheese from my cock.

I wanted him. I wanted to suckle on his foreskin, sipping its hidden juices and clots of blond *fromage.*

He drew a breath. On purpose, he drew a breath, dislodging from between his pecs the bead of sweat that slowly rolled down the maze-way of his gymnast-carved abs, not straight down, but following the hard-flexed muscle groups, left, then right, like a silver pinball. I imagined buttons on his slender hips that flipped flippers. I wanted to shoot the bead of sweat back up his torso, hitting his nipples, scoring points, lights flashing, bells dinging, with the same concentrated intensity with which a champion pinballer passionately keeps his silver ball in play.

I must have looked like a fool standing on my own tongue. When the sweat bead reached his navel, it dropped in, stopped, stayed. He smiled and flexed his washboard belly, popping the bead up and free, rolling down toward the band of his shorts. I dreaded its absorption into the white nylon.

He was even better than I thought. At the last possible moment, as the sweat rolled to his waist, he pulled his hand from his crotch. He fingered into the waistband and triangled it open and the sweat bead ran down, disappearing into the almost visible blond bush growing around his big jock cock. He flipped his finger, snapping the waistband closed like a slingshot, and for the first time, he opened his mouth and laughed the deep laugh that comes from loaded stud teenage bullballs.

I will never love anyone as much as I loved him that moment. If my whole life ever flashes before my eyes, I hope the film gets stuck on that one frame: where the blond, muscular boy laughed as the bead of hot sweat ran down the length of his ten-inch cock. He had everything. Even *that:* a big dick. Blond. Blue-eyed. Built. Sweet-natured. Innocent. And a ten-inch cock. Two inches more than Sebastian, I might add, and one inch more than me.

Was I in luck, in love, or w-h-u-u-t?

There is only one sin in life. When a Bavarian Methodist minister's muscular son invites you to suck his big, blond, uncut, ten-inch cock, and you will not do it. Me? I'm no sinner. *"This could be heaven,"* the Eagles sang on "Hotel California," *"this could be hell."* I was going down on that boy. I was going to swallow him till his foreskin came out my asshole.

With all due respect to the genius of Anne Rice, I dropped her Beauty for his. He was the perfect blond Aryan youth who sang "Tomorrow Belongs to Me" in *Cabaret.* He was the lean-muscled ideal Dr. Frankenfurter sang about in *The Rocky Horror Picture Show:* "In just seven days, I'll make you a man!" He was the perfect, sculpted blonde the Marines put on recruiting posters.

And he hadn't been around the block. He had an innocence. He was not one of the village boys who worked the beaches and hotels where the likes of Thomas Mann and Tennessee Williams once spoiled them with too much of everything, making them mercenary, hard, and liars.

I was tired of rough-trade German and Bavarian boys force-feeding me the cheese pastry from their thick European foreskins.

I wanted the minister's tasty son.

I wanted his fresh innocence.

I wanted his innocence to give rebirth to mine.

The only hitch was Sebastian. He wanted whatever I wanted more than he wanted what he wanted. Ever since that bed-and-breakfast night we spent in a freezing castle in Transylvania, Sebastian had turned into the Bride of Frankenstein. You know how some gay guys are: they latch onto a schtick and can't let go, repeating the same act or the same catch phrase like "See how you are," or, worse, "Thank you," a million times a day as an answer to no matter what you say.

Just so Sebastian. He was a film queen. He'd forced me through a truly gross week at the Cannes Film Festival. I saw more films than I wanted to, and Sebastian saw none. He spent the week cruising like a human mattress up and down the sand, Gauloise in one hand, champagne bottle in the other. No matter what happened to us, or who we were with, or what was the conversation, he continuously spouted non sequiturs: "Just like Susan Hayward in *I Want to Live!*" or, "How Bette Davis!"

Transylvania was his latest affectation. Why he identified with Elsa Lanchester, the female monster, and not with the male, puzzled me. Sebastian was masculine enough. At least on the outside. Through the chatty haze of his martinis, he thought he was terribly clever as, without realizing it, he was driving me farther away. Our summer tour had been meant to bring us closer together. It took Transylvania to make me realize I hated Sebastian.

"You and this preacher's kid haven't a chance. You're just Sandra Dee in *A Summer Place*. And he's Troy Donahue and I want his foreskin." He sipped his thousandth martini. "We agreed what was mine was yours and what was yours was mine."

"Here's a new word, Sebastian. *Disagreement.*"

"You so piss me off."

"You're so easy to piss off. You're a queen."

"You're a cocksucker."

"Better a cocksucker than a queen. When I get up off my knees, you're still a queen."

That didn't end the argument, but it ended the conversation.

"Here's your hat," he said. "Don't let the door hit you when you leave."

"You're a real shit-psychic," I said.

"I don't need to be a psychic shit to know where you're going."

I sped our rented Peugeot through the village streets, heading to Dieter's house, the parsonage and school, where he lived with his mother and father and three younger brothers, who I knew would make returning to this village every summer for the next six years a delight.

I drove, remembering that first day at the outdoor café, how it had happened, how Dieter had stood up at his table and stretched his full body in the blinding sun. His dick and balls hung transparent in his white nylon running shorts. He was hard. He winked at me. I rose from my chair, forgetting Beauty on the table, and walked toward him. His beauty grew with each step nearer. My hard cock made me drag my leg like one of Jerry's kids.

He put out his hand to me. I took it. His gymnast palm was cool and calloused from working the parallel bars. His grip was firm. Not rough. Not soft. Just right. He smelled the sweet smell of young men who have not yet begun the long menu of grownup poisons and addictions.

He smelled, his strongest smell, after the first sweaty waft from his hairy blond armpits, of smegma. He held my hand long after the handshake ended, and then, right there in front of God and everybody, he placed my hand on his hard cock, guiding my fingers to his two-inch foreskin on his ten-inch cock, stretching it between my thumb and index finger.

"It's all yours," he said.

Back in Kansas City, we always laughed about the "PK's," the Preacher's Kids who were wilder than anybody else in town. I was about to find the same thing in *Zeider bei der See,* Bavaria.

He led me from the café to the ancient stone gymnasium, built in the fourteenth century, with his father's present high-vaulted church set upon its foundation at the turn of this century. Fantasy and charm.

"No one uses it anymore. Just me. And, sometimes, my brothers."

He smiled making me imagine him taking his younger brothers one by one to the cellar gym for a workout on the rings and the parallel bars, naked, always nude, their growing young dicks flopping on turns and tumbles, all four brothers with matching thick foreskins they'd strip back after their workouts, exhausted, to let the sweaty heads of their cocks breathe, laughing, dipping their fingers into their foreskins and feeding each other their steaming headcheese like chip dip. Once he had tied together all four 'skins, his and his three brothers, wrapping them with rawhide and making them play tug-of-war. "So they will grow up to be men," he said, "tough as their foreskins."

Uncut!

Uncut!

Uncut!

The way Sebastian wanted the uncut versions of movies, I wanted the uncut version of males. That's why he was a bride, and I was a groom, born to groom uncut dick, groom uncut horse dick.

Some men are lucky enough to know that their destiny, their purpose in living, lies hidden in the tight foreskins of young men.

I know me. Dieter recognized me. He saw my face. His foreskin twitched. He knew me for the true-blue "Skinner" I was.

"We are brothers," he said, "under the 'skin."

No shit, Sherlock!

I drove the Peugeot quietly up the drive, heading to the back of the church where I knew the door to the gym would be unlatched and he would be waiting for me, sweaty from his workout, his hungry uncut cock arching up, wanting service.

He stood naked under a single light next to the parallel bars. He said nothing. His eyes spoke all. I moved closer. He turned, placed his chalked hands and taped wrists on the shoulder-high wooden bars, and, without so much as the tiniest jump from his feet, lifted his whole body using only his arms.

The movement tightened the definition of his muscles.

He was hard as a rock and he was rock hard.

He held his position. I knew mine. I crawled between the bars and knelt below him, my face a foot under his Thuringer cock which stood out and up forty-five degrees above the horizontal. He did not move. I leaned forward and sucked his toes, first one, then all of them, licking the salt-sweet soles of his feet and tonguing his hard heels. His strength was amazing. I leaned up and opened my mouth, wanting his foreskin-cock reigning above me. He began to do slow dips, lowering his shoulders down almost to where his hands gripped the bars. He raised his legs at the knee behind him and crossed his feet. Each dip brushed the tip of his 'skin across my face, going down, going up. He lavished me with his tube of 'skin, teasing me.

"Give me your innocence," I begged.

He laughed, as well he should have. "Then I give you my cock." He dropped slowly to the floor. "Suck my foreskin."

I pulled the two-inch tube to my nose and breathed in its heady aroma. I stretched the 'skin open and fit it tube-tight around my nose, snorkling deep inside the clean, cheesy darkness, snorting like a pig for truffles of smegma. Big young meat always tops itself with clots of melting cheese. His aroma was so sweet and strong, I almost hyperventilated.

"You will eat it now," he said. His voice was sweet but commanding.

I let go of his foreskin. It closed down tight. Its iris-eye stared me straight in the face. Its folds wrapped in soft flesh rings around the huge head of his hidden cock. A long strand of clear gleet drooled from the iris. He took hold of the 'skin and stretched the two inches to three, then four.

"It is big, yes? Bigger than you imagined? I have trained it. I have disciplined it."

He put his calloused hands on his long, thick shaft, and stripped the foreskin back, slow, slow, so slow, slow as the most expert skinner. The big lip suctioned back down over his mushroom cockhead. Its rosy blond crown shined with 'skin juice. His smell was clean, dirty, athletic, angelic. My tongue hardened in my mouth and parted through my lips like an MX missile exiting its silo. I sucked his piss slit. I sucked his head, cleaning the boy out. He kept his fist wrapped tight below the corona of the head.

"Eat it," he said. "All of it." His passion made him fierce. *"Fresse dich!"*

I vacuumed his dickhead into my mouth. I beat my own meat, sticking its licentious head out though my own foreskin. Maybe Sebastian had been right about putting down the minister's son. "Probably a neo-Nazi pervert tease." Dieter definitely wasn't that. He was merely an over-sexed village boy with a ten-inch cock and a two-inch foreskin who liked games he could only play with tourists.

"Kneel closer. Open wide." He said it and he smiled. He mounted the parallel bars once more, raising himself effortlessly using only his arms. His strong lean pecs striated. His pink nipples hardened. The light down of gold boyhair on his body glistened with sweat. As he rose on his magnificent arms, his dick passed my waiting mouth. I almost went for it the way a suckerfish dives for the biggest worm. The kid was tasty, we'd say back in Kansas. He liked to take things slow and easy. He knew the world. He wanted no part of the fast lane, not even on the Bavarian Autobahn. He knew how to savor a moment. We knew we had no more than three times together. My Lufthansa ticket was waiting. We wanted them to count.

Stretched tall above me, held aloft by his arms, he smiled down at me. "I want to kiss you, but from here I can't. Keep your mouth open."

I obeyed.

He worked his rosy cheeks back and forth, his blue eyes shining. He parted his lips and let a long strand of gossamer drool start its slow descent from his mouth to mine. No nectar, no champagne, no sacred wine ever tasted better than his spit. I swallowed his juice into me the way I had cleaned the cheese from his foreskin. I know it's become unfashionable and unsafe since, but, back that summer, sex wasn't sex without exchange of bodily fluids. We partied foreskin to butthole.

I hated Sebastian. He was cynical but he was right about vacation romance. Somewhere in the world some radio station was playing Percy Faith's "A Summer Place," as Dieter began the first of his long slow dips aiming his hard cock deep into my mouth. He was strong as an engine, pistoning his rod deep into my throat.

He made me part of his gymnastics routine.

Rising, pulling his ten-inch cock from my mouth. Lowering, driving his cock deep past my choke point. Starting slowly. Picking up steam. Like a locomotive. Great hard iron wheels slowly moving, driven by the long lateral rods that turn them faster and faster. He picked up the clip of his dips. Sweat poured from his face, his chest, his hairy blond armpits, ran in rivers down to the spout of his cock. Salt-sweat burned my eyes, my throat.

He was what I wanted. He was what I got.

I dove onto his cock, sucked him down tight in my throat, held him captive, pulling on his cock against his strong arms, a tug of war, until he let me win, and dropped to his feet. He took my hair in both his hands and pulled my head back freeing his cock. I gasped for air. His foreskin slipped up tight around his ten-inch cock.

"Now," he said, not letting go of my hair, holding my head in place.

His tight foreskin became the nozzle on a firehose. The long yellow stream blasted my face with all the hyper-force of piss shot through the hose of a total hard-on. His hot wet hardly quenched my fire. He aimed straight for my mouth, and, still streaming, rammed his cock down my throat. He was pulsating, near to coming. My own cock threatened to come before he did, and, if it shot, I did not know if I could still handle the force of a very young man determined to throat-fuck me silly.

He yanked my hair, pulling my nose deep into his sweet groin. He was soaked with sweat. I was soaked with piss. He held me in place, and rammed. Rammed. Rammed his cock deep into me. I could feel his foreskin slip and slide over his cock in my mouth. He began groaning. He was close to coming, and just as I thought he would choke me to death with his huge load of sperm, he pulled out, quickly gripped the tip of his huge foreskin, jerked his cock three times in rapid succession, moaning, grinding his teeth, coming, not in me, but inside his foreskin. The 'skin ballooned full of his huge dripping load.

"Drink," he said.

I moved in tight next to his foreskin. His fingers released the first sweet taste. I took my cock in my hand.

"Suck my cum from my foreskin," he said.

I put my mouth to the iris eye pinched between his fingers. I put my lips around the cum-balloon of his two-inch 'skin. His fingers were in my mouth. And then they weren't. He released his grip and the whole thick white gelatinous load of his cum, condomed in his foreskin, spilled like burning lava into my mouth. I worked it cheek to cheek, staring up at his great beauty, beating my dick.

"Swallow," he said. "Swallow and come."

His was an easy order to follow. I swallowed his million clots of seed and shot my own all over his beautifully formed feet, shouting, "Oh, God, Dieter, I'll love you forever! Forever! I will!"

"There you are, you bitch!" The shock was operatic. Abrupt. And very Transylvanian! Sebastian entered the room voice first, fangs second. *"Forever,* for your info, ends with a nine o'clock flight tonight."

Now I know why handguns should be outlawed, ones with silver bullets, to kill the monster bitch Bride of Frankenstein.

Tricktych

Pansy Bradshaw

1. "what i really want..."

out cruising...i meet up with this man...he is...maybe...fifteen or twenty years my senior...well past six feet...military coif...shaved on the sides...short on top...salt and pepper...his rugged face bears a five o'clock shadow at two a.m....there's a paratrooper's tattoo on his left biceps...a pack of smokes rolled up in the sleeve of his t-shirt...narrow at the hips...broad at the shoulders...he looks like an illustration by blade...he's a major buck...i've seen him around...

he releases smoke from his lungs and suggests his place...cool i say...we walk silently the approximate ten blocks down market...then into the tenderloin...four flights up sour dimly lit stairs...along a dingy corridor...he shoves me against the wall...his tongue probes my mouth...i recognize the flavor...cigarettes and too much beer...

he lights a smoke...flicking the still-lit match to the floor...i want to yell fire...and run screaming from the building...but i do not...he blows smoke into my face...through the haze i see my father...staring back...as an afterthought he turns and unlocks a door...

as i follow...a line from an old song wafts...through my mind...where you lead i will follow anywhere that you tell me to...

a freakshow light cast by a street lamp outside the only window...fills the room...the space is small...chaotic...with a mattress on the floor...filthy sheets thrown everywhere...there's a dresser...drawers partly open...with clothing appearing to explode from within...a single open door reveals the toilet...i think he smells like his room...he sprawls...fully clothed...on the mattress...

take yer clothes off he says...his voice is loud...though he is not shouting...what i really want is to suck his dick ok...but he has other plans...obviously...

i pull off my boots...taking time with the complicated laces...setting them aside...i unbuckle my belt...unzip my jeans...standing first on one foot...then the other...i remove my pants along with my shorts...stop he says...he stands...towering over me...i feel...on display...lift yer arms he grunts...i do this...even while wondering...might he have some ill...purpose...in mind...for me...

he's got another cigarette...dangling...dangerously...from the corner of his mouth...will he burn me...will my friends and co-workers read about me in the papers...how my badly decomposed body was discovered...in an abandoned tenderloin rat-trap...will my brother be able to...identify...my mutilated remains...

he blows smoke on me...and then with surprising gentleness...lifts my t-shirt off me...i lower my arms...but he takes my wrists in each of his hands and raises them again...placing his mouth first against one armpit...then the other...he kisses and tongues them...he is making sounds which i can only...imagine...as animal-like...i respond with my best...guttural vocals...

his lips are on mine now...we kiss each other hard...i bite his upper lip...he stands back from me...takes a deep drag off his smoke...flicks the butt out the window...as he exhales...he punches me in the gut...

i drop to my knees...i cannot breathe...fuck you he grunts...he slaps my head with the back of his hand...i'm trying to breathe...he kneels in front of me...grabs my face with both hands...puts his mouth on mine...blows air in...and releases...i exhale violently...still trying hard to breathe on my own...he lets go of me...calmly lighting another smoke...inhaling deeply...he grabs my face again...he exhales smoke into my mouth...forcing it into my lungs...i black out...

when i come to...he is lying next to me...naked...i wonder if i have been...used...while unconscious...but i sense no...violation...back there...you ok he asks...gazing at me with something bordering on...indifference...i manage a meek...yeah...my stomach is sore...roll over he tells me...when i do...he straddles me...and begins to stroke my back...his hands are large and rough...they move over my flesh with a familiar deftness...i know him somehow...yet...i do not...every so often...he slaps me...hard...deliberately...and it burns...

he climbs off me...and the mattress...and walks into the toilet...i can see his backside...i see his balls hanging through his legs...will he let me at them...or what...he's pissing up a storm...i am jealous of the porcelain bowl...he strolls back to the mattress...kneels at my head...look at this he says...his cock and balls are in my face...the odor of smoke and shit...emanates from his crotch...i breathe in this divine essence...the skin over his dickhead is pulled back...just enough...to see the slit...glistening...in the room's bizarre light...open up he orders...i do...and he places his cock in my mouth...

he tastes like piss...cheese...and someone else's ass...he pushes it in more...he slides the foreskin back...and i gather the full benefit...of his natural treasures...i close my eyes and suck...he fucks my mouth steadily...taking his time...every so often pulling out completely...he whispers...come on boy...clean daddy's cock...or...lick me faggot...i wonder to myself...can it get any better than this...

he pulls back from me...and crawls around between my legs...his hands are on my ass now...each hand envelopes one cheek...he spreads me apart...slowly...thoughtfully...i can feel the rush of his breath against my butthole...then his tongue...causing me to shudder...i want to ask him if he can touch his nose...with his tongue...but i do not...it's rough...wet...he continues to probe my hole...he shoves his face in for more...i push back so he can...have at it...

he stops now...to readjust...he spreads my legs further apart...grabs my hips...and with one swift motion...lifts me...into a kneeling position...with my face still...prostrate...in his filthy mattress...i wonder...am i facing mecca...he speaks softly now...almost a whisper...tell me what you want...tell daddy what you really want...

2. "afternoon on the hill..."

all in all...it had been a dull morning...so up the hill i went...with a full load in my pocket...sunny...with a cool breeze...it's so different in daylight...first of all...you can see...and what i was seeing...wasn't pretty...i must admit to a little apprehension...as a frequent visitor to the hill...at night...i mean...like...what kind of...holes...was i sticking my dick in...when i couldn't see nearly so well...as in broad daylight...oh what a dude will do to get his nut...

just shy of the peak...there is this shelter...of low-hanging trees...with horizontal trunks...and a sandy floor...covered with the remnants...of past tawdry moments...i parked my ass against a tree...and whipped out my...thang...when it's soft it doesn't look like much...and it takes me some time to...get it up...it amuses me to pull on it...i just love to...spit and pull...until it gets wicked hard...right there in broad daylight...with the air...and sun...touching me...it's hard to keep from...blasting off...if you know what i mean...

i noticed some guy...crouching...in the bushes...just past the entrance to my...special...place...he was wearing glamour sunglasses...for fashion's sake...reminding me...a bit...of jackie onassis...i was not in the mood for calling up the...memory of any of the...dead kennedys...of course if it had been...john john...that would be different...i decided to ignore him...he split...only to be...replaced immediately...by another man...

this one was like...a construction worker...he crouched...just like jackie o...an impersonator i thought...even though he looked...the type...work boots...jeans and t-shirt...with a black baseball cap...for effect...all of him seemed...respectfully...dirty...the visor of the cap...pulled down so low...i could hardly see his eyes...

i shook my piece pretty hard...causing my precum to...whip through the air...like a serpent about to strike...its heavy liquid...leaving an...s...shape...in the sand at my feet...

well...he got down and...crawled...through the brush...towards me...up close...he smelled of funk and dirt...my favorite cologne...his eyes...blue...his skin...deeply tanned...from working outdoors i guess...though it might have been...salon induced...goddamn that's a big fuckin' piece of meat you got there...he says grinning...i just stare at him...i let go of my cock...just so he could...catch a look...at the big picture...he grabbed it...giving me a couple of good pulls...then...unbuckling his belt...and unbuttoning his jeans...he unleashed...a fucking whopper...i mean...fuck...ok...i had not expected that...and all the while...he kept talking to me...about my own...big manmeat...and shit like that...but my eyes had seen the glory...so i leaned toward him...so close...my lips...could feel the heat off his body...and i whispered in his ear...can i suck your dick man...he looked at me kind of surprised...then he said...yeah buddy...go for it.

so i pushed my pants down...around my ankles...and knelt...as shakespeare said...before the god of my idolatry...i yanked his pants down too...i opened my mouth wide...and swallowed hard...i gave him deepthroat but good...burying my face in his sweaty pubes...pulling my mouth off of him...to lick his balls...he tasted just like sex...

he slapped me with it...smearing...that juice...all over my face...its force of impact made me whirl...using his thumbs...he opened my mouth...further...his cock...flapping about...as if it had a life all its own...he pushed the fingers...of one hand...into my mouth saying...suck 'em...and believe me...i sucked...while he slapped me...with his free hand...tears streamed down my face...i was sure i would gag...but he knew this...warning...don't you dare fucker...withdrawing his fingers...and sliding that...mean ol' pecker of his...down the...abyss of my throat...

i swallowed...as fast as he would feed me...looking up into his eyes...i could see...he knew...exactly...what i needed...so he gave it to me...he spit right in my face...i went down more...willingly...after that...his cock swelled up...he grabbed my ears and...fucked my mouth...the way his pelvis pounded my face was...like a punch...i was beginning to feel dazed...when he suddenly pulled out and shouted...fuckfuckfuckfuckfuck...aiming that nasty...thing...at me...and shooting sperm...all over me...

i was still...pulling on my own...piece...while he was beginning to relax...after being wracked by orgasm...i felt like saint theresa...treated to a...vision...of almighty ecstasy...while the urge welled up in my balls...he let go a stream of hot piss all over me...and that did it...i tried to...catch...as much as i could...while it splashed on my face...poured down my neck chest and stomach...drenching me...i blew my wad in the crotch of his jeans...

later...walking down haight street...even the street punks say...i smell like piss...when i catch...my reflection...in a shop window...i see...i look like shit too...

3. "chainsaw fuck..."

recently...i took a big risk...i let a stud from hell...fuck me gently...with a chainsaw...and no condom...you can imagine my thrill...feeling the icy hot metal...rip into my...flesh...blood and feces flying in every direction...my last words to my trick...before he set the saw in motion...fuck the lube...i want to feel this sucker inside me...at first i thought the risk was mine alone...but as i watched an arc of blood...from a badly severed artery...squirt him in the eye...too bad he didn't have goggles on...well...it was then i wished i had a safety monitor to tap one of us on the shoulder and say...excuse me...but i really care about you...and i think you're taking too great a risk here...the thought was rather touching...as last thoughts often are...it was at that point...the saw made contact with bone...causing the chain to slip off track...backfiring...is that the right word for what those chains do...when they whip off...and slice up the dude holding onto the handle for dear life...whatever...i thought...as he bled to death before my eyes...too bad i won't find another guy like this one...

Palladium

D. Travers Scott

Erik took six steps away from Lev and planted himself in the bath-room doorway.

"Come here," Erik repeated, breath rolling over teeth.

Lev continued jacking off slowly. He moved his head from side to side.

Never get to do this with Dwayne, Lev thought. He savored this: playing the resistant stud, flaunting his sex to tease this gun-shy guy. Sweet, actually. He leaned back into the right angle where Erik's mattress met the wall.

Erik returned to Lev, one step at a time. He stood beside the mattress.

Lev looked up at him, palm gliding up and down, and his impassive face grew into a mild smirk.

Erik wiped his palms down his khakis. As he folded his arms across his chest, Lev glimpsed damp patches in the pits of Erik's white polo.

That's so cute, Lev thought. He's all nervous.

"I said come here." Lev fixed his grin and looked Erik in the eye. Yes—make him beg for it.

Lev remembered Erik's startled expression as he'd been interrupted mid-sentence, their house-job-when'd-you-move-to-town small talk gagged short by a kiss. He'd run his tongue along the roof of this pensive boy's mouth, pressed himself against this bar-corner lurker. Erik had sat still, then kissed back, leaning forward and touching his tongue to Lev's.

Lev had broken the embrace, kicking back on the mattress and pulling out his dick like he owned the place.

Yes. Make this guy really want it. Dwayne always has to be snuggled for hours into arousal.

Erik's metered breaths whistled through his nostrils. He scuffed the sole of his left engineer boot with the toe of the other.

Lev closed his eyes, basking in a sultry haze. Warm cock in palm, he felt like the prized center of attention, like the eighteen-year-old pornstar he'd never been.

Erik stared down at Lev. Brow furrowed, he looked back into the bathroom.

Lev bent over his dick and brought a lubricatory wad of spit to his lips.

Erik's fist slammed against Lev's cheekbone.

Lev gasped, choked, his breath gone. The spit-string, still connected to his mouth like an umbilical cord, swung around and splattered back over his cheek. He released his dick and fumbled to regain balance on the mattress' edge.

Erik resumed his stance in the doorway.

Gingerly, Lev touched his cheek, parted his lips, rotated his jaw. Erik had deftly secured his attention with more force than Lev had ever experienced—but he hadn't injured him. Through the stunned pain Lev felt dimly impressed by Erik's finesse.

"Now." Erik breathed deep, sighed. "Will you come here before I have to beat the shit out of your pussy ass?"

Erik indicated the cold linoleum between his black boots. "Come here. Put your head on the ground. Right here. At my feet."

Lev wiped the spit off his face. His mind struggled to construct situation appraisal, a rational flow chart of damage and risk assessment with an outline of future strategy, but Erik's fist had shattered his reasoning gridwork like a mirror. His willpower crumpled and collapsed like Oakland's Nimitz freeway in the 1989 earthquake.

A red glow swelled inside Lev, as if someone had switched on a torch deep up in his bowels. The beam blazed up his spine, illuminating vertebrae crevices and nocturnal rivers of spinal fluid, a searing spotlight penetrating his skull and cauterizing his limbic, reptilian brain to the aristocratic cortex.

He pulled himself to the doorway—unthinking, instinctive, obedient.

Erik paused in slipping his black leather belt through the khakis' loops. He held the strap of leather by its cold chrome buckle in midair, arm's length from his body. The tongue of the belt clung to his waist through one remaining loop, barely hanging on. Only his eyes moved, tracking as Lev settled his face onto the pallid bathroom floor.

"There," Erik whispered. He spit out a thick wad of saliva. It dribbled between his boots onto the side of Lev's penitent face.

* * *

Lev peered into his compact, one watchful eye on his cubicle entrance. The bruise and scratches on his neck mercifully didn't show, but his improvised facial cover-up was an odd milky-yellow. His and Dwayne's medicine cabinet hadn't had any Cover Girl for years, so he'd mixed a concoction of calamine lotion and bronzer, dusted with Dr. Scholl's foot powder. Who knew what toxic compounds were seeping into his skin.

Pressing down on him, Erik raised his flat palm suddenly as if to strike Lev's chest or ribs again. Stiff horizontal plank rose up, slicing the air, stiff fingerspalmwristsiegheil taut tendons in the soft wrist underside parallel tubes like interior plumbing. Vein tendrils, bulging blue creeping across around under and through like cracks in concrete, all poised tense midair. Paused, steadied, flew up an inch or two higher, swooshed down kamikaze crash-land toward Lev. Millimeters from Lev's skin, a pause, a stop, a traitor to the Empire.

Erik's fingers curled into a fist, the knuckles red, white. The fist jerked back into the air. Lev felt Erik's body flex against him. Lev braced himself. The fist pummeled toward home. Again, hesitation. No; as if Erik were holding back, fighting the urge to release his full reservoir of anger and violence.

It was excruciating, but Lev couldn't bring himself to beg out loud for Erik to complete the blows.

Erik saw Lev arch his back, raise his chest and ribcage slightly in encouragement. "Cut that shit out," he hissed.

Lev returned the compact to his desk. He eyed report folders. He listened to the hum of computers, their keyboards' muted crackle like that of a far-off fire. He examined his nails: he needed a manicure.

"I can't believe your boyfriend's never fisted that ass. So fuckin' sweet."

Lev's extension rang. Lev smoothed his tie, wiped sweat from his upper lip. "Advertising, this is Lev."

"Hey, babe! Sucking up that overtime again? Called home this morning at like seven, but you'd already done gone and left."

Lev swallowed, struggled to keep the guilt out of his voice.

"Mm-hm. I took myself out to Kornblatt's for breakfast. It's so boring in the apartment alone."

32   D. TRAVERS SCOTT

*"Aw, don't act like you don't want it. Sweetie. Little
faggot-boy."*

"Well, now, won't be much longer, hon. I'll be back next week."

"Oh, damn—guess what we have to endure again upon your return."

"Huh?"

"Dinner with Ivan and Jung."

"Aww, no!" Dwayne moaned. "Man, how'd that happen? We never call them back."

"I know, I know. Don't get me started. Truth is, I have to admit I actually called them. The Mac crashed again and took my past year of diaries with it. I had to call Ivan to see if he could salvage anything."

"Did he?"

"Like a pro. Took him only like fifteen seconds. Of course, by then I'd already promised to take them out to dinner, paint their house and give them our first-adopted child if he retrieved anything."

*Erik finally let Lev come. Lev choked back sobs, gasping as
his semen shot out over his chest and face.*
*Erik smacked a red handprint onto his shoulder and cheered,
"Ay, piece of cake!"*

"Computer-geeking with Ivan and Jung," Dwayne sighed. "And here I was all worried about how you'd be fucking half of Portland while I was gone."

Lev dry-swallowed.

"Lev? Lev? Hon, that was a joke: ha-ha. Don't go telling me it's not."

Lev forced a chuckle. "Why don't you just come home," he muttered. "I miss you."

* * *

Lev lingered in the alley's shadows, peering through umbrous smoke and steam across the street to the Offshore Café. Through misted panes of glass, dripping sweat beads like a nervous forehead, Lev saw Erik, black hair neatly slicked, gliding about in a crisp white shirt and dark apron. So cool, so professional. Sweat rained down all around him as he poured ultramarine margaritas for a cadre of laughing women. Tiny pink lights in black shells hung delicately above their heads, casting each woman in a fleshy, overripe glow.

Lev crouched against the brick corner. A liverish, wet wind kissed his face. Its sane coolness counteracted his flush, like the soothing endorphins released after the eleventh or twelfth bite of Erik's belt.

The dopamine rush calmed the pain panic, placated fear with an intoxicating, unconditional bliss. Lev knew it wasn't love. But Erik had made him feel overwhelmingly...grateful. Only he hadn't known what for.

Erik rested against the wall. He raised his right arm without looking at Lev, who instinctively crawled into his grasp. Erik stared up at the ceiling, reflective. Lev breathed in his armpit, the acrid hairs damp against his nose. "Wish I was young enough to keep hustling. I know that's fucked, I mean people treated me like total shit, but I hate this holding a real job. Don't know how you computer slaves do it. Absolutely sucks."

Lev licked Erik's wet pit, small tastes. Long, steady laps, as if washing him. He covered the pit and worked out toward the nipple. "Good boy," Erik murmured. "Good doggie. Get it all, real nice like."

This is stupid, this is so stupid! Lev, you are going to completely ruin everything that's good in your life.

Lev's nose wrinkled with distaste, smelling the rancid grease in the restaurant's exhaust. He skipped over an oily puddle, not seeing the swirls of his rainbow reflection, hurrying to catch his train.

Never will I cheat on Dwayne again.

* * *

Lev jut out his jaw, furrowed his bushy eyebrows. He pushed his shoulder's weight into Dwayne, prodding him.

His lover offered no resistance, but rested limp against him, arms happily draped around his neck.

Gasping, Lev fell forward.

Erik jerked his arm away from him, avoiding his collapsing embrace. He pulled his pants up and stepped out of the bathroom. Lev slumped on the bathroom-sink counter, his sweat-slick back cold against the mirror. He wiped the tears out of his eyes. They stung the scratches across his face. He struggled to speak but only made rasping sounds.

Erik turned back around to face him.

Lev looked at him, confused, questioning.

Erik bristled. He jerked his head toward the bed. "Don't worry, you'll get some affection in there, like last time. You know how it goes. C'mon now, get up off the floor."

Lev gazed down Dwayne's familiar back: the gentle, parallel slopes of muscle on either side of his spine. The undulating plains of brown, cocoa, ebony, coal. A thousand shades of shadow, he'd memorized them all.

The pink scar on his left shoulder shaped like Florida.

He wanted to shove Dwayne away.

Dwayne sighed contentedly. "Mmm...get that shirt off, babe."

Lev wriggled out from under him. He glared at Dwayne and pulled back, tauntingly out of reach. His arms bowed out at his side, flexed defensively.

How do I tell him to hit me?

"Take it off me," Lev challenged.

"Oooh, grrr!" Dwayne's expression stretched into a rubbery scowl. "Yassuh, Massa Grumbles!"

Dwayne snatched the hem of Lev's T-shirt, pulling it up over Lev's head and face. He twisted it closed over the top of his skull.

"Sack o' kitties!" Dwayne crowed. "I's got me a sack o' kitties to take down to da river!" He tickled Lev's ribs with his free hand. "Gotta drown dem kitties daid!"

Lev put his hand on the gate-handle. He hesitated, turned back to Erik. Erik turned away awkwardly. He squatted down, inspecting asparagus in the narrow garden alongside the high, wooden fence.

"Don't kiss me good-bye out here," he muttered, "it'll embarrass me." He tore out a tiny weed. "I'll see you next week, anyway."

Lev wrested away, throwing himself down onto the bed beside Dwayne's feet. His breath was hot and dank inside the shirt.

"What's up, hon? Work that bad?"

* * *

"Hey, y'all, I know a place," their friend announced. "Let's go to)ffshore!"

Lev froze on the curb. Erik's café.

"Huh?" Dwayne said. "What's that?"

Ivan and Jung spoke simultaneously:

"It's—"

"—this *cute* little ole bar and grill—"

"—right over on Third—"

"—*fantastic* desserts—"

"—and this new *bartender*—"

"—*hot* new bartender—"

Lev interrupted with a loud tsk.

"Oh, that place. It is so intolerable!"

"What?"

"I have to go there constantly for work lunches," Lev pouted. "It's all that whole yuppie het uptight polished brass scene."

"Don't sound that bad," Dwayne chided.

"Oh, come on, I have to go there all the time." Lev folded his arms across his chest.

Ivan and Jung looked to Dwayne in deferment.

Dwayne turned to Lev. "Well, where else can we go?"

Lev skirted his tongue across his teeth, thinking.

"Let's do Lac Vien. Some good, solid Vietnamese food. How can we go wrong?"

Ivan and Jung exchanged camouflaged frowns.

Lev walked ahead. "Come on, it's just down the block and they're a good price. You guys'll love Lac Vien; we go there all the time."

Dwayne stepped up beside Lev. Ivan and Jung flanked their sides.

Lev sighed. "Trying to get a bunch of queens to decide where to eat. You'd think we were negotiating Gaza here."

Ivan and Jung shrugged at each other.

Dwayne chuckled.

Erik chuckled, deep into Lev's ear from behind. He stuck in his tongue. He pressed both his hands down, squeezing Lev's wrists held firmly at his side. Lev whimpered.

"Yeah, you took all that pretty good, but you could've taken more." Erik was still hard. He pushed his torso up, locking his elbows and pressing Lev's hands down hard. He arched his back and thrust his cock in deeper, pushing with all his remaining force against Lev's ass, feeling his cock plow deep up inside the man's gut. "And I've got more for you," he whispered.

Lev had come long ago. Erik had forced it so Lev wouldn't enjoy as much what followed. Erik shoved his still-hard cock in again, deep. Lev cried and Erik let go of one of his wrists. Erik slapped the side of Lev's face. Lev whimpered, his free hand limp at his side. Erik sighed, ready to switch gears. He flexed his abs and pulled his cock out of Lev's ass. It flopped in the air when free, flinging off drops of

cum that landed on the back of Lev's thighs, white globs
catching in wiry black curls. Pretty, Erik thought.

Lev smiled perfunctorily. Without looking both ways, he bounded off the curb, leading the group at a decisive clip across Third Avenue. Out of the corner of his eye he saw the rosy glow of Offshore.

* * *

Lev sweated under the pale pink lights.

"You just missed him."

Lev glanced over his shoulder out Offshore's window, hoping Dwayne and the others wouldn't question his lengthy absence.

"What?"

The waiter tossed off a sigh.

"Yesterday was his last day." He balanced a fifth martini onto his serving tray and carefully lifted it.

"Well? So then, where did he go to?"

The waiter sucked in his stomach to squeeze past Lev. The white linen towel grazed the ridge of Lev's ear; the heavy glasses floated precariously over his head.

"He left town!" the waiter snapped. "Some gig at a karaoke bar in Eugene."

"No one's ever done all this to me," Lev announced, voice
cracking. He stared down the slope of Erik's abdomen at his
dark, cropped crotch hair. His view rose and fell with
Erik's steady breathing. "I know that," Erik said, his voice
resonating through his chest into Lev's ear, sounding
underwater. "You've been good, though. You could still take
a lot more, and you want me to give it to you. You want a
hell of a lot more, don't you?" Lev nodded. He breathed in
the starchy dried cum and sweat on Erik's gut. His face,
back and arms stung. Erik rested a hand on Lev's sweaty
hair. "You're a good boy, aren't you? A real good boy. Are
you mad I held back? It's not 'cause you're bad or anything.
I just—I can't, these days. I'm kind of..." He dug his
nails into the soft sides of Lev's scalp. "If we go much
further, I might not be able to hold back."
Lev closed his eyes, dreaming.

Lev slipped out of the restaurant, retreating to Dwayne and their friends.

"Enough change?"

"I put in plenty." Lev sat back down at their table at Lac Vien. "The meter's full."

He brushed his slacks. He ran fingers through his hair. He drained his ice water.

Dwayne nodded, smiling.

"Dwaynito was just about to tell us how you had sex with Isabella Rossellini?" Jung said dubiously.

"Isa-fella Rossellini," Ivan murmured.

Lev frowned, startled. He rolled his eyes. "Oh, God," he laughed quietly.

"You tell it," Dwayne urged. "Go on, hon. You tell it so much better."

Lev surveyed the table of expectant faces. "Oh, well, okay. Okay. Um—here goes."

He rolled up his eyes and licked his teeth, composing himself with a deep breath. He smiled at Dwayne with determined affection.

"Okay. So, now, let's see: Dwayne and I had just begun dating—"

"So this is *after* the public john in Dallas?" Ivan queried with exaggerated politeness.

Dwayne beamed. "Already told them that one!"

Lev pushed his tongue along the inside of his right cheek, tossing his lover a look of fond reproach.

"Dwayne is such the romantic. As I was saying: it was only our, oh, fifth date or so. Now, this was years ago, you see, back when *Twin Peaks* had just come on and was ridiculously popular? I was constantly being told by people how much I looked like Kyle MacLachlan—"

"Ooh, he really did—wasn't getting all gray then—"

"Hello? I'm telling the story here?" Lev held out his upturned palms. "So everyone thought I looked like Kyle MacLachlan, including Dwayne, who was so kind as to bring it up on our very first date. So we made this running gag over dinner about the scene in *Blue Velvet* where Kyle's making it with Isabella Rossellini and she goes, "Heet me!" and then David Lynch cuts to this close-up of a candle loudly sputtering as it's blown out."

Dwayne blew a raspberry on his thumb.

"Like so," Lev nodded, indicating Dwayne with his left hand. "It was such a goofy, non sequitur, David Lynch kind of thing to do, we did it all through dinner at totally unrelated things: we'd be all worked up gabbing about some ACT-UP demo, all very serious, then one of us would jump in the other's face and go—"

"Heet me!" they both gasped. They covered their thumbs in a spray of noisy spittle, grinning goofily.

Ivan and Jung's faces held steady, expectant.

Lev's eyes darted around the table, fell.

"Maybe you had to be there."

Lev's expressive storytelling face blanked, switched to vacant introspection.

Jung and Ivan glanced at each other.

Dwayne shuddered.

A waiter set down a jiggling tray of Vietnamese iced coffees.

Dwayne clapped, abruptly bright. "Sin time!" he cackled. "I ordered you one, too, babe."

"Oh?" Lev frowned as the waiter distributed the tall glasses, layers of condensed milk, sugar cubes and ice spheres, metal coffee strainers balanced carefully on top. "Dwayne, you know I'm trying to cut back—"

"Ooh, shit! I'm sorry hon—"

"It's alright," Lev sighed, "I'll live, I'm sure."

"Want me to send it back?"

Lev shook his head, ran his fingertip along his glass' side, cutting a path through the condensation.

"Yeah. Cut your side open with this belt then piss in the sores."

Lev set his jaw, straightened in his chair.

"Anyway," he announced, "Dwayne and I were over at Dwayne's place on, oh, only our fifth date or so—" He arched his eyebrow and placed his right index finger onto his left pinky-tip.

"Sluts," murmured Ivan. Jung elbowed him.

"And I was forced to retire to the bathroom with a nosebleed—"

"Was this when you broke the light in there?" Dwayne interrupted, unscrewing the floral thermos of hot water.

Lev cocked his head in remembrance.

"No, I believe that was when I was demonstrating for your roommates that scene from *Triumph of the Will*—"

"Oh, yeah," Dwayne nodded and poured hot water into each man's tiny tin strainer.

"Anyway, when I returned to the bedroom, there was Dwayne: sprawled out and ready for the taking, dangling all over his zebra-striped futon—and wearing this enormous, black curly wig!"

"Heet me!" Dwayne hissed through the rising steam.

Lev's face set grimly into a deadpan double-take. "I've often said that was the Point of No Return in our relationship. The fact that I stayed there and actually had sex with this man—"

"—in the wig—"

"In the wig, this man who looked more like Rick James than Isabella Rossellini, instead of running from his apartment in sheer terror, was a sign that we were going to be stuck together for quite some time."

He clamped his fingers around Dwayne's warm shoulder in closing.

Ivan and Jung smiled benignly. "You two are so sweet."

Ivan stuck a spoon in to stir Jung's coffee.

Lev's jaw clenched. Dwayne's tendons writhed under his fingertips. He tried to cover, forcing a quick, fractured smile.

"We ever told y'all about the time we played *Carmen?*" Ivan held out the spoon for Jung to lick.

"Oh, no," Dwayne groaned, capping the thermos' steaming mouth.

Lev's fingers flew off Dwayne's shoulder. He cringed in mock dismay, resting his forehead on his fingertips and rocking his head slowly.

Jung and Ivan launched into their tale, describing the University of Texas at Dallas in the early eighties: new wave dance clubs and masochistic industrial bands....

Lev, head lowered, stared into his dessert coffee. His face fell blank again. The scalding black liquid dribbled into his glass, melting the hard geometry of the sugar and ice, their neat, precise volumetric shapes eroding and mixing. Drops hit the placid surface of the condensed milk, black and white absolutes staining, streaking, swirling, mixing. Clean met lactate met bitter met sweet; hot and cold likewise, until none were distinct nor separate. Individual properties succumbed to adulterated dissolution.

* * *

Lev pinned Dwayne's itinerary to the bulletin board above their living-room desk. He studied the flight numbers and times. He looked at the calendar on his Mac's screen below: regimented rows of blank, white squares.

"Fucked him like I'm fucking you now," Erik muttered. "Held his arms back tight just like this. You like it like this?"

"Yes."

"Well, he got better than you. I gave him more. After I finished fucking him, I took him to the hospital 'cause I'd broken his fucking arm."

Lev fingered the CD-ROM tray. He launched SelectPhone and instigated a search: Karaoke Bars, Eugene, Oregon, USA.

How many karaoke bars could there be in Eugene?

* * *

Lev checked the clock, wrinkling his nose at the bus station's dull, yellow stench. Dwayne got back into town in thirty hours. Minus two hours for the ride back, add two hours for Lev's working-late excuse. As long as he made the 5:45 p.m. bus back to Portland, he'd be safe.

* * *

Dwayne squinted at the clock radio again.

11:20 p.m.

Shit. Okay, now it's late enough to worry, but when do I get on the phone? How come he didn't leave me a phone number?

* * *

"Damn," Erik hissed through grit teeth. He wiped his tears on the red-splattered sheet.

social relations

Scott O'Hara

Fuck. Pull out. Beat it to get it hard again. Re-insert. Fuck. This time, after a minute or two, it slips out on its own. Beat it. Re-insert. Fuck. This time the director calls a halt. "Let's do some dialogue and reaction shots," he says, wearily. "Then we can get back to this after you've had a rest."

Believe me, the process of shooting a pornflick is nothing like the product.

Tommy and I were actually hitting it off rather well: he was an enthusiastic bottom, and I was in a relatively toppish mood, so my dick had twice managed to achieve that upcurved-banana look that is so riveting to viewers. Nice. Fact is, I think they'd already gotten plenty of useable footage, but directors always want extra to play with. My first director told me they liked to work with a three-to-one ratio—three minutes shot for every one used in the video. Mind you, I've seen some of his subsequent videos that looked like they were one-to-one, but I understand about ideals not always being the same as results. And hey, I'm a performer. ("Talent," they try to call us, a term that makes me shudder.) I know how difficult it can be to get useable footage.

So Tommy and I got to relax awhile; when we spontaneously started playing with each other's tits, the director knew it was time to get back to shooting. And this time, for some reason, I was really into it, I guess, because it felt like we'd initiated the sex ourselves instead of being directed; and my dick got really super-hard, and I managed to

plow him from every angle for about twenty minutes before the director finally asked his cameraman, "How much tape do we have left?" A
good director always asks that before he tells the performers to give
him a cumshot. And there was plenty of tape, so he nodded to us, and
we both started working up to shoot our loads. Tommy, as I said, was
enthusiastic: he was one of the few bottoms I know who really stayed
rockhard during the whole fuck. Didn't have to beat off or anything.
Fact is, he should've been a top. So I rolled him over on his back, bent
over and went down on him: directors always like that number, and it
turns me on, too. And he went wild and started bucking up and down,
fucking himself on my dick and fucking my mouth, and within about
thirty seconds he started moaning that he was gonna shoot, and at
the appropriate moment I pulled off and let him spray all over his
stomach, while I was ramming against his prostate. And then a few
seconds later I pulled out and mixed my load with his. Perfect double-
cumshot.

And then, while we were still in position, it was time for reaction
shots—all those "oh, fuck, yeahs" and "aw, shit, I'm gonna come's!"
and grunts and groans and moans and facial contortions, while I'm
pretending that my dick is still hard and that I'm still fucking him. And
then finally, five minutes later, we could move. I just slumped down on
top of Tommy and kissed him, real deep. He didn't seem to mind in the
least. Far too many of my co-stars, once the work is over, just want to
get into the shower and get outta there. Tommy seemed to share my
love of the work. I think he was really just doing it because it ensured
a steady supply of big dicks up his ass. I can understand the feeling,
even though I don't share his obsession with size.

So we lay there smooching, and got comfortable on the dingy old
ripped mattress (we were supposed to be in a back alley somewhere,
and there were trash cans on both sides of us), while the techies took
down the lights and reflectors and other equipment, moving it all into
the next room for another set-up; and we talked. He asked me, curi-
ously enough, about my family.

"They're Mormons. Nothing much more to say about them. Haven't
seen them in years. Lots of brothers and sisters, teeming hordes of
nephews and nieces. When I told them I was doing porn, Mom told me
I was going to hell. And yours?"

"Oh, about as opposite as you can get. My mom collects all my
videos. Dad died when I was a kid, Mom got a great life-insurance set-
tlement and decided to spend the rest of her life having fun. I swear,

every time I go home, she's got a new young stud hanging around the house. Nowadays, some of them are younger than me. She writes, too. Romance novels."

This rang a bell, somehow. "Where did you grow up?" He looked at me funny.

"Southern Illinois. Why?"

"Like, in Cairo, by any chance?" And I pronounced it right: Kay-ro.

"Yeah..."

"I think you lived just a couple blocks from me. You were two years younger, we never saw each other at school, but I remember my mother spewing fire and brimstone about that terrible loose woman down the street, how she ought to have her child taken away from her, all that noise. I guess she never succeeded."

The light was dawning in his face. "I remember you now! And I remember one summer at the city pool, when you and I were the last ones out of the shower, and you..."

I'd been hoping he'd forgotten that particular episode; I found it a little embarrassing, in retrospect. But he obviously didn't; he described it in excruciating, and lascivious, detail. Hey, we were— what, maybe nine and eleven? I'd just shot my first load of cum a few months before, and I was eager to show my new-found talent to anyone who I was sure wouldn't tell my parents. And Tommy (I don't think I even knew his name, but I'd seen him around, knew where he lived), given his background, seemed like a good candidate. To my surprise, however, he proved to be way ahead of me. "I always wondered why you never wanted to play with me again, after that." There was a slightly vulnerable, childlike look on his face, now; I guess I'd penetrated one of his earliest insecurities.

"And I, well, I guess I felt guilty about 'seducing' a kid as young as you. I thought about you a lot. But then, you know, we moved West the next summer."

"Yeah, I know." Tommy was looking at me with a semi-worshipful gaze, which then turned thoughtful. "Did you ever do anything with Buddy?" Buddy was my younger brother, Tommy's age in fact, and when I was growing up he was just a pest to me; I never much thought about him even having a cock and balls until suddenly, on one of my visits home during my college years, I saw him come out of the shower—I shared his bedroom on these visits. And he was...well, stunning. I didn't put the make on him or anything, I didn't have that sort of self-confidence, and he was a butch bruiser who could easily have decked me by that time, but I did spend the rest of the visit watching him pretty closely. And that was the visit, right at the end, when I came out to my family. They weren't thrilled. They didn't quite kick me out of the house, but that night they suggested that Buddy go sleep over with one of his friends, and he seemed quite eager to leave. I left early the next morning, and haven't been back since. I'd like to see what Buddy's developed into—he's the only one of my siblings still unmarried, so he probably hasn't developed a potbelly yet—but I don't feel like braving the fires of hell just to find out. I assume he's away at college somewhere—he was always an intellectual sort—but I don't know where.

I told all this to Tommy. A smile hit his lips. "You know, I played with him. The same summer you and I met in the showers. We used to meet out behind those sheds, down by the river, and beat off together. And he's the one who taught me how to suck cock." Now he was grinning broadly, perhaps at the open look of shock on my face. "Of course, I don't know if he turned out queer, but he sure liked playing with my dick."

Suddenly I realized that I was humping my quickly stiffening dick against Tommy's thigh. A wave of lust surged through me. I kissed him, hard, sucking his tongue into my mouth, and he responded with a moan deep in his throat. I pulled back. "So, get down there and suck his big brother's dick, cocksucker," I growled in his face, and pushed his head down.

Tommy was, without a doubt, the most eager cocksucker I'd ever met. He didn't poke around, licking and kissing and teasing. He dove for the whole banana, taking it right down his throat. Even when, as was the case right now, the dick was too hard to bend down his throat, he still forced it right down there. I suspected he might have sprained it, but at the moment I didn't care. I just started fucking his throat, holding onto the back of his head and slamming it home. Suddenly I wasn't exhausted any more. You'd never think that I'd shot a load just half an hour previously. Imagining him down on his knees, doing this to Buddy—when he and Buddy were just nine years old, yet!—had really awakened something in me that I'd effectively suppressed for years, and suddenly I wanted to plant a load where my younger brother's had gone. (Had he been able to shoot yet, I wondered?)

Tommy forestalled me. After a couple of minutes of serious cock-diving, when he was wheezing and gasping and his eyes were running with tears, he pulled off and looked up at me with a half-wild, half-mean expression on his face. Guess I'd aroused something in him, too. "You know, I didn't just suck Buddy off," he said, in a knowing way, his voice suddenly huskier, deeper. (Was it so obvious what I was fantasizing? I guess it was.) "I fucked him, too. We had a blanket that we'd spread out on the riverbank, and he'd lie down on his stomach and stick his ass up in the air," and Tommy was stroking my upstanding dick while he was relating this, and with his other hand he was rubbing my asshole, which suddenly, unexplainably, felt empty, "and I'd lick his asshole until he begged me to put my dick inside him. I bet I shot about fifty loads of cum up his ass that summer. Sometimes I'd shoot twice without stopping."

I moaned. Yes, he'd hit a mental spot as sensitive as any prostate. Almost without thinking about it, almost without volition, my body heaved itself over, and I was on my stomach; and quick as a flash, Tommy was behind me, with his tongue slathering spit all over my butthole.

Now, being rimmed has never been one of my biggest turn-ons. It's enjoyable, but it doesn't send me into the stratosphere, the way it does with some people. But I wasn't myself any longer: I was my little brother Buddy, that hunky teenager I'd watched for a week as he changed and took showers, until I almost couldn't stand it any longer. I was that boy, and I'd never felt anything so incredible as this tongue squirming its way up my ass.

In what seemed like no time at all, my asshole was spasming and opening so that Tommy's tongue was going in with virtually no resistance; that was when he scooted forward and slipped his dick in. And there wasn't any pain, just the sensation of a space having been finally filled, the other half of the puzzle supplied, the whole joined. The smooth slide of one slippery, spit-covered mucous membrane against another. I swear, I could feel his dick against my heart. And he didn't fuck, right away: he just lay there, moving in and out a little bit, holding me while I shook with sudden, wracking sobs.

After a few minutes of that, my ass started reacting of its own volition. It began humping up against Tommy, trying to take every millimeter of him, right down to the pubic bone. That's when his sadistic streak started coming out. He pulled out to the point where just the head was inside my ass, and kept it there. No matter how frantically I pushed back, I couldn't get any more of him inside. Then, about every ten seconds, when I was clawing the mattress and crying in frustration, he'd slam it balls-deep and grind it for a few moments, flattening me to the mattress, and then pull out again. God, he knew how to make me crazy. And then, while he had me pinned to the mattress, he leaned down next to my ear and whispered, throatily, "This is the way I used to make Buddy crazy," and slammed it in with that extra-hard hip-twist that rocketed my prostate right into heaven and made my cum start spilling out all over the mattress, even though my dick wasn't even all the way hard. "And this"—shove —"is the way"—shove—"I shot my cum up Buddy's butt"—and I could feel his cum-tube pulsing, and he grabbed me in a ferocious bear hug, and for once in my life I was very glad there wasn't a director leaning over us telling us where to shoot our loads, because from a cinematic viewpoint, we'd clearly fucked up big-time. No cumloads visible. But oh, I liked where we'd left them. I swear I could feel his load swirling around in my guts, practically percolating: all those spermatozoa beating frantically against the walls of my asshole, trying to find someplace fertile.

And we lay there contentedly for another ten minutes (we could still hear the sounds of the next scene being shot in the next room over), kissing and stroking each other and breathing hard; as our heart rates slowly returned to normal, Tommy eventually rolled off me, and I scooted down so I could suckle on his dick. There's nothing like, for me, the act of sucking on a dick that's just come out of my ass: sucking the remnants of a cumload out of it, cleaning my own shit off it (What does my shit actually taste like? Although I've sucked dozens of dicks after they've come out of my ass, I still couldn't say), letting him know that I really worship his dick, that I appreciate the pleasure it's just given me. And Tommy was looking down at me with a curious mixture of pride and wonder; and I guess I could have predicted what he said next. "You know, that's exactly what Buddy used to do after I'd shot a load up his butt. Do you suppose these things run in families?"

"No, not really," I mumbled around my mouthful of dick. "I just think I know my brother well enough that I knew, subconsciously, just what he'd like. That's what relations are. People you know better than you want to."

crescendo

SIMON SHEPPARD

The first mighty chords ring out, filled with the majestic power of a flowing river, the ominous on-rush of fate. An elderly, blue-haired usher dressed in funereal black closes the door. The two men are alone in the box.

One man, well-dressed, distinguished-looking, gestures to one of the overstuffed chairs, red velvet glowing softly in the muted light from the stage. The other man, who's wearing jeans, T-shirt and sneakers, takes a seat. He's perhaps ten years younger than his host. And, by the looks of it, a lot less rich. "You don't really want to stand through all five hours of *Götterdämmerung,* do you?" the older man had asked just moments before. German accent. "There's an extra seat in my box. Come up and join me?"

The younger man, Daniel Levy, had grabbed up his program and his leather jacket and left his standing-room place at the rear of the orchestra section. Pick-up line or no, this was an offer not to be turned down. Not when the house was sold out and the chance of grabbing an empty seat at intermission near zero. And how much could happen in a box at the Opera House, even during Wagner?

Compared to his accustomed standing-room vantage point, Daniel finds himself astonishingly close to the singers. Perched right above the orchestra pit, he figures he could spit on the tympanist's bald head. Whoops, pay attention! "The Twilight of the Gods."

The three Norns, soprano, mezzo, and contralto, are weaving the ropes of fate. Re-telling the tale of Wotan, ruler of the gods. His magic spear. The destruction of the sacred ash tree. The on-rushing doom of Valhalla, the home of the gods.

The rich solemnity of the music is punctuated by a cloying waft of too much perfume. Giorgio, probably. Why did rich women insist on wearing unbecoming dresses and too much Giorgio?

A stirring brass fanfare heralds the entrance of Brünnhilde and Siegfried. And the arrival of the older man's hand on Daniel's knee. "Mr. Schiller..." Daniel begins in a whisper.

"Hans. Please call me Hans," his host whispers back. He moves his hand up Daniel's thigh. The swelling vocal lines of the chubby soprano and chubbier tenor pledging their love are matched by an unplanned swelling at Daniel's crotch. The man is suave, all right. His hand creeps upward, massaging, backing off. His pinky reaches Daniel's dick just when Siegfried pledges to do great deeds in battle and Brünnhilde ecstatically accepts the gift of the magic ring. The magic ring made of the gold from the River Rhine. The cause of all the bother. The leitmotif of the Rheingold has been heard throughout the preceding umpteen hours of the Ring Cycle. And it will be heard again and again until the whole shebang goes up in flames.

O heilige Götter! Hehre Geschlechter! Weidet eu'r Aug' an dem weihvollen Paar! The chubby soprano implores the gods to feast their eyes on her and the tubby tenor.

The familiar, spirited strains of Siegfried's Rhine Journey accompany Herr Schiller's first decisive squeeze on Daniel's basket. And the Prologue comes to an end.

* * *

The scrim goes up, revealing the castle of the Gibichungs. Hagen and Gunther, two basses up to no good, are busy planning evil in ringing tones. A woman enters the next box over. Very late. Another whiff. Not Giorgio, Shalimar this time. Hans' hand, which has been ceaselessly kneading Daniel's hard cock, retreats at last.

Hagen's dark voice is filling in Gunther and his sister Gutrune on how the giant dragon—*Wurm*—was slain by Siegfried's mighty sword, when Schiller whispers in Daniel's ear. "Come with me. Now." They rise from their chairs. Schiller leads the younger man back through the red velvet curtains separating the inner and outer rooms of the box. The auditorium is hidden from view. No one can see them. Hans Schiller flips the lock on the door to the outer corridor. The orchestra, just slightly muffled by the heavy drape, crashes to a crescendo as

Hagen, insincere as hell, greets Siegfried with a hearty *Heil!*

Schiller and Daniel are face to face, inches apart. The German grabs the Jew around his waist, tugs T-shirt out of jeans, pulls it off over Daniel's head. Schiller runs his hand over the triangle of wiry black hair on Daniel's chest. Pinches a nipple. Hard. "Sit over there!" He indicates an ornate armchair, all gilt and red velvet, in the corner of the little room. Wagner's music rolls on and on, ebbs and flows. Evil doings in the world of the gods.

Daniel, who might be apprehensive if his dick weren't so hard, feels velvet against the naked skin of his back. Schiller picks up a black leather case leaning against the wall and reaches inside, pulling out a handful of neatly skeined rope. At its first touch against his skin, Daniel's cock gets even harder, starts dripping as Schiller binds first one hairy forearm, then the other, to the arms of the red velvet chair. Within a minute, coils of rope tightly restrain Daniel's arms, his hands tied firmly in place.

Schiller kneels and pulls off Daniel's sneakers and socks, then ties his hairy ankles to the carved legs of the chair. Working quickly and gracefully, Schiller winds rope around jeans-clad legs until Daniel's lower body is securely restrained.

Several eye-bolts have been set into the wall to either side of the chair. Schiller takes one last long piece of rope from the bag and runs it through the eye-bolts and across Daniel's naked chest, back and forth and back again. He tugs hard until the web of rope presses into Daniel's naked torso. A square knot, and the young man's body is immobilized.

Schiller reaches into the leather bag once again and pulls out a ball-gag and a blindfold. "This is so you won't make noise," he says as he fastens the gag in place. "No one likes a noisy opera-goer. And this blindfold will help you concentrate on the music. No distractions, you see." Daniel can't see a thing.

But he can hear. The music of Wagner, craftsman, anti-Semite, madman, genius. Music of dark, insinuating power. The glimmering leitmotif of the Magic Fire. The doom-laden chords of the Curse. Then the ceremony of blood-brotherhood. Gunther and Siegfried sing *Treue trink' ich dem Freund.* In his mind, Daniel translates. "I pledge my faith to my friend. Happy and free may blood-brotherhood this day spring from our bond!" Daniel feels his jeans being unbuttoned. He never wears underwear. His hard cock springs free, stands straight upward, throbbing against his belly. He feels Schiller's hand stroke it briefly, squeeze the hot shaft. Then the feeling of cord, looping around the base of dick and balls, cinched down tight, tying up ballsac, stretching it taut, winding again and again around hard dickshaft, tight against swollen flesh. Siegfried and Gunther row off down the Rhine in search of the rock where Brünnhilde sits, having lately been awakened by Siegfried's kiss. Sudden pain sears Daniel's nipples. Tit-clamps. Schiller has put on tit-clamps. The pain segues into pleasure. The orchestral interlude between scenes, ending with a bit of Wagner's greatest hit, the "Ride of the Valkyries." Schiller pulls the chain connecting the tit-clamps, ties it, Daniel surmises, to the rope around his dick, so that even the slightest shift of position sends a pleasant jolt of pain through his tender nipples. Dah-da-da DAAH da!

"Now then," Schiller's soothing, masculine, slightly taunting voice says, "let's just listen to the music, shall we?"

And listen Daniel does. Stripped of control over his body, unable to move, the pain in his nipples becoming waves of pleasure washing over him like a river, Daniel listens. And hears things in the music he's never heard before. The awful, aching longing for transcendence. Power beyond good and evil. The lonely death of the gods. A place where "pain" and "pleasure" no longer have meaning. Beauty so absolute it somehow approaches horror. He can see how the Nazis could have loved Wagner. And yet, and yet...he loves, he needs, he becomes one with this music.

Teilen den Taumel. "Share the frenzy." A hand on Daniel's hard cock. A wet hand, stroking, squeezing hard. His dick strains against the cord that grips it tight. "Share the frenzy which has made you mad."

Waltraute, one of Brünnhilde's Valkyrie sisters, sings in a forceful mezzo of the distress of Wotan, king of the gods. "So sits he, speaking not a single word, silent and solemn on his sacred throne." Daniel's body strains against its binding. He's let another man do this to him, possess him, use his body, take away his will, give him what he's always secretly wanted. *Walhalls Göttern weh!* Waltraute cries out. "Woe to Valhalla's gods!" And Daniel is lost in the richness of the music once more, until a burst of applause yanks him back. The end of Act One.

* * *

Intermission. Without a word, Schiller strokes Daniel's face, then firmly inserts earplugs into the standee's ears. Now Daniel is deaf, blind, dumb, half-naked, tied down to a chair. Only a sudden draft of air alerts him when Schiller leaves the box. Leaves him alone. Alone.

Time has become elastic, stretching and contracting. Seconds or maybe many minutes crawl by. Daniel is lost in a place of darkness and silence. No, not silence: the music of Act One courses through his mind. He's lost in remembered music. Till he feels the gag come out. Schiller's come back. The edge of a glass touches Daniel's lips. Icy champagne fills his mouth with its dry bite, its piercing bubbles. Wine flows over his tongue, down his parched throat. Next, a strawberry, its ripe sweetness flooding his heightened awareness. Its juice still fills his mouth when Schiller brings his hand down, hard, on Daniel's cheek. The sudden, stinging pain brings tears to Daniel's eyes. The gag is replaced, the earplugs removed. And Act Two begins.

* * *

The rasping, insolent voice of Alberich. The evil dwarf, starved for love, scorned by the Rhinemaidens, is plotting to bring the whole world to a fiery end.

A sudden tug and the blindfold comes off. Daniel blinks in the unexpected light. In front of him, an ornate little table holds a bottle of rubbing alcohol, cotton balls, several spools of dental floss. A surgical clamp. And perhaps two dozen gleaming hypodermic points, each still contained in its sterile wrapping. Needles. Daniel is afraid of needles. Sweat starts trickling down his sides. "Even my curse is blunted on that fearless hero, for he knows not the ring's value and makes no use of its unique power." Alberich's voice is blacker than night. "Laughing in the heat of love, he burns away his life." And the blindfold goes back on.

A gorgeous passage heralds the dawn's glowing light spreading over the Rhine. Schiller removes the thick ropes from Daniel's bare chest. The woody smell of rubbing alcohol fills Daniel's nostrils. Dabbed onto the skin of his chest, it evaporates quickly, leaving a chill. A men's chorus sings out: "We come with our weapons, we come armed!" The first needle slides beneath Daniel's skin, just above his left nipple. "What is the danger? What enemy is near?" Another, above his right nipple. Schiller is guiding each needle's point beneath the upper layers of skin, through flesh, then out again. "We come armed with our sharp weapons!" Needle three, above the first. And needle four. Sharp little bursts of pain. The masculine, hypermasculine sounds of men headed off to war. The voice of the Nuremberg Rallies. "Hagen, what do you command us do? What must we do? What do you command us do?" And something else: where each sharp burst of pain has been, glowing warmth spreading outward. "Once the animals are sacrificed, what must we then do?"

And Schiller inserts the tenth needle. Amazingly, Daniel is lost in pleasure, a feeling like, he imagines, being stoned on opium would be. Afloat in a stream of astonishing well-being, he feels only his dick, hears only the music, welcomes only the next needle. Waits for Schiller to have his way with him, whatever the man wants. Whatever the magician wants. Whatever his god wants. Red dawnlight sets the River Rhine afire.

Helle Wehr! Heilige Waffe! sings Siegfried: "Shining spear, hallowed weapon, enforce my eternal oath!" The music gleams like fire, like a blade, like a needle through flesh, like Daniel's bound and swollen dick. "Where blade can pierce, there can you pierce me."

Once again the blindfold is removed. Daniel looks into the mirror. Perhaps a dozen sharp needles, perhaps more, have been pushed through his naked skin. Schiller takes a spool of dental floss. Expertly he winds it from needle to needle, forming an intricate webbing across Daniel's chest, anchoring the web of floss to a series of small hooks unobtrusively set into the wall behind the chair. Every new loop of floss around needles brings new pain, new feeling. At last the bondage is complete. Schiller steps back.

Daniel is mesmerized by his own reflection. The man in the mirror is him, yet not him. It's a wild-eyed man, pierced by silvery needles, bound to a red velvet chair. Bound as firmly as the magic fire had bound Brünnhilde to a rocky bier. And yet he's as free as the astonishing possibilities of the human voice. A man is singing, "May those whom love gladdens be made as happy as my joyful heart!" And for that moment the voice belongs not to a chubby tenor in an ill-fitting wig, but to Siegfried, great hero, last best hope of the gods. Just as the body in the mirror belongs not to Daniel Levy but to his captor, his master, to Schiller. Schiller, who stands before Daniel, straddling his legs. Who unfastens his gag and pushes his crotch against Daniel's face. Who unzips his fly and pulls out a hard, uncut dick. Who shoves it into Daniel's hungry, waiting mouth.

And while the evil Gibichungs convince Brünnhilde that Siegfried has betrayed her, while they plot to gain the ring of power, while they plan the hero's death, Schiller fucks the young man's mouth. Every thrust, every shifting of bodies, makes the floss tug against the needles. Presents of pain. Dark music. The gift of Schiller's dick. There are tears in Daniel's eyes, running down his cheeks. He can take no more. But he wants this never to end. His trials have brought him, like a warrior killed in battle, to Valhalla, home of the gods. Dark music. Dark music.

Sterb er dahin, swears Hagen. "Die he shall, the handsome hero!" The brass section blares music for a marriage procession. Siegfried and Gutrune. A marriage founded on deceit. One that can bring only doom. Daniel wants to choke on Schiller's dick. "Choke me," he thinks, "choke me, please." Crashing chords. And Act Two comes to a close.

* * *

Once again the earplugs are in. Daniel is, as far as he knows, alone again. He expects more strawberries, more champagne, but they don't arrive. Then he expects nothing at all. Dissolved into his own tiny world, hearing only the pounding of his heart, the high-pitched whir of his nervous system, he alternates between meditative calm and mounting panic. Every time the panic shows itself, his dick throbs.

At last the hint of a breeze signals that Schiller has returned. But Daniel is unprepared for what comes next: the cold press of metal against his hairy upper thigh. Then a sawing, a feeling of rope and fabric giving way. The German is slicing through Daniel's jeans, a serrated knife blade cutting through denim. Within minutes, the job is done. Daniel feels his shredded jeans being pulled from his body. He's never felt more vulnerable. Or more at peace.

The earplugs come out. The blindfold comes off. Applause for the conductor making his way to the podium. And in the mirror Daniel sees himself, handsome, bearded, bound, gagged. A blue-eyed Jew. With a look in those eyes that he's never seen before.

The music begins. The trumpets call. The man in the mirror stares at the traceries of webbing zigzagging between the needles in his flesh. The leitmotif of the River Rhine, a theme first heard way back at the beginning of *Das Rheingold*. The man in the mirror's tied-up dick is still mostly hard. The Rhinemaidens, guardians of the river's golden treasure, sing *Weialala leia,* mourning the theft of their golden hoard. Schiller stands before Daniel, blocking his view of himself. A horn signals Siegfried's approach. Hans Schiller reaches down, deftly unties the rope around Daniel's dick. Freed of its bounds, it begins to get soft. The Rhinemaidens flatter Siegfried, hoping to tease the magic ring from his finger. "So handsome! So strong! So desirable!" Schiller kneels and takes Daniel's dick in his wet, skillful mouth. The harmonies of the Rhinemaidens ebb and flow. Blood rushes into the young man's cock. He shuts his eyes in pleasure. He can feel the power of the music running all through his body. And he's quickly close to coming. He moans behind his gag, and the wet mouth pulls away. "Not yet," whispers Schiller. "Not yet." *Kommt Schwestern!* sing the Rhinemaidens. "Come, sisters! Let us leave this madman! Though the hero thinks himself clever and strong, he is like a blind man, or one who is bound." They prophesy doom, a doom set in motion a long time ago. A fate which will sweep both mortals and gods along in its remorseless path.

Men's voices, threatening, harsh. Hagen and Gunther. The orchestra churns itself into a downward spiral of evil fate. Schiller snaps a leather cock ring around the base of Daniel's dick so it will stay rock-hard. Siegfried's heldentenor voice now, retelling the story of his quest for the ring, his battle with the dragon, his braving the magic fire to find his bride Brünnhilde. At last the tit-clamps are removed. A rush of pain. Daniel winces. Schiller dabs alcohol on the tied-up Jew's nipples. Ravens circle above Siegfried, then fly off to the Rhine. Schiller has a needle in his hand, point against the tender flesh of Daniel's left nipple. Hagen cries out for revenge. The needle enters flesh. Hagen plunges his spear into Siegfried's back. Pain. Daniel cries out, his voice muffled by the gag, as the orchestra crashes out the theme of the hero's murder. "Hagen, what have you done?" sing the vassals. A second needle penetrates Daniel's other nipple. The searing pain takes Daniel even further into the dark. Siegfried sings out his dying words, a farewell to his love. The onrush of pain over, Daniel sinks back into pure sensation, a place beyond pain or pleasure. The familiar, stately strains of Siegfried's funeral march carry him on his way. Doom-laden, swirling brass. The comforting beauty of violins. And Hans Schiller kneels and plants a long, deep kiss on Daniel Levy's mouth. Homeward to Valhalla. Carried along on the music's incredible power.

Schiller is standing at the little table now, as Hagen drags Siegfried's corpse home to the hall of the evil Gibichungs. Schiller picks up the surgical clamp, which has triangular openings at its tips. Brünnhilde is singing, her voice brim-full of grief and vengeance. Schiller kneels, squeezes the flesh of Daniel's dickhead in the clamp, locking it shut. On stage, vassals are erecting Siegfried's funeral pyre. Schiller pulls the gag from Daniel's mouth. "You will not make a sound," he says, "however much you may want to. Nobody likes a noisy opera-goer." *Ruhe, ruhe, du Gott!* sings Brünnhilde. "Rest, rest now, o god!"

She pulls the ring from Siegfried's finger as the vassals lift the corpse onto the pyre. On the table, a small, shining gold bar tipped with gleaming metal balls sits next to a thick piercing needle. Schiller picks up the needle. "Accursed ring, terrible ring, I take your gold and give it now away!" Schiller places the tip of the needle against the clamped-down cockhead. Brünnhilde grabs a torch and sets the pyre alight as the needle enters Daniel's flesh. The Jew sees his own face contort in a rictus of pain, mouth open in a silent scream. Brünnhilde jumps on her steed and rides into the flames. The Valkyries' leitmotif: Dah-da-da DAAH da! Biting pain, burning pain. The rising Rhine, in flood, overflows its banks. Electric shocks run through Daniel's convulsing body as the needle makes its slow and agonizing way from one side of his dickhead to the other. Valhalla itself is aflame. He wants to scream, jaws straining, mouth wide open. But no scream comes. Instead, music comes out, music of the most amazing power and beauty, the sound of the destruction of the home of the gods. One long rush. One endless orgasm. Like the "Liebestod" from *Tristan*. And Daniel's pain is extinguished, becomes joy, becomes bliss. Amazed, stoned calm in his tear-filled blue eyes. The needle is followed by the little golden bar, one end-ball refastened to hold it firmly in his cock.

Gods and mortals, good and evil, Hagen and Brünnhilde, all have met their doom. To strains of overwhelming beauty, power, clarity, the dying flames become the rising dawn. Final chords of peace regained. From everywhere and nowhere, a torrent of *bravos* floods Daniel Levy's mind. Somewhere beyond the red velvet drapes, someone is tossing bouquets at the performers.

* * *

"How's it feel?"

"A little sore. Feels good." Daniel Levy, lying in his lover's arms, looks down at his dick, his new ampallang piercing. Golden balls gleam at either side of his cockhead. "Looks good, too."

"You did really well. I was afraid you wouldn't be able to take it, but you did. You did yourself proud."

"Thanks, Hans. Like Siegfried says in Act Two, *Mich freute die schwelende Brunst.* 'I enjoyed the soaring flames.' "

Dawn is creeping through the windows of their penthouse apartment. Arms around one another, the two men are ready to drift off into sleep.

"And you enjoyed the opera?"

"Wagner's never been so...intense. But Hans..."

"Yeah, Dan?"

"Next season, I'll be top."

cocksuckers' tango
Justin Chin

1. Queen

The Cock of Last Resort. I am in an alleyway, a basement let-in, the leather blindfold firmly in place, gripping my eyes until I can feel the moist condensation of sweat between the fragrant leather and my short-sighted eyes. The puffy eye pads press into my eyeballs so tightly that I see green and purple spots as if I were on acid watching a Grateful Dead lightshow, but there are no unwashed hippies here, no skanky flower-children that never grew up nor teenage converts to the nostalgia trip, just the sound of shoes and boots scuffling around me, flies unzipping, the smack of cocks in hand, the ale smell of crotches and unwashed pubes, the occasional grunt and cough, the sticky smack of semi-dried lubricated cocks against flesh.

The Cock of No Contest. There are those who will grab your head and there are those who will grab your ears like a teapot handle. There are those who will hold your shoulders and those who will try to reach down and pinch your nipples. There are those who you will feel nothing but their cocks in you as they are busy pinching their own nipples as hard as they can. Then there are those who have absolutely no idea what to do with their hands.

The Cock of Dreams. Cocks fill my mouth, caress my tongue, poke blindly at my lips, slap against my cheeks, one by one they drip their load into my face, in my hair, dribbling down my chin, down my throat, on my lips, on my tongue and I take it in like so many deep breaths, the last gasp of a drowning dog. The very first time I had a cock in my mouth, I gagged so hard, I vomited so much I scared myself. The man I was sucking fled the toilet stall. At that moment I decided that I would never gag again, no matter how large or mean or deep the next cock got. I practiced with fat marker-pens, broomhandles, shampoo bottles, beer bottles, carrots, cucumbers. I practiced on the dog to make sure that I could tolerate even the most disgusting cock. I practiced hard and, like musicians training for the symphony, I got good.

The Cock of Wine & Roses. Once I was falling so fast that I woke up in a pool of piss. Once I was falling and when I woke I was falling and when I got up, I was still falling. There is a Chinese boy who I meet with sometimes, our relationship is wholly undefined, he is not a hustler, at least not in my eyes, but someone I pay. But that is a different story altogether. We agree on a number and it is his job to get me that number of loads. We use dice for this, sometimes one die, sometimes two. He blindfolds me and puts my wrists and ankles in shackles and ties me to my bed, he puts a gag in my mouth, he saves his load for the last one of the session. In the meantime, he gets on the phone and calls phone-sex lines and party-room conferences, he gets on the computer bulletin boards and invites anyone to come and feed me. He takes pictures of the men who come through to feed me. I know, I can hear the click and whirls of the Polaroid camera, I can see the flash through the edges of the blindfold. After the session, after he empties his cock into my mouth, he unshackles me and holds me while I cry like a whipped child. He whispers into my ear, describing the men who I have eaten from. He never shows me the pictures, though, in my imagination, I like to think that he masturbates to them in private, maybe he sells them to other people, saying, look, here's a picture of a pig, a real pig, (oink oink) do what you want to do to him, here's his address.

The Cock of Understanding. When did you learn how to suck cock? The artist Louise Nevelson was once asked how she created her art, and she replied in her croaky Bette Davis voice, "Honey, how do you eat a peach?" Sucking cock is nothing like eating peaches. It is nothing like sucking, even as the prominent verb/continuous tense of its namesake suggests. Suck: to draw into the mouth by inhaling; to draw from in this manner; to draw in by or as if by suction; to suckle. In my youth, terrified by the crudeness and suggestiveness of language, we called it "eating ice cream." But it is nothing like eating ice cream at all. It is nothing like breathing, it is nothing like art. It is its own act, its own tense, transitive verb, noun, dangling pronoun. It is its own universe, not made of atoms but of stories, so many stories you wish you were deaf.

The Cock of Love. Once, I considered pulling all my teeth out. I had met a man who promised me nothing but load after load of jism from his beautiful cock and I had partook of it enough to believe him, it was his suggestion. The gumjob, the selling point of men who have gotten so decrepit that that's the best they can offer on phone-sex lines, sight unseen, all that's known is a mouth, void of teeth, just a fleshy wet slobber to face-fuck and a voice that cries, *Please.* I chickened out at the last minute. More likely, I couldn't make the sacrifice of having a wound in my face, unable to suck cock for weeks while I healed. Sucking cock has nothing to do with monogamy, I recalled telling myself and I got on my knees in the backroom of another bar and I never ever saw that man again. It is no loss. Not yet.

The Cock of First Offense. There are two kinds of hell. One is an icy world where sinners are lodged in a lake of ice, their heads two-thirds popped out of the lustrous sheet, mouths trapped beneath the frozen solidity, the air is dry as meat lockers. In the other, the more common version, hell is the fire-and-brimstone land that children are told they will be sent to if they misbehave, don't obey or tell family secrets. Here, demons rip out the glutton's bowels and drape their intestines on pine trees that are on fire. Liars are fed hot coals. Idolaters have their eyes poked out with blunt pencils. Those who love gossip have their eardrums perforated with biting insects. We're told that it is the hottest place that anyone will ever experience. The hell you want to go to, though, is that place somewhere between the two hells. Here, there is no sand, as all the sand has melted into glass. But, unlike the fiery hell where melted sand remains in liquid-glass puddles collected on the floor like clogged storm drains in New York City, rank and foul-smelling, floating with the flotsam of discarded memories, the melted sand in this place, by virtue of the clashing temperatures, condenses into a sparkling expanse of glass that you may walk on. It is like walking on an eternal sheet of shattered windscreens, cracked, shattered as an exquisite spider web but still holding to each chip, smooth as the underbellies of lizards, the size of a desert. The fierce light from the Fiery Hell and the coldest intense light from the Ice Hell light this place and the waves of light sneak through the cracks in the glass and make it radiate into a quintillion spray of light. It is a hell worth going to.

The Cock of Heaven & Earth. Someone's beeper goes off, someone is chatting to another in the background, someone is preparing for another shot, someone pops open a canned drink, someone can't get hard, someone has the cold flaccidity of a tweaker, someone I recognize, someone has brought a friend, someone is being re-acquainted, someone has a new piercing, someone has a fever, someone has strange bumps on his cockhead, someone is severely deformed. This is democracy in action. I take it all. I accept it all. I accept them all. Like a mother of a nation, I hold them all dear to me. Here on my knees, in this alley this basement let-in with this blindfold in place, here at the wee hours of a new dawn, week after week, I am queen, and I will rule here forever and ever. Watch my coronation, watch me ascend the throne.

2. Pisser

You tell me that this kiss means I'm your boy and that your lover doesn't understand your craving for young smooth boys to play dead for you, the bear of a man that he is and how you now cannot bear the sight of his face nor his body nor his cock, you need a boy to lie across your lap *tell me a secret* you whisper in my ear *tell your daddy your secrets* and I spit my spirit of transaction into your ear. This is such a fucked-up way to score but—shit—what's a person to do when your dealer changes his phone number and doesn't give it to you—you either take it personally, take it as a sign from the almighty to get clean or you improvise, easy choice when the only voice on the other end of the line plies your ear with sweet promises in some adult bookstore, yeah desperation and dependency can make me fake it good, yeah, I can fake that virgin-shit, that innocent-fuck-shit, that I-haven't-had-good-sex-until-you shit, being a bespectacled chink helps and he wants to know a secret so I tell him about how my uncle buttfucked me when I was ten which explains my daddy-fetish and *oh daddy daddy, feed me your cum daddy.*

I lie like mad, and he laps it up like a stray mongrel licking Sizzler throw-outs *feed your boy your cum, daddy* I whisper and he feeds me with semen, sweet greens, money, gifts, promises. Oh he feeds me good and he feeds me like I was some starving Third World child touched by the blessed golden hand of Sally Struthers and the Christian Children's Fund and he feeds me and oh, I eat, I eat and I eat like I was that starving Third World child wide-eyed visited with the blessing of All-You-Can-Eat, every meal was like the last meal on death row, belly full, and I shat the whole day to keep up with my feeding schedule and I ate till I puked until I kissed sweet sleep.

But like the well-fed, contented with my buddha-belly filled with yummy treats, hips swelling fat, I learned to give it away for free, I thought I found my twenty-four-hour open-all-night 7-11 of satiation, yeah, I gave it away, I thought I found the high road to all that I couldn't bear, every wisp of grief that I couldn't bear, my heart, my lungs, my liver, my guts, my eyes, my ears, my heart.

I give it away all the time and I also take too much, but the buffet table doesn't go on forever, nothing ever does, and he moves on to some little Latino kid who satisfies him better than I could.

I see you through the glory hole at the adult bookstore, you have him in the black sheer crotchless panties that you once offered to put me in. He is sitting on your lap, you are masturbating with one hand, one hand free to feed the tokens, he is curled on your lap, your head is buried in his skinny chest, he is curled silent as an aborted foetus and you are stroking him and cooing like a pigeon on speed. I do not notice that I am kneeling in a pool of someone else's cum. After you leave, I sit on the small stool and bring my knee up to my mouth and suck at the fluid in the fabric, sucking out someone else's cum that I say is yours, that you put your dick through the hole and left your cum just for me and now I am feeding on it like a hungry mosquito, like a baby hungry for a spurt of teat milk.

But nothing goes on forever, not that craving for some consecrated high in slosh and grind, not for anonymous cum, nothing goes on forever but this bursting in my chest, this new addiction that I hold in my ribs, this bursting this little pisser desire, this queer desire, I take a swig of my heart and baby, lean in, let me tell you one last secret, if I were to leave my body and never come back to it, if I were to leave my blood and never again taste the metal of it, if I were to leave my semen in some stranger's rectum, leave my brain in some discarded pool of my past, I will know that in the crux of any reckoning, this queer desire defines a locus wider, more than where my dick has been and who it has regretted.

Heat wave

Kevin Killian

Carey heard a chuckle, and turned around on Sixty-eighth Street. The man was gone, the place where he'd been now an empty space filled with sunlit air. Some kind of optical illusion, perhaps? Like the silhouettes they showed you in the service: are you looking at two vases or a woman's head? Carey could have sworn he'd seen a man, sandy or auburn hair, slinking behind him, then again maybe it was just his hangover. "Next I'll be seeing little green men from Mars."

The sun was high, and the top of his head felt warm. He stood and watched with quiet eyes down the warm pavement that lay behind him. All was quiet as in a dream landscape. Silver sunlight and the black patches of adjacent alleys—nothing else could he see. Then from out of the silence, very close by, there came once more a low, throaty chuckle, louder and closer than before. There could no longer be a doubt. Someone was on his trail, was closing in upon him minute by minute. Carey stood like a man paralyzed, still staring at the ground that he had traversed. Then suddenly he saw him. Maybe fifty feet down the street, a man, studying a shop window with minimum interest. A young man with red hair, a shock of it standing on top of his head like a rooster's red comb. Idly the man turned from the window display and looked inquiringly at Carey, who averted his head.

Carey stepped into a restaurant he'd never been to. Just to see if he'd be followed. The maître d' was stern and authoritative. "Table for one?" he asked, holding a pink finger up in the air to summon a waiter.

"I'm not really hungry," Carey thought, but he sat down at a booth, feeling the tight friction of the leather seat against his thighs like a warning or a caress. A slight breeze waved a plummy perfume from a large bouquet of red roses standing at the center of the table. He'd been seated at the last booth from one to the men's room, by no means a choice placement. Bearing a fly-specked menu, the waiter approached. The wallpaper was flocked with water spots that streaked through a design of mallard ducks rising up out of a reed-strewn horizon. Carey read from the menu, "Victoria's Canadian Tea Shop."

"Thanks, that'll be all," he told the waiter, handing back the menu. "I'll just have a bowl of soup."

"No soup today," replied the waiter, without emotion. "Too late, mister."

Carey took back the menu as expected. "Ain't that the story of my life."

Then the front door opened and in walked a man, a man with bright red hair the color of fire. Carey opened the menu and covered his face with it. Prices and entrees swam before his eyes.

"Mister, what you like?"

"I'll have the Salisbury steak," he said quickly. "Maybe a couple of vegetables. I don't know, go away and let me think about the vegetables."

But the waiter wouldn't leave. Steadfastly, he stood there with his palm out like maybe he was expecting a tip.

"People steal our menus," the waiter observed, with a vast shrug. "I don't know why."

With a guilty start Carey passed the menu to the waiter, who nodded imperturbably, and added:

"Irving Berlin used to eat here and write his tunes on our menus. The owner's got a couple of them framed in there—" pointing to the men's room, which more and more seemed to be the heart of the restaurant. "Some men like a tea room, it brings something out in them. Maybe you agree, mister?"

Carey jumped up. "I'll take a gander," he said brightly, slipping into the alcove. "Irving Berlin...'White Christmas,' right?"

"Right, mister."

Carey could see the red-haired man approaching the maître d' with a question in his eyes. He saw the man take a photograph out of a card-case and display it. Lingering no longer, he pushed open the heavy door to the men's room and hurried in. He tried to lock the door from within. But the catch was broken, and dangled loosely from the clasp.

The restroom was fairly large, about thirty feet long and ten feet wide. An elderly gent stood whistling at a sink, patting his face with some kind of green unguent: liquid hand soap. He stopped whistling when Carey barreled in.

"Look like you just saw a ghost," said the old man.

"The prices scared me," Carey said. "The prices on the menu."

"Wait till you hit my age, sonny boy," said the geezer to Carey. "Nothing scares a man of eighty but a flu bug or a warm pussy." The old man chuckled and turned the tap with a great flourish. Cascades of faintly red water steamed out of the tap and soaked the old man's green, slimy hands.

Four urinals lined the wall to their right, one a little shorter to accommodate child patrons. On the left a row of stalls stretched to the far wall, in which was set a window—one window, too small to climb through, covered with a fine metal mesh. Street noise. Irving Berlin's lyrics to "Heat Wave" hung, framed, next to this window. Very nice. Very nice decorative bullshit. One of the doors to the toilets was ajar, and Carey slipped inside it.

"Yessirree," called the old man. "When you hit eighty, you're not scared of the Devil himself."

"I bet," Carey called, over the partitions. Then, breathless, he examined his surroundings. One door, two marble walls that stopped a foot from the floor, a toilet built into the far wall with a flush handle. The walls were covered from top to bottom with messages from other men. Graffiti, that lined the gray marble from top to bottom. Just the kind of reading Carey preferred in lighter moments.

In the stall, Carey sat down on the cracked black wooden seat and put his head in his hands. He needed pictures, though, pictures more vivid than the graffiti. Lifting a hip, Carey reached back and took his wallet from the back pocket of his slacks. He'd had this wallet since the service, and it looked it. "I'll buy you a new one," his wife had said.

"You buy too much," Carey had said.

The money he opened to now had come to him from his wife. All in all, there must have been sixty or seventy dollars in the wallet. "I don't want you arrested as a vagrant," she said.

Fuck *vagrancy*, Carey thought, in the toilet stall. From an inner compartment of the scuffed brown wallet he pulled out a fistful of mementos and pictures. This was his past: somehow it felt correct to bring it out now, here, amid the pungent scents of Lysol and men's piss. This handful of memories and impressions. A subway token clinked on the damp tile floor—Carey let it lay where it fell.

"Yessir," called out the old man, "when you get to be my age, every day you wake up to some new terrible thing."

Carey shuffled the stack of cards and papers from hand to hand, while listening with one ear to the sound of the tap water and the old man whistling Irving Berlin's "White Christmas."

"So long, sonny boy," called the old man, finally finished cleaning his old palsied hands. Carey heard the restroom door swish open and shut. Then, in the sudden gray silence, he pulled out a card—"any card," as the jokers in the bars tell you to—and turned it over from back to front. It was a picture of himself at eighteen. He looked frank, confident, alert. Now he was thirty-two. Carey took a deep swallow and waves of feeling washed over him in deep, regressive movement.

He was sitting there, his cock draped across his palm neither soft nor stiff, with its usual dead weight and perplexity, when he saw the hole in the wall. When he noticed it wink at him.

His eyes widened forcibly, as though he'd been given a jolt of electricity or shock treatment. Again he saw the wall blink, or appear to blink, its gray solid surface part and join again. There *was* a hole in the wall, and someone was standing in its light, in the next stall.

The wall that separated the two stalls was a thick slab of Italian marble, and in its center a hole had been drilled in the ancient, sexual past; through this hole now a finger poked, nail upward, and then twisted to measure the dimensions of the space it was in. Three-inch circle? Something like that. Carey gazed steadily at the moving, questing finger, thinking to himself, "It's the red-headed guy."

The finger continued to probe, leaving fingerprints all over that portion of the inner wall it touched, greasy fingerprints, as if left from liquid hand soap or semen. In his fantasy that finger wanted to stretch to an unimaginable length to touch the very tip of his penis, which he held firm in his own right hand. He looked down at himself, and his cock slid forward in his lap, gaining on him. He felt his balls tingle, and grow warm.

The finger withdrew and Carey next saw an eye staring at him, a placid green eye that blinked once or twice but otherwise made no signal. Carey smiled at the eye politely.

The eye closed, then withdrew. In a moment Carey heard the sharp sound of a zipper descending, then the soft ribald fold of cloth. He began to tremble in his loneliness and his longing, waiting for what he knew must come. Next an enormous cock, bigger than his own, appeared through the hole, inch by inch, to come to rest, ringed in a nest of soft, crisp, orange pubic hair, like a birthday corsage for a little girl, a toy. Finger, eye, cock: finally Carey put together the various parts of the body that had been shown him, figured they were all one male. This sum of addition made Carey swoon; if this wasn't the man who'd followed him into the restaurant, Carey would eat his hat. In sexual life, he'd always had a weakness for redheads. Why not go for it? *Here I thought I was being followed. Hell! I was being cruised.*

A strip of ripped toilet paper, ringed with gray moisture, floated to the wet floor. Carey read the words. *Touch it.* Then they dissolved.

He raised his left hand shakily, to the bobbing cock, felt its satiny heat with two fingers. In response it lifted its weight to meet his tentative touch. The ringing in his ears vanished, his headache with it. The cock shot forward; Carey put his mouth to its head and kissed it. Inside his mouth the cock had little volume of its own, but a great suggestion of propulsion and questioning. Carey's nose hit the marble wall, which deflected it…"I'll make it easy for you," said the man in a low throaty whisper. Bent in two, Carey sat back onto the toilet seat sideways as, from under the marble partition, two bare knees came forward, followed by long white thighs, then the whole crotch was squatting directly into his face. An athletic guy, obviously, confident, bouncing on his heels with his pants and underwear drawn down to his ankles. *I could pick his pockets in twenty seconds,* Carey thought obliquely, as he leaned down to the floor to suck Red's dick. Down so low his face felt damp and clammy, and the muscles in the left side of his face started to harden and contract, as he pressed his mouth over the large head of Red's expansive cock. "Red" spoke the familiar words of praise and contempt.

"That's good, Carey," he said. *How'd he know my name?* "That's as good as a woman any old day, I guess."

Athletic guy—mysteriously knowing guy—and a guy who really knew not only what he wanted but how to get it out of Carey. *How'd he know my name?* All in all Carey had to hand it to him, but now wasn't the time or place. The thick stern hardness in his mouth was smooth to his tongue, to his throat, filled him to the tonsils. He was breathing through his nose like a drowning man.

Carey reached up through Red's legs and his hands passed through the light growth of hair on the thighs, till he felt the creamy weight of the ass in his hands, then the delicate filigree of the balls. Red was practically sitting on the floor he was so excited. "Is your dick hard?"

"A little," Carey replied, and the sound of his own voice unnerved him. Again the hardness in his mouth throbbed, as though he was hitting some kind of nerve. "Mount me," the voice said. Obediently Carey let Red slip out of his mouth, which instantly felt hollow. "Slide under," Red commanded, and Carey, oblivious to the piss spilled on the tile, slid his crotch into the crack of the freckled butt, which glistened from exertion and summer heat, his smooth cheeks pulled neatly open with most of his fingers and from sheer will. A pale hand, coated in some shiny invisible glop, guided A to B. From there nature took its course. Carey grabbed Red's waist with both hands; inside, Red's asshole was sweeter and warmer than Carey would have thought possible. From every surface it sank around the column of Carey's dick, and together, through some unspoken physical signal, the two men began to heave slightly, in and out, in a 3-D tangle of limbs and swollen distended muscle. Carey's lungs started to expand at approximately the same rate as his cock. "Don't cream in me," Red pleaded.

"Maybe I will," grunted Carey.

"Don't come in my fucking ass," Red begged, with a long gasp between each syllable. "Don't shoot no big wad up my hungry hot hole."

"And maybe I won't," Carey said.

After a while, Red rose, adjusted his clothing and left. Carey lay back against the stubby toilet and panted. The cards and photos he'd taken from his wallet were spread on the wet tile exactly as they had fallen. His hands were grimy, thick with sweat and shit, urine and cum.

Outside, from the dusty corridor, he heard a pleasant chuckle. *"We're having a heat wave,"* sang a whiny tenor. *"A tropical heat wave."* Only other thing Carey heard was running water, the white sound of water through underground pipes.

when the cat's away...

Lawrence Schimel

My boyfriend was in Los Angeles for two weeks on business and by Wednesday of the first week I was desperately lonely and missing him. And I was horny as hell.

We lived together, and while we didn't have sex every night, we did have intimacy every day, the low-key domestic intimacy of holding each other as we watched the news, of brushing against one another in the bed we shared, even the simple fact of having each other in the same space. Now that he was gone, I realized how much I missed picking up after him, since it meant that he was here, had been here, for me to pick up after, even if I didn't see him at that very moment. In the few days that Kevin had been in Los Angeles, I had long ago cleaned up any casual indicators of his presence; sure, all his stuff was still here, but it was all too neatly in place—where I had placed it, since Kevin was so cavalier about his living environs—and I missed the small messes he made to show his presence, like coming into the bathroom and finding a string of dental floss floating in the toilet, waiting to be flushed away.

I didn't just miss his presence and constant companionship. I missed his body. I missed waking up next to him and feeling his early-morning piss boner pressing against my thigh. I missed waking up before him and lifting aside the sheets, licking my way down his flat abs to that boner, aching for release, and sucking him awake. And some mornings, after drinking his cum, I kept his dick in my mouth as it went soft, wouldn't let go until he'd unloaded his night's bladder down my throat, washing away the sweetness of his cum with the brine of his piss.

His body was always so present. He liked to strip to his T-shirt when he came home from work, leaving his suit, shirt, and tie rumpled on the couch or floor, wherever they had fallen. He even stripped off his underwear, childish BVD briefs he still wore, out of habit, though he was certainly no longer a boy. His thick, floppy cock attested to that, and all evening long I'd get glimpses of it, dangling low and peeking out from beneath the edge of his thin T-shirts, worn almost sheer with age. I couldn't get enough of him, of watching him, of feeling him, even after having lived with him for four years.

We'd settled, as it seems all domestic couples eventually do, into not having sex all the time, letting the tension and pressure and desire for each other build, to make the sex more intense. Watching him lounge about the apartment, though, careless in his nudity, always brought an ache to my balls. Kevin was so unselfconscious about his body, which is one of the qualities I found most appealing about him. Of course, he had a nicely shaped body, smooth and lean, developed by years as a runner in high school and refined by regular workouts at the gym. But there were plenty of guys I knew with seemingly perfect bodies who didn't have his ease, his naturalness with himself and his sexuality. I certainly had nowhere near that level of comfort, although I was perfectly at ease being naked with him, and tried to be in that state whenever possible. So, sex might happen at any time of day or night, in any room of the house. Now I spent every night alone on the couch, wanting to feel him lying next to me, and though I stared at the television set, I didn't see the news. Instead, my mind replayed images of sex we'd had together.

As he'd stood at the stove one night, sautéing onions and other vegetables for a sauce, I came up behind him and cupped the cheeks of his ass, ran my fingers over the layer of short coarse hairs that covered them. Squatting down behind him, I pressed my face into the crack, inhaling the scent of the light sweat that covered him from the heat of the stove. My tongue darted forward as I used my hands to pry the mounds apart. I licked up and down, my tongue flickering across the sensitive bud of his asshole and moving on, wetting down the entire region thoroughly before narrowing in on my target. His cheeks clenched involuntarily as I struck home, and he thrust his hips forward, pushing himself towards the stove.

"Careful of the fire," I murmured into his ass, though I don't know if he heard me.

My tongue darted back to his hole, working deeper and deeper inside as his muscles relaxed into the pleasure. "Mmm," he groaned, pressing his entire body back against my tongue as if he were trying to impale himself on it.

When I'd worked him for a while, I stood up and reached around for the jug of olive oil. I poured some on my cock, which had been eagerly at the ready ever since I'd first seen his naked buns calling to me as he cooked. I pressed my slicked cock against his ass, rubbing it back and forth along the crack and over his asshole, spreading the oil. Kevin lowered the flame under the vegetables and continued to stir them as he leaned forward, lifting his ass for me. I took aim and slid my cock slowly inside him, pushing until it had disappeared from view. We stood frozen like that for a long moment, and Kevin squeezed with the muscles of his ass. He let go of me, and I began to pull out, slowly still, so that he was aware of my cock's every inch and movement, aware of the void it left behind and aching for me to fill him up again.

Which, of course, I did. Soon, Kevin was gripping the edge of the stove with both hands to balance himself as I pumped in and out, fast and hard. Sometimes I'd pull nearly out and jab with just the swollen glans of my dick, letting his sphincter thrill the thick sensitive crown. And then I'd thrust inside of him again, filling him as deeply as he could take me until we were the same being, my chest pressed against his back, our bodies slick with the sweat from our fucking and the heat of the stove. My cock was planted far inside of him, and I was content to leave it there, no thrusting or friction, just the firm squeezing of his ass against the base of my cock. I grabbed his cock in one hand, squeezing it tight, and tickled his balls with my other. We ground our hips together, a slow gentle twist that sent a totally different thrill through my cock than the swift thrusts.

I felt Kevin's balls tighten, and I increased my grip on his cock, massaging its length. My other hand I flicked across the underside of his balls, which had pulled up until they were nestled on either side of his cock. I stood on my tip-toes, shifting the position of my dick inside of him, as if I were going to lift him off his feet on my cock. That pushed him over the edge, and he began to shoot. The first spurt arced onto the stove, where it sizzled. I pulled at his cock, pointing other spurts onto the oven door and floor, away from the dangerous flames. But something about hearing the sizzling cum, or the smell of his semen mixing with the aromas of dinner, or the pulses his ass sent through my cock as he orgasmed, sent me over the edge, too, and my balls unloaded themselves inside of Kevin, long exhausting, exhilarating pulls of semen shooting from my body into his.

"That was really hot," Kevin said, twisting around to kiss me, my cock still inside of him. Then he pulled off me, turned fully around and kissed me again, and told me to order take out. Dinner had burned while we fucked. Hot, indeed!

How I wanted Kevin here now! How my cock wanted Kevin here now!

I switched off the television. I'd been stroking myself, idly, through my sweat pants. Without Kevin, and his ease with nakedness, I'd reverted to wearing loose clothing when lounging about the house.

I stood up, my cock tenting my sweat pants. It had no doubts about what I should do now, with or without Kevin. But I was tired of jerking off. I'd done that two or three times each day the weekend that Kevin had left. Now I wanted the connection with another body that sex provided.

When Kevin and I had moved in together, solidifying our relationship, we'd established certain ground rules. Sex outside the relationship was permissible—with caveats. We must always practice safer sex, and this included no sucking someone else off without a condom, even though unprotected oral sex was thought to be very low risk. We had each tested negative for HIV before we moved in together, and again half a year later, and these ground rules were our way of establishing and maintaining the trust that allowed us to have unprotected sex with each other.

If we had sex outside of the relationship, we had to tell each other, immediately, especially if we slipped up and did something unsafe. That had been a touchy subject, but necessary.

One time I just couldn't help myself: I was fooling around with this guy who suddenly slipped his dick up my ass, and I was enjoying it so much I didn't make him stop. I didn't let him come inside me, of course, but it was still a definite risk, especially since the guy's cock had leaked so much precum. I'd been torn about whether to tell Kevin, but I realized I couldn't not. It wouldn't be fair, especially if I had actually caught something which I might pass on to him. We had a huge fight, which was good for us, because it let us show our commitment to each other. If we hadn't meant for it to be okay to have sex outside of the relationship, we shouldn't have made it possible, but we both enjoyed the occasional trick, it kept our own sex life revitalized. We were fighting not because of what I'd done, but because of what it meant for our own sex for the next few months. We would have a fear of fluids for the next half year. No more languid sixty-nining. No more heat-of-passion fucking, either; now everything had to be more planned: we had to have condoms handy, and water-based lubes.

And for the next six months, Kevin and I practiced safe sex. I was still able to suck him off and even swallow his cum, because Kevin had been well-behaved. But since we didn't know my serostatus, everything related to me was latex-wrapped. When I tested negative again six months later, we decided it was safe enough to go back to fucking without condoms again. I don't know what I enjoyed more that night, the feel of Kevin's tongue on my cock, slick with saliva, or the feel of my cock up his ass without a condom. They were both heaven. And I was determined not to lose those pleasures again.

I'd never been much into anonymous sex. I'd flirted with it before, of course—how could you not, visiting any bar with a backroom, the curiosity to check it out was too strong to resist—but I had never felt much need for it. I'd never had a problem finding tricks to pick up, but that required so much more investment than what I wanted right now. I wasn't looking for a fling. I just wanted to feel a body next to mine, to hold a cock in my hands. I'd love to feel a cock in my mouth, but I wouldn't, not tonight, and I knew that.

I untied the string on my sweat pants and let them go. They started to fall, but got caught on my erection, which held them up in front, leaving my ass bare. I laughed, and undid the fabric, stepping out of them completely. My balls were already pulled tight against my body, aching for release. I pulled on jeans, not bothering with underwear, and tucked my erect cock down the left pants leg. I buttoned the jeans and then stroked the bulge through the denim. I was so aching for action, I wondered if my cock wouldn't stay hard with anticipation even during the long subway ride to the bars.

I pulled on a white T-shirt, and my leather jacket, which I planned to check as soon as I got where I was going. Kevin and I weren't bar hoppers, since neither of us were heavy drinkers—wine with dinner, of course, and socially, but not just for the sake of getting plastered, and hardly ever beer. But we had friends who were still single, intentionally or otherwise, and they kept us up to date as to what bars were happening and which were duds, and of course there were the local rags. One bar in particular was touted for its downstairs backroom, an entire floor devoted to the pleasures of anonymous flesh.

The subway seemed jam-packed with good-looking men. Of course, it was just that I was horny, so I was focusing on what it was about every man I saw that made him attractive. It might be something as simple as the bulge in his crotch, or something as ineffable as the way he held his hands in his lap, that made me want to feel those hands dancing across my skin. I flirted with some of the guys, just to pass the time, but wasn't seriously cruising any of them. I wasn't interested in that right now, actually, much as I was desperate to get laid. I didn't want to go through the effort of picking someone up, of dealing with someone as a person. I wanted just a warm and willing body.

At the bar, however, I cruised in earnest, looking for someone to bring down into the lower level and undress. But my pursuit came up. fruitless. There's something different about cruising on the subway or the streets, places whose express purpose isn't built around sexual attraction. In those locales, cruising is exhilarating. Even if I'm rejected haughtily, or being cruised by someone who doesn't interest me, there's that moment of recognition of sexual interest that I find so comforting. In some ways, it's like gaydar, but there's something a little more active in cruising, an outpouring of energy, of affability, of sexualizing energy and appreciation. In a bar, however, cruising is a more desperate affair. There's a single-mindedness that I find off-putting. Besides, I wasn't finding anyone I'd want to pick up.

I wandered to the lower level. At the bottom of the stairs was a short hallway, with bathrooms to the left and a door to the right. A black sheet was hung across the doorway, and I pushed it aside and walked through. The area beyond was a dimly lit room whose walls had been painted black. I paused near the threshold, waiting for my eyes to adjust to the almost-light. Someone brushed past me from behind, coming into the room as I had just done and unable to see me as his eyes hadn't adjusted yet. However, as his body came into contact with mine, he reacted, instinctively, and reached out to touch me, to feel my back, the muscles of my arm, groping. His hand dropped down to touch my ass.

I walked away, ignoring him. He didn't follow. I stepped towards a wall, and again a hand reached out and touched me. I looked into the darkness and realized there were people lined against the wall, dark shapes against a darker background. I shied away from this new hand as well, and looked for a bare space to lean against. Twice I accidentally brushed against another body, which turned towards me like a flower turning towards the sun, eager to engage me in sex. Each time I pulled back, not yet ready.

I'm not sure what was restraining me. Perhaps it was seeing the crowd upstairs, and knowing that this group must be made up of men pretty much like them. I'm not a body-fascist, in that there are many different types of men I'm attracted to, and many things about men that I find attractive, but overall I'm pretty visual, I think, and I like to see a man I'm having sex with. The idea of putting a cock in my mouth that I couldn't admire first, couldn't hold in my hand and appreciate, just didn't appeal to me. Which was fine, since I wasn't going to be putting any cocks in my mouth. But I wanted to feel one in my hand, wanted to feel another man's hand on my own cock, pressing against my asshole or up inside it, twisting my nipples.

As my eyes grew accustomed to the dimness, I began to see the men around me. Like me, they mostly stuck to the edges like a bunch of wallflowers. In one or two cases, backs faced me. I realized I was staring at two men who were engaged in some sort of sex. I watched the thrusting of hips towards the wall, wondering what the guy against the wall must feel like, wondering what it would feel like to have someone stand in front of me and rub his crotch against mine, on display to everyone. I think that's part of why I wasn't yet hard, really, the idea of other people watching to get off on my having sex. I've been part of orgies before, but in those situations everyone's taking part, and you can see all that's happening. You're meant to, there's an exhibitionism to it all. There was a different feeling about this sex around me, though, as if so many of these men were here not just to have sex, although that's what we all were hoping for, but to be in the presence of sex. And I was one of them. I had this desperate yearning to be part of the sex, but right then all I could do was be in the presence of sex, which had its own sort of fascination.

I watched the men cruising the wallflowers, some walking around with their dicks out, stroking themselves. I could see the motion of arms pumping among the wallflowers as well, men jerking off from being in the presence of sex, keeping themselves hard to be ready in case an interested hand or mouth came near, or perhaps to attract someone over with the motion. Any sex drew attention. Watching one of the cruising men suddenly connect with a wallflower near me, everyone in the vicinity suddenly shifted. We were all aware of the sudden union, and focused on their coitus. Men moved in to reach out towards the pair, to touch an ass or chest, as if hoping their sexual success might rub off on them, like patting the belly of Buddha for luck. Sometimes it was to encourage the pair in their endeavors, or to encourage the pair to reach out and embrace an additional partner.

I, too, was drawn to the sex nearby. I looked for silhouettes, for the outline of a cock being jerked in someone's hand. As I was watching one cluster of men, having stepped away from my place along the wall to get a better view, a hand reached from behind to grab my crotch. My back stiffened, but I stopped myself from pulling away. I didn't encourage the guy, exactly, but I didn't stop him. His hand drifted up and down my crotch, trying to work my cock to stiffness. I don't know if it was his hand or watching the silhouettes of the cocks before me, the cluster of bodies, of men who'd abandoned themselves to sex, that did it. I started to get hard. I stopped being someone who was here to be in the presence of sex, became someone who was here to have sex. It didn't matter who I was having sex with, it was having sex that mattered. So people were watching; it's not as if they could see much anyway. And what the fuck if they could? That's what we were all here for, that's what we were all here doing. I felt suddenly liberated, and thought I understood some degree of Kevin's unselfconsciousness about his nudity.

Thinking about Kevin suddenly brought my cock to life, and the guy unzipped my pants and drew my swollen dick out into the air. I felt as if the attention of the room focused on it for a moment, and I relished that attention and admiration. I let my own hands reach out and feel the crotch of the guy who'd been groping me. His cock was already out of his pants, and kept at attention by a leather cockring that thrust his balls forward. His cock was thin, the size of two fingers, more or less, but enough length to stroke. It didn't matter. I wasn't looking for perfection, I was looking for contact, pure and simple. He was uncut, and I spent some time playing with his foreskin, rubbing it back and forth over the crown of his dick, letting the precum spill over onto my hand. I ran my slicked fingers down the length of his cock until they bounced against his balls. I dropped his shaft to tickle his balls, wetting them down with the almost-dry precum.

I felt a hand on my own balls then, and realized that the guy had not let go of my cock. Someone else had joined us, and I reached out to feel who it was. I connected with a solid bare chest, a T-shirt whose front had been pulled over the guy's head, and I began to stroke his bare pecs. My fingers grazed against stubble, a triangle of hair he shaved to show off his muscles. A ring of stubble surrounded his nipples, and the left one had a ring in it. I twisted the tit with the ring between the fingers of one hand, and squeezed the other guy's cock in my other hand. Both of them were playing with my own cock and balls, and a hand was rubbing across my ass. I wondered where the first guy's other hand was, but it didn't matter. He was probably stroking the other guy. Which is what he should be doing, I thought.

Still pulling on the first cock with one hand, I let my hands drift down the chest of the other guy to his crotch. I wanted a cock in each hand as I was getting jerked off. I sprung the button on the guy's pants, and his crotch fell open; he'd already unzipped the zipper. I reached into his boxers for his cock, feeling a nice hefty one through the fabric. I pulled it through the slit in the boxers, wishing for some light so I could take a look at it and admire it. I glanced down to see its shape, but couldn't see anything against the dark floor. It didn't matter. I could see with my fingers, which were now gazing at a Renoir or Matisse painting, a great work of art.

I let go of the other guy's thin cock and brought both hands to play on this new one, the better to see you with, I think, and I smile even though no one can see me. I turn towards this second man, positioning my body against his. Pairing off. The first guy who engaged me feels slighted, I guess, but I don't care. He got to feel my body for a while. He got to touch my cock, massive compared to his, though certainly no monster compared to some I've been fucked by in my time. We had no promises of completion. This was not a pick up, where we've implicitly agreed, in going home with one another, to try for a mutual ejaculation.

The first guy's hands still reached for me, reached around my back for my cock, but I didn't care. My attention was focused on the guy before me, and he held my complete attention. Or I should say, I held his attention, quite literally, squeezing along his cock with both hands. There's something about a cock of a certain size that's a marvel just to feel and hold. It doesn't have to be gargantuan, but it needs to have a certain heft to give this feeling. And this guy's cock certainly was big enough to delight. I would've loved to sink down to my knees and take him in my mouth, but I knew I couldn't. I didn't know anything about this guy, who he was or what his serostatus was. I didn't even know what he looked like. But I held his cock in my hands, and he was tugging on mine, and that was a wonderful thing to be doing.

He suddenly let go of my cock, though, and put his hands on my shoulders, pressing down. He wanted me to suck him off, and I wondered how he'd sensed my desire. But I shook my head, and shrugged his hands away. He stopped, and I pulled on the tip of his cock, my fingers thrilling the sensitive crown. After a moment he pulled his beautiful cock out of my hands and tucked it back into his pants. I felt, for a moment, as crushed and rejected as the guy I'd turned my back on just a moment before must've felt. My fingers curled around empty air, remembering feel and heft, and I was jealous of the next man this guy paired up with.

I looked around, seeking sex again. My cock was still hard, and still out of my pants. A short, heavyweight guy walked past me, and his fingers groped my crotch. They closed about my cock, and I tried to pull it out of his hands. I wasn't interested. Having held that beautiful cock in my hands, I was now looking for perfection again, not just contact with anyone. But the guy didn't let go; he sunk to his knees and before I could pull back had wrapped his lips around my dick.

He knows nothing about me, I thought. But I knew I was safe, and my guilt didn't last long as his tongue worked its way up and down my shaft, slicking my cock down. His lips clenched tightly around my dick, and worked their way all the way down to the base before pulling back. He wasn't someone I would ordinarily have wound up having sex with, but it didn't seem to matter. Tonight I just wanted a mouth on my cock and a cock in my hands. I might want a cock in my mouth, want to sink down on my knees and take any hard cock into my mouth like this guy had done. I wanted that beautiful thick cock I'd held, wanted to suck it and feel it inside me, but I knew it wasn't to be, that I'd never do it because I wouldn't feel safe doing it, wouldn't want to take that risk. But that was fine. Right now I had a mouth on my cock, which was exactly what I wanted. I reached out and grabbed the guy's head, and began to fuck his face, not merely taking a blowjob off this stranger, letting him decide to suck me off, but taking the active role in this encounter.

He murmured something, but it wasn't a complaint so I didn't stop. I pounded into his face, pushing deep into his throat, hardly giving him a chance to breathe. I pulled out all the way and lifted my cock away from his face. He whimpered, as if he were a child whose favorite toy I'd just taken away. "Lick my balls," I said. My voice was not loud, but in the quiet of the room, the utter silence except for the rustle of clothing as men shifted, waiting for sex, and the sounds of fists and mouths pumping cocks, it commanded all attention. Men drifted towards us, as the guy on his knees did as I told him. I slowly stroked my cock, slick with this stranger's saliva, as he took each testicle into his mouth and then let it go. Men stood nearby, their crotches poised at the ready for the cocksucker to do them next. Hands reached around to cup my ass and squeeze my tits, and I pointed my cock down the guy's throat again. He started pumping away on my shaft, and I let him go at me like that, enjoying the admiration of his worship on my dick and all these hands on my body. Letting him suck me off, instead of actively fucking his face, left my hands free to roam, and I sent them each in search of a cock. I wanted to hold a cock in each hand while this guy sucked me off, to connect in sex with three strangers.

I undid zippers and fondled crotches, looking for those two cocks. The guy's mouth kept working, up and down along my cock. I grabbed onto a cock with my right hand, held it tight as if it were an anchor, and thrust my hips back and forth into the stranger's mouth, pushing my crotch upwards until his nose squashed against my belly. My other hand found a cock that was already out of some guy's pants and hard, waiting for some action, and I began to tug on it. I felt, for a moment, like a kid, trying to pat his head with one hand while making circles on his belly with the other. And I felt childish glee at being able to do so. I was in sensory overload, and I was in heaven.

The guy who was sucking my cock pulled off to catch his breath. Almost immediately, a guy who'd been standing nearby moved forward, thrusting his prick in front of the guy on his knees. I guess he hadn't really needed to catch his breath all that much, for he swallowed this new guy's prick immediately. I was disappointed that someone had stolen my cocksucker, but right then my hands were both busy, stroking and pulling on two nice cocks, and I didn't want to risk letting go of either of them, so I didn't have a free hand to take my cocksucker back.

It turns out not to have mattered, because the guy whose cock was now being sucked suddenly leaned forward and began to suck my dick. The idea of this daisy chain, of someone whose cock was being sucked sucking on my cock, really turned me on, and I felt my balls tighten. I began to tug harder and faster on the cocks in each of my hands, and I heard breaths quicken all around me. The new cocksucker was even better than the last one, or perhaps it was just that my cock was harder since I was so close to coming, but it felt great. I wanted to feel a cock in my own mouth, and I imagined sucking off Kevin, thought about having sex with him the moment he came off the plane. The image of Kevin's cock in my mouth brought me close to the edge.

"I'm gonna come," I said, thinking it a courtesy to warn the guy whose mouth was on my cock. He didn't know me from Adam or Steve, after all, and he had no way to know I'd tested negative and practiced only safe sex. But the guy didn't pull off my cock, as I'd expected, but pushed even deeper onto me, thrusting my dick deep into his throat. Whatever, I thought, and knowing I was negative I didn't feel much guilt as I pulled on the cocks in each of my hands and thought about sucking on Kevin's big cock and suddenly felt my balls let loose and my hips buck as I shot my cum down this stranger's throat, a stranger whose own cock was being sucked as he sucked on mine. He bobbed up and down on my cock, milking it of every drop of cum. Only when I had begun to go soft did he let it fall from his mouth and stand up. He started pumping away at the face of the guy who was sucking on his own dick. I turned my attention to the two men whose dicks I still held in my hands. Not for any desire of reciprocity, but because I wanted to feel their cum rushing over my fingers, wanted the satisfaction of having brought them to orgasm.

I'd have to bring Kevin here sometime, I thought. The idea of being on hand while some guy sucked Kevin off, to have some stranger give us a tag team blowjob, to have two guys suck each of us off, to kiss him while each of us was being sucked off, to be here in the presence of sex and for me to suck him off while he held another man's cock in his hands—there were infinite possibilities, all of which seemed intensely arousing just then, and I felt my cock begin to stiffen with renewed life.

southern sheriff

GARY BOWEN

It's late, it's dark, it's after the bars have closed but people don't want to go home. I take a turn through the state park as I do every night about this time. The park is closed; nobody is supposed to be here after dusk. But kids like to come and party, and occasionally more nefarious things go down. Once I found a body. So I patrol the park.

I'm running with the window open, night breeze giving me goose bumps under my tan shirt. I think about putting on my jacket, but it's muggy too, and I decide to wait a while. I pass the playground and the first picnic area: empty. I shine my spotlight over the restrooms and lakefront beach: no motion. Satisfied, I roll on. The woods wall me in, trees blotting out the sky. I have excellent night vision, I turn off the lights. I want to be able to see whatever there is to be seen when I roll into the second picnic area: the furtive dropping of little baggies, or the quick zip-up of pants. I want to loom suddenly—out of the night, all six-foot-three of me, every white boy's nightmare: a black man with a badge. I'll scare the living daylights out of whoever is there. If anybody is. Most nights it's quiet.

I turn off the engine and coast the last few yards to the edge of the trees. I can see the picnic area before me: the parking lot is full. It's a small lot, it only holds twenty cars. There are few empty slots. Some of the cars are rocking. Beside them, off to my left, are picnic tables where men sit and smoke or drink from silver cans. Some guys are strolling among them, giving each other measured looks. Right in front of me, on the closest table, two guys are necking.

"Faggots," I think. I should clear them out. But I don't. Instead I sit and watch, mesmerized.

I have magazines at home, I've heard stories, I've even busted a hitchhiking hustler. They haunt my dreams, these promiscuous men who meet for anonymous sex. They give me uncomfortable nights and sticky sheets. I've never done it with a guy. I've looked at the men around me and I just can't imagine doing it with any of them. The men in the magazines are just models, they aren't really doing it either. It's all talk, none of it real, like Bigfoot stories. Sure, lots of people claim to have seen Bigfoot, but I don't believe them either.

And yet, there it is, right in front of me. I have imagined furtive couplings in the dark, but I have never imagined kissing. Yet these two are sitting fully clothed, one a white male with black hair, approximately five-ten, one hundred seventy pounds, mid-twenties, wearing a blue and white windbreaker. The other is a white male, red hair, six-foot, two hundred pounds, early-twenties, wearing a jean jacket. I describe them to myself as if they were suspects, but they don't act like suspects. They act like lovers. Their eyes are closed, oblivious to the world, giving each other the most languid, intense lip massage I've ever seen.

The dark-haired one, a Jew by the looks of him, sucks the other's lip between his, rakes it gently with his teeth, lets it go and teases the redhead's lips with his tongue. The red-haired boy sticks his tongue out, and the tips meet, touch lightly, then disappear as their mouths come together. Their arms wrap around each other, the Jewish boy pulling the other boy close, hands slipping up under the jean jacket. They shift position, the red-haired boy's hands coming up between them and slipping inside the windbreaker, *CFL Colts* across the back.

Their lips part as suddenly as the Jewish boy's pants. I can't figure out what's happening, the redhead's hands are nowhere near his crotch. The Jewish boy squirms, then strips off the windbreaker like he was suddenly overheated. Now I can see his arms, which are firmly muscled and dark-haired. He wears a short-sleeved white dress shirt like he's an office worker somewhere. I try to imagine him as a pansy male secretary, but my imagination fails as he strips out of his shirt, revealing a well-developed chest. He didn't get those pecs at a desk job!

The red-haired boy bends his head and kisses his nipple. The dark-haired boy watches, eyes liquid in the darkness, his lips parting. I can hear him panting now. The redhead clings to his chest, sucking his nipple like it was a tit, and the dark boy is cradling him in his arms, fingers stroking through the bright hair in mindless motions as he moans his pleasure.

The sound makes me squirm and I'm glad I didn't put on my jacket; it's definitely warm tonight. The red-haired boy sits up, his hand replacing his mouth on the other boy's nipple. He tweaks it with his fingers, then rolls it back and forth between his thumb and forefinger. The dark boy arches his back, muscles hard and ridged, sweat starting to gleam on his face. His sharp breath comes clearly through the night. I've seen women like that. I never imagined a man could feel that way, too. I find my nipple under my breast pocket, squeeze it gently. Fire suddenly flows in a line straight to my crotch. I shift in surprise, twist harder, feel the spark leaping from nipple to groin. The fabric slips beneath my fingers and I lose the nipple. I find the other one, it's already erect. I twist it, panting in arousal, my cock straining against the seat belt.

The red-haired boy is using two hands now, working two nipples, and the Jewish boy collapses sideways, leaning against the table top. The torment doesn't stop, two hands keep the pressure on him, and his hair is starting to curl from the sweat gathering on his brow. I clench my hands on the steering wheel, keeping them away from my body, keeping them away from temptation to do as the two boys are doing, but I can't stop feeling what I feel. I should have flipped the lights on when I first came in, I shouldn't have waited, shouldn't have let myself be tempted.

I want the Jewboy.

I admit that to myself. My fantasies are going from the realm of the abstract to the realm of the flesh. I have seen a man that I want, and want badly. I unbuckle the seat belt, I reach for the car-door handle. I hesitate. They will run at the sight of my uniform. I stay put. All I can do is watch. The red-haired boy drops to his knees before his— *trick?*—the word sounds so tawdry. Call them *lovers*. The red-haired boy is making love to him. They might not know each other, but it doesn't matter. They know what they want.

The dark boy sits on the bench and opens his knees and the red-haired boy leans between them, pushing his crotch up tight into the V of legs. They're still dressed, but I can't stand it, I have to open my fly and grab my cock. They're kissing again, kissing with their groins grinding together in slow motion, hands clamped to each other's bodies. Get on with it! I want to see them fucking, I want to see the dark boy roll over on the bench, his ass jutting back as he drops his pants. I want to see the red-haired boy mount him like an animal—I want to mount him like an animal. I want to throw the red-haired boy aside and sink my horny cock into his backside and fuck him until I have a heart attack.

But I don't. I yank my prick so hard I hurt myself but it doesn't stop me from spraying cum all over my uniform.

Geezuz Christ.

In front of me the red-haired boy is unzipping the fly in front of him, reaching for the long, swollen cock, his mouth closing over the tip and slurping it up. I'll never have what they have, not even for the briefest moment. In a fit of jealousy, I hit the light. If I can't have it, they can't either.

Red and blue lights flash across the clearing, and suddenly guys are zipping up and hiding joints and trying to pretend nothing's going on. I step out of the car, flashlight in hand, and shine it across people. I use the bullhorn, though it's not really necessary in such a small space. "Everybody move along. The park closed at dusk and it's two a.m. Go on home."

Guys shuffle to their cars. They eye me warily, but I stay by the car. I'm not busting anybody tonight. Cars pull away, squeezing past my patrol car. "And don't come back!" I yell.

"Redneck sheriff!" somebody yells. Somebody else hushes him. I do nothing.

A Ford Taurus maneuvers carefully past, and for a moment I meet the driver's eyes: the Jewish boy. He blinks and turns his face away because my flashlight has blinded him.

He's handsome, this boy. Wavy black hair, large nose, brown intelligent eyes, strong chin, heavy shadow of beard. A nice normal guy, you see them all the time. "Move along," I tell him unnecessarily. He has no intention of stopping. He gives me and my car wide berth, and is gone in a blaze of red taillights.

I still want him. Want him more, now that I've seen the shadow of his beard. Things are clicking inside me, and my desire is growing clearer and stronger. I like men. I like working with guys. Female cops are okay, if they do their job, but I wouldn't want to share a locker room with them. I like sweaty hard bodies and rough camaraderie. I like pulling pranks on the other guys and trying to outwit them when they retaliate in kind. I want somebody who can take it as rough as I give it, somebody who gives it back in spades.

I flick off the flashlight and jump into the squad. I throw it into reverse and fly backwards down the narrow road, not taking time to turn around until I hit the previous parking area. Driving backwards at speed is one of the fun parts of being a cop. I'm chasing a suspect, I'll do whatever I have to do to stay with him.

I keep my lights off, eyes scanning for traffic. Taillights. I follow at a discreet distance. At the exit from the park he stops at the sign, properly legal, then turns left, away from civilization. The road is straight here, and I sit at the sign while a couple of cars back up behind me. He disappears over the crest of the hill. Line of sight broken, I know he thinks he lost me, if he ever noticed I was behind him. I turn left, snapping on my headlights and roaring away from the stop sign, trying to overtake him. The guys in the cars behind me know I'm after someone, and thank their God it isn't them.

I brake as I crest the hill; a speeding car attracts attention. There before me, going over the next crest, is a set of taillights. We are the only two cars on the road. Yet it might be a different vehicle turned on the road between him and me. When it disappears over the rise I speed again, playing Red Light, Green Light, like a kid. If you catch me moving, I lose. If I catch you, I win.

My balls are aching, my chest is aching, a migraine is starting behind my eyes. I need him, I have to do it, I can't stand the suspense of wanting anymore.

I'm closing on him; it's the same make of vehicle, only one person in it, it must be him. I continue closing, then he turns down a tree-lined side road. It winds, and I wonder if he's trying to lose me. I catch up, pace him, check the radar gun. He's doing exactly the posted limit on each curve. Nobody drives that neatly unless a cop is on their tail. He knows I'm there.

He takes another turn, down a dead-end road to the quarry. He didn't see the sign. Or did he? During the day the road rumbles with trucks, but at this hour it is deserted and will stay deserted. I pop the lights.

It takes a moment, but he pulls over. I pull behind him and switch off my headlights. I don't call it in. The radio crackles, an officer needs backup. I'm far far away, someone else will cover it.

I take a deep breath to steady my nerves, then get out. My jack boots crunch on the gravel. He is rolling down his window, offering his license to me. "Is something the matter, officer?" he asks, trying to sound innocent.

I accidentally deliberately bump my nightstick against his car door and he flinches. "Evening," I say, polite as always. Cops are always polite. I peruse the license. I should have called it in, he might be wanted for something. You never know. More cops die making traffic stops than anything else. But he looks like such a nice Jewish boy. And Jeffrey Dahmer looked like such a nice white boy.

"Martin Siegel," I read by the light of the flashlight. "That Jewish?"

He tenses. Southern deputies are infamous bigots. "Yes." He answers reluctantly.

I almost laugh at his fear. I read his address aloud. "This your current address?"

"Yes."

I memorize it.

Then I shine the light over his face. He holds up his hand to shield his eyes, so I lower the flashlight beam.

"Sorry about that. Could you step out of the car, please?"

"Why?"

The stars are very bright through a ragged hole in the tree tops, the crickets are chirping, and a ground fog is creeping about my ankles.

"Just routine," I say. It isn't. I step back, giving him room to get out of the car.

He hesitates, torn between arguing and obeying, not sure exactly what his rights are, not sure what I'm up to.

That makes two of us.

I move off about twenty yards. "Walk towards me, please." There is no yellow line or I'd make him walk it.

"Oh." He's relieved. He thinks he knows what this is about now. He gets out confidently. He hasn't been drinking, he'll have no problem passing a sobriety test, and then he can get back into his car and go home, and tell his buddies how he got off easy.

He walks straight towards me, with a natural gait, almost cocky. I move the flashlight in a little circle. "Now the other way." He turns and walks away from me. I admire the way his butt moves under tight gray slacks.

He reaches his car, turns and faces me again. I'm getting hard, so I shine the light at him. I'm a dark shape behind the glare and he lifts his hand to protect his eyes. His night vision is shot.

"Turn around and put your hands on the roof of the car," I say.

"Sir?" he squeaks. He's scared again. I'm weirding him out, this big, black, laconic, bigoted deputy that he thinks I am.

"Please turn around and put your hands on the roof of the car." I'm polite, but firm. He can't accuse me of rudeness or hostility or anything. I'm hassling him, but I'm within the limits. I haven't done anything I can't defend to my supervisor.

Using one hand I frisk him in a business-like way, pulling his wallet and his condoms out of his pockets and throwing them on top of the car. He holds utterly still, rigid beneath my hands. My touch is feather light on his body, tracing the lines of muscle, feeling the tension of his body. I want to kiss away the hardness of his body, want to see him melt under my mouth like he did the redhead. I can't, it's an awful impropriety. My hand lingers a bit, sliding up the inside of his thighs, caressing him, but I can't help it. I frisk his crotch, fondling his balls while my own erection grows. He can accuse me of lewdness now, but it won't stick. Nobody will believe him. Sam, Deputy of the Year, groping a faggot? No way.

I flick off the flashlight and lay it on top of the car. I'm using both hands now, sliding them into his pockets, my breath hot on the back of his neck. "You have anything else in your pockets?" I breathe. It's supposed to be a demand, but it comes out a whisper.

"No sir," he gulps. He wears no underwear. I feel him through the thin fabric of the pockets, my fingers tracing the shaft folded over to the left, and cupping his balls from the right. I am definitely out of line now, but there's no proof, my word against his. I pull his cock gently, feel it lengthen in my hand. His shoulders bunch and release, and my mouth comes down on the back of his neck.

I kiss him fervently, my hands masturbating him through the cloth and he starts to pant, his cock coming up quick and hard. The strangeness of the encounter has us both in its grip; he is frightened about what I might do, but relieved that I am not arresting or beating him. His confusion makes him vulnerable to my will.

My hands withdraw from his pockets and move to his belt. "I'm gonna have to strip-search you. You wouldn't believe where some people hide contraband."

This is risky, it might produce physical evidence: a bit of mud on the pants where they fall around his ankles, a scratch as I accidentally clip him with my fingernail. I don't stop. My hands caress his ass, tracing the firm cheeks and running through the dark hair. One hand slips in front to clasp his shaft as one hand slides into the crack between his cheeks.

"Bend over and spread 'em," I order.

He bends obediently, ass jutting towards me. I put my nightstick between his legs and bounce it between his thighs a couple of times. "Wider." He spreads them as wide as the slacks around his ankles will allow. His balls are visible, hanging between his legs. He's sweating, the moisture gathering in the crack of his ass. He's scared out of his wits and horny as a stallion. He will do whatever I want him to do.

I could slap him on the ass and laugh. "I really had you going, didn't I?" Then he'd cuss me out and maybe make a complaint to my supervisor.

Relations between the gay community and the sheriff's department would continue at their usual sour rate. The other deputies would tell me I had a crude and nasty sense of humor. Life would go on.

It was intolerable that I should continue with this aching in my body, this need in my heart, never to find satisfaction.

"Now hold real still, this won't hurt a bit." I spit on my hand and stick a finger into his asshole. He jumps and clenches, gasping in surprise. "I believe in thoroughness."

I probe him inside, find his prostrate and stroke it. It's round and smooth and nice to touch and he moans in response. He quivers and thrusts back against my hand. I pump his cock with my other hand. He doesn't know what to think, this deputy jacking him in the middle of the night, his cock so hard and balls so full that all he wants to do is come, and he has no idea if it's going to happen or not.

I caress his leg with the nightstick, and the way he flinches sends a thrill along my spine. I kiss his neck again, nibble his ear. I slide two fingers into his ass and he bucks wildly.

"Now boy, I can't have you resisting my search. I'm gonna have to handcuff you."

I pull his arms behind his back and he doesn't resist. I clamp cold metal around his wrists, then put my hand between his shoulder blades and force him forward until his chest touches the car. He pushes his ass backwards towards me, wanting it. My hand tells me his cock is harder than ever. Some guys are like that: put the cuffs on them and they get stiff.

His fingers fumble, then he grips my hard-on through the uniform pants. I lean into it, letting him feel my size and shape, the large uncut head distinguishable even through the fabric.

"If you're going to do it, just do it!" he cries.

I pick up one of his condoms and he tenses as he hears the foil rip. He knows what that sound is. His hands work quickly, unzipping my trousers and fishing inside for my meat. I watch as he produces my length from inside my briefs; he's had practice undressing men. I put the condom on, then his hand pulls me to his ass. I set the point against the wrinkled flesh and brace myself. This is the moment of truth, this is the felony crime, this is the ruin of my career if word gets out, this is the temptation too fierce to resist.

I slide into him. He's tight, but the condom is lubed, we fit. I grip his hips tightly, overwhelmed by the feeling of a man's muscular ass milking my cock. His muscles are tightening and relaxing around my prick, sending a buzz of sensation through my body. If I move, I'll lose control, I'll bust a nut like a schoolboy. I bite his neck and he cries out in pain. Good. I can tell the difference. I was afraid I wouldn't know if I hurt him.

I start with long slow strokes and he squirms, panting and thrusting back. I hold his hips, not letting him impale himself on me like he desperately wants. I have to keep control, have to make it last, have to savor every sensation: the smell of two men rutting, the wriggling of his ass, the sweat sticking my shirt to my back, everything must be blazoned in my memory. It can't be over too quickly, it has to take enough time to matter.

But I can't last, not the way he's panting and moaning and trying to get it. I grind into him, feeling like the top of my head is going to blow off, and I move my hips in a circle, trying to circumvent the need to go for broke.

He's swearing and grabbing my shirt with his metal bound hands, trying hard to make me give him what he wants.

My resistance melts, nothing is left but the short strokes, and I pound him, fingers biting deep enough into his hips to leave bruises, but neither of us care. I slam into my climax, jerking out of him and ripping off the condom, spurting strings of white all over his ass. I have to do this, I need visible proof that I have fucked a man. I have to see it with my own eyes. If I'd spurted inside him it would have been one more used condom on the side of the road, and nothing but a wet dream to haunt my nights. But the white stuff glows palely against the dark hair of his ass, saying, "This is real. I did it."

I squeeze my cock, pumping the last drops of cum from my slit, wiping it off by rubbing it up and down the crack of his ass. I want to put it back in him, but I'm losing it. I've come twice already in the last half hour, I'm not as young as I used to be. Number three will take a while.

He moans in helpless frustration, cock jutting before him, bound hands rubbing the cum into his skin. I think about leaving him that way, squirming with need so that he jumps the first man who comes along. But I haven't got the will. There is something else I must do.

I turn him around and kneel before him. I slip the circumcised tip of his cock between my lips, tasting the sour precum oozing from the slit. He might be diseased, this might kill me, but I have to know what another man tastes like. Otherwise I could of bought one of those inflatable dolls. My hat brim bumps his belly and I take it off, dropping it on the gravel beside me. My knees hurt and I shift, brushing gravel clear from a spot.

I return to contemplation of his cock. With my tongue I trace its veins, circle the hairy balls. I fit one of the balls into my mouth, feeling its size and shape and texture. I pick hair off my tongue and concentrate on the hairless shaft instead. He's long, not particularly thick, curved a little to the left. I cup his balls in my hand, feeling their weight and liking it. I press my nose against the sac, breathing in the musky male scent of sex and sweat and fear. But he's not afraid of me anymore, though the tang of it is still on his skin. He watches me with wide eyes, my dark hand against his hairy pale crotch, my mouth exploring his flesh.

I open my mouth and pull his hips forward, taking as much of his length as I can manage. There is a trick to it, but I don't have it. I can only get it halfway in before I gag. I slide it back and forth, trying to ease it a little further down my throat each time, and he's breathing hard, hips moving with me, propelling his cock into my face.

I hold still for a moment, and he pumps in and out of my mouth. I've fucked a man and now he's fucking me. I close my eyes tight and make a great effort to suck down the whole cock. He surges forward, forcing me to take him, and I do. I choke, stop breathing, then realize my nose is buried against his hair. I'm doing it, and he's coming.

I jerk him out of my mouth, and he shoots over my shoulder, splattering my back. Some of it is in my mouth and I know I should spit it out, should minimize contact with possibly contaminated fluids, but I don't. I savor it, tasting the flavor of a man's passion in my mouth.

When he catches his breath I stand up. Only now do I kiss him. This is awkward for me. I've never fantasized about kissing a man, never craved it until I was crazy, never risked my job and my reputation for a kiss.

His mouth opens under mine, and his tongue meets mine in the middle, caressing mine with the same arousing motion his hands made on my cock when he was trying to get me to fuck him. It's interesting, this masculine way of kissing. I keep on kissing him, tasting his lips and his teeth, his tongue and the inside of his mouth. Hesitantly I slip my hand up and find his nipple underneath the shirt. He moans into my mouth and I know I've found the right spot; I toy with it experimentally.

"Jesus Christ," he mutters. "You're making me horny all over again." It's a dark and lonely road. No one will come here all night. We can keep going. But the radio is squawking in the squad car, and belatedly I wonder how long I've been out of touch. "I know where you live," I tell him. "Come by," he answers. "I get off at six. Will you still be up?" Six a.m. Daylight. Normal people get up then. "I'll be waiting." "Good." I unlock the cuffs. He pulls up his pants and collects his personal items. He gets unsteadily into the car, and pauses to look back at me. I lift my hand in farewell. He pulls away, making a U-ee back towards the main road. Only when he is gone can I bring myself to lift the radio and mutter some excuse into it. Will I go? Or will dawn restore me to my senses and send this all to the realm of half-remembered dreams? My cock is hot in my lap and I put my hand down to cover it. It stirs. I won't be able to forget. I put the cruiser in gear and pull back onto the road.

steel gray

KEN BUTLER

The bar was dark, and I searched for a seat as my eyes adjusted to the light spilling over from the dance floor. I found an empty stool at the bar and slid onto it. The guy on my left was lucky that the bartender hadn't carded him—if he was twenty-one, I was a straight arrow. Since I'm attracted only to older men, I ignored him. After an initial gawk and hesitation, he actually had the guts to cruise me with his eyes, but one hard stare from me and he quickly turned away. I ordered a beer and took a look around.

The guy on my right seemed much more interesting, even though I couldn't see his face. He was in a fairly intense conversation with the man to his right, and all I could see was the great shock of silver-gray hair covering his head. But his shoulders were wide and his waistline was just perfect as far as I was concerned—not fat and not fit. A small paunch had begun to creep over his belt and the butt on the stool had begun a little spread of its own. Just my type.

I didn't have a chance. In a few minutes, he stood and left with his companion after calling a good-bye to the bartender. The voice was a relaxed baritone that sent a wave from my gut down to my cock. I cursed my luck as I watched his back leave the bar. Damn, not even a glimpse of his face, I thought, as I signaled for a beer.

The bartender, who couldn't have been farther from my type but assumed that I must be attracted to him simply because he was good looking, sauntered over with a longneck for me. Tony was taut, muscular like me, and wore only a worn pair of chaps behind the bar, his sizable meat swinging freely between tree-trunk thighs.

"Who was that, Tony?"

"Don't know. Haven't seen him before. Good tipper, though, especially for a Friday." He sauntered away, sure he had broken my heart once again.

The next week, I was at the bar a half-hour earlier in the evening, but that shock of silver-gray was nowhere to be seen. The same the next week, and the next. I decided I'd give him one more week. Hell, maybe he was a travelling salesman with a month-long route. I couldn't believe how obsessed I was becoming with a man whose face I'd never seen, but that wasn't going to stop me from sitting on that bar stool for at least one more Friday.

I had to work late that Friday, so I didn't have time to change clothes, but drove straight to the bar, still in my suit and tie. The shoulders I'd memorized were not in evidence, though, so I found a stool and didn't even look up to acknowledge Tony when a beer appeared.

"Thanks," I mumbled.

"What's with you?"

"Nothing, I guess."

"Yeah, whatever," and he was gone, seeking adulation from another.

After a bit I headed to the bathroom and caught a flash of gray hair at the front door out of the corner of my eye. I backed up a step to peer around—and there he was, paying the cover charge. He was alone, and I willed my bladder to relax. I wasn't going to let him out of my sight again.

He spoke to a few men at tables and nodded to a kid on the dance floor, but settled onto a stool by himself. I willed myself to walk over slowly to the stool on his right. He was watching Tony's ass jiggle as his martini was shaken, and I waited until Tony placed the drink down; then I took a deep breath and said, "I'll have another beer, Tony."

Tony cocked his head quizzically, then looked at my eyes and didn't have to ask why I'd moved down the bar. "Sure, Jerry, coming right up."

The object of my fascination turned to me, I think to say good evening, but the words never made it out of his mouth. I was about to make my standard self-deprecating joke, but I took one look at his eyes and was equally tongue-tied.

They were like none I'd ever encountered: large, somewhat rounded at the corners, a bright gray that stopped me cold. They sparkled like highly polished stainless steel, and the thick lashes that encircled them were the same silver-gray as the hair on his head. So was the bushy mustache hanging over his lip, and his ruddy complexion made the intense gray even brighter. And despite the gray, I guessed he was no older than fifty.

He was as surprised as anyone is when he first lays eyes on me, I guess—I'm living proof that they grow 'em bigger out in the Midwest. Indiana-born and raised, I grew up in a farming family and never felt out of place physically until I moved west. I'm six-foot-seven and weigh about three hundred twenty pounds, the last twenty of which is extra weight, gained when I stopped working out, trying to break the jock image I was afraid I'd never shake because of my size and the circumference of my biceps. I have straw-yellow hair, fair skin that reddens instead of tanning, and blue eyes that are considered piercing in their own right, though nothing like the pair staring back at me.

He regained his composure first. "Forgive me, son, I didn't mean to stare, but it's not often you turn around to see a linebacker next to you. I hope you won't take offense."

"None taken," I said, pleased I could speak again. "And I hope you don't consider this a cheap pick-up line, because I don't mean it to be, but I've never seen eyes the color of yours. They're beautiful." I started to blush. I embarrass easily. I tried to cover up by sucking down half my beer.

"I'll take it as a compliment, then," he said with a wink. "Thank you. My name's R.J., and yours is Jerry, right?"

"Right. Jerry Sanders."

"R.J. McIntyre." He offered his hand.

"I saw you here a month ago," I said. "I hoped you'd come back. I wanted to meet you."

He raised one bushy eyebrow. "I don't remember you, and I think I would."

"I sat next to you at the bar, but you were really involved with some guy."

After a beat, he said, "Oh, him. What a waste of time."

"Sorry." I grinned.

"So, Jerry," he said, "I'll be obnoxious. Just how big are you, son?"

"Six-seven, three-twenty." At least he hadn't beat around the bush before he asked. "Does that make some sort of difference to you?"

"No, son, not at all. I'm just curious, and crass enough to ask. But I suppose everyone asks you that."

"Sooner or later. I've got all the comeback lines down pat."

At that, he reached over and patted my forearm, squeezing its muscled firmness gently before reaching back for his drink. I went for more of mine, too, only to find the bottle nearly empty. Tony walked by, and R.J. said, "Another beer for my newest friend, bartender."

Tony smiled. "Sure thing."

"So," R.J. said, "tell me a little about yourself." That was always the next question, after they'd asked about my size. By now, I had an honest, pat answer.

"Midwestern. Farmer. 4-H blue ribbons to prove it. Football and wrestling at Indiana University. Excelled at neither—no killer instinct, my coaches said. Degree in computer science like everybody else in the mid-eighties. Moved to the Silicon Valley just in time for the layoffs to begin. Moved north and managed to get into computer games at just the right time. I make a comfortable living, but don't have many friends.

"And I'm not a top," I finished. "Surprised?"

"Yes, but not disappointed." My heart beat a little faster. "Okay, my turn. California. Common as dirt. No college. Worked for my pop's construction business until he died; that was years ago. Took it over, became very successful, but hated it, so I sold it and live on the dividends. I'm lazy, I guess." He chuckled. "Actually, I raise money for charities, just to keep myself from drying up and blowing away. You gotta do something when you're my age, or your brain just quits."

"You sound like you think you're old."

"I am old."

"Fifty isn't old."

He patted my arm again. "Bless you, son. You sure know how to stroke an old man's ego."

"How old are you?"

"I just celebrated my sixty-second birthday."

"Bullshit."

He reached back and pulled out his wallet with a little sigh, like maybe he too had done this often before, and opened it to the first cellophane window. "Read it and I'll weep for you." Sure enough, the birth date read June first, 1935. I was impressed, and said so.

"Don't be. I've just got good genes. God knows I don't take care of myself like you do." I blushed and he noticed. Slapping his forehead with his hand, he said, "Shit, Jerry, I'm sorry. I just keeping chewing on that foot in my mouth, don't I?"

"It's okay," I said, because I sensed that he was truly contrite.

"It's just that you're so damned built. Good-looking, too." My blush doubled and he chuckled. "So, go ahead, ask me something personal—anything."

I knew just what I wanted to ask. "Is the hair on your body the color of your mustache?"

"Well, why don't you reach over, unbutton my shirt, and find out for yourself?" And he stared into my eyes with those killers of his.

I was flabbergasted. No one had ever been this direct with me, and my cock started to grow in my slacks as I shakily reached out to finger the top button of his cotton shirt. It slipped out of the hole easily, and I ran my hand down to unfasten the next button, and the next. I then used the side of my hand to pull back the edge of the shirt and was rewarded with the gray forest for which I'd hoped. Tony walked by, acted like he was going to say something, then walked on silently.

I sucked in a breath. "Like what you see?" he asked.

"Yes, sir."

"Well, boy," he replied, lowering his voice slightly, "if you've got a place, you could see the whole package."

I was shocked at his candor, but turned on by the direct proposition. I blushed yet again.

R.J. put an arm on my shoulder and kneaded it gently. "Boy, you're just about the best-looking man I've ever seen. Doesn't everyone say that to you?"

"No, they don't.'"

"They should." He stood, left Tony a ten-dollar tip, straightened something that seemed cramped in his pants, and started off through the crowded bar.

He stopped outside. "Where are you parked?"

"Right over there. Do you want to follow me?"

"No, son, I want to ride with you. That way you can't just kick me out the door if you don't like me," he said, laughing.

"Don't worry. I like you. Very much."

R.J. reached up and caught the back of my neck, pulled my face down to his, and kissed me. I could feel the heat in my face as he let me go, and was glad it was dark enough that he couldn't see my now perpetually red face. I couldn't believe how bold he was, kissing me like that out in the open, but I liked it. I knew he simply didn't care who saw.

I opened the door for him, then walked around and got into the Lincoln, one of the few cars large enough for my frame.

My house isn't far from the bar, but the ride was memorable. As soon as I pulled out of the lot, he grabbed my hand and placed it on the crotch of his pants. The bulge beneath the cloth was sizable and rock hard. I kneaded it carefully, gauging its size, then reached down to cup his scrotum and gently squeeze his balls. He sighed and unzipped his pants.

I tried to extract his cock from the folds of cloth.

"Wait," he said. He unbuttoned his slacks, pulling back the edges of the fabric, then reached down into his boxers and pulled out his cock and balls. The car swerved slightly as I looked over in fascination.

R.J. guided my hand to his thick shaft, and I gently pumped him a few times, then kneaded his balls again. I'm especially fond of testicles, and his felt fat, just like the cock above them. I was slightly surprised that he was circumcised, but filed that question away for the future.

"Now, pull on my balls." I complied, and he sighed again.

I pulled into my driveway and had no sooner stopped the car than he was getting out, holding his pants with one hand as he stroked his shaft with the other. I prayed that none of my neighbors were looking out their windows, and moved quickly to open the front door.

He walked right in, then turned to face me as I locked the door. He opened his hand, and his pants fell in a heap at his feet. I stepped forward and pulled the boxers down with a jerk. He kicked off his loafers and stepped out of the heap around his feet. "R.J." I began.

Those beautiful eyes narrowed. "What happened to 'sir'?" There was no menace in his voice.

"I'm sorry, sir."

"Get on your knees." I obeyed. He loosened my tie, slipping it out from around my button-down collar. Then he tied it tightly around his cock and balls. I gasped as his cock grew another inch before my eyes, then looked at him in wonder and lust. "I like that look in your eyes, Jerry. We're going to enjoy this, aren't we?"

"Yes, sir."

He grabbed me gently by the neck and guided my face to his cock. I opened my mouth, saliva collecting in its crevices. In one smooth motion, he buried most of that cock down my throat, backing out gently to let me lube him with spit. Then he plunged roughly down my throat again, and we both moaned in pleasure.

"When I first looked at you, I didn't think I'd have a chance. But when you said that you weren't a top, I knew I was going to have you, boy." I groaned around his shaft, and he continued. "I didn't think you'd unbutton my shirt, but you did. That's when I knew I could probably do whatever I wanted with you. Right?"

I tried to nod, and he backed out so I could get a breath of air. But he plunged back in before I could speak, and I looked up at him as he said, "You don't need to talk, Jerry. I know all about you. I'm gonna work you over good, boy, and we're both gonna enjoy it." A tear slid down my cheek. This was what I so desperately needed and never seemed to find, and I couldn't believe that it was happening to me with this gorgeous man.

He looked down, saw the tear, reached to brush it away, then backed out of my throat. "Stand up." He took me in his arms and I leaned to kiss him. The kiss became passionate, and my breath became ragged as it continued for the next minute.

He broke. "Where's the bedroom?" He stripped off his shirt as he followed me there, then collapsed onto the bed. I turned on the lamp on the dresser so I could get a look at him naked.

He was covered in that beautiful gray hair, and looked as if he had once been muscular. Time and a thin layer of fat, along with all that hair, had softened the outlines of his body. He turned me on naked more than he had clothed, but I found myself constantly drawn back to his eyes.

"Strip for me, boy. Let's see what's under that suit." I pulled frantically at my coat. "Slower." Off came my coat, then, slowly, my shirt, then my loafers. Then I unbuttoned my braces and unhooked my pants, letting them fall as I pulled the braces up over my shoulders. That left only my undershirt and my briefs, which were tented out uncomfortably in front of me.

"That's far enough for now. I want to make you sweat before I peel those briefs off of you." His sexiness made my balls ache.

"Come to me." I walked to the edge of the bed and placed one knee on the mattress, then lowered myself beside him, took him in my arms while he kissed me—for a long time. I was panting again before he let me up for air.

He backed out of my embrace and casually lifted an arm. I attacked the pit without being asked, pleased that he wore no deodorant, and licked and sucked the skin clean, revelling in his musk. He lifted the other arm into the air; I worked my mouth across his hirsute chest, paying attention to both erect nipples before plunging into his other pit, snorting in the thick nest of hair and sweat.

When he was clean, I got up on my knees and licked down his chest, cleaning his navel along the way. My forehead bumped against something and then my lips found the base of his cock.

I made a hard arrow of the tip of my tongue and jiggled it up his shaft, plunging down over him with my mouth when I reached the tip. The wide head bumped against my soft palate and I fought the urge to gag. I forced myself down farther, and the tickle subsided as the shaft penetrated deep into my throat. I held him as long as I dared, then swiftly expelled him, sucking in a deep breath. But his hand found the back of my head and he shoved down, hard. I took all of him again, and we groaned together again as my nose bumped against his soft, fleshy scrotum.

He worked my mouth around his cock, pushing with his hand and urging me on with shallow thrusts from below. I started to sweat. At some point my pelvis began to thrust of its own accord, and soon I felt a knuckle kneading my asshole through my briefs. I backed against it, eager for the pressure. A hand landed on my ass, hard. I groaned louder.

Then R.J. pulled on my balls through the cloth, and groan turned to plaintive moan.

"Like that?" I nodded furiously. "So do I." Still sucking his shaft, I reached around my head to grab his scrotum. His balls had a nice heft, and I pulled them out and away from his cock. I was surprised at how far the flesh stretched, but finally the skin tightened. I pulled my mouth away, then let myself fall on his sword yet again, swallowing hard as my nose touched the tightly stretched skin. I twisted the testicles a quarter turn, and this time the groan from above was half an octave deeper.

"Oh, yeah, Jerry. I like that." His grip on my testicles was merciless, and the bunched cotton cloth was rough against my now-sensitive sac. He released me suddenly.

"Stand up. Take 'em off." I grabbed the hem of my undershirt and pulled it over my head. He gasped when he saw my chest, which I keep hairless despite the fact I'm not working out anymore. It's one of my best features, and he sat up to run a hand over my pecs.

Then I hooked my thumbs in my briefs, turned to face away from him, and bent over as I slid them over my thighs. I wanted him to know my ass was his if he wanted it, and was rewarded with his thumb against my hole.

I also keep the hair around my cock clipped short, which makes my average endowment look just a bit longer. When I turned, he grabbed my cock so hard that I fell to my knees on the bed beside him, and he pumped it several times before letting go.

"Get back on my balls."

I scooped them into my mouth, sucking and chewing for a long time, until precum leaking from his cock ran down the shaft to wet my cheek. He smoothed the fluid into my skin with a finger while a knuckle found my hole. I impaled myself on the folded digit.

"A condom, Jerry. I'm gonna fuck you." I stumbled to the bureau to dig out my stash, chose a black condom, ripped the package open and rolled it down his fat firm cockflesh. Then back to the drawer for lube, which I squeezed over the condom, rubbing until it was slick and shiny. My silk tie would be ruined, but I didn't care.

He stood. "On the bed, on your knees." I crawled up, leaving my ass hanging over the mattress edge. He picked up the lube, went to rummage in the drawer, found a latex glove. He skinned it on over his right hand and squirted a sizable blob of lube into his sheathed palm.

Seconds later, a finger went up my ass with no preamble. "Tight," was all he said, as I sucked in air to quench the fire in my ass. I don't get fucked often, but he calmed me by working the one finger until I was open to it. Then he pulled out, put two fingers together and slowly slid them in.

It felt good this time. I moaned with pleasure, groaned at the shadow of pain. "Tell me," he ordered.

"They feel big. I don't get fucked much, so they're really stretching me out."

"Can you take three, son?"

"Yes, sir." Two were removed, and soon three fingertips were poised at the edge of my butthole.

"Tell me what you want."

"Your fingers in me, sir."

"How many?"

"As many as you want, sir."

"My fist?"

"I've never been fisted, sir. But for you, I'll try anything."

He chuckled. Three fingers pushed inside me to the second knuckle. He stopped briefly, pushed again, and a fourth firm digit bumped against the back of my balls. R.J. rubbed and stretched my hole, and I bucked back to meet them, twisting my pelvis in pure pleasure. My moans mounted in intensity—it was then he slid the fourth finger in.

I was hotter than I'd ever been. I wanted him in me, and was willing to do anything to get him there. I whispered: "Please fuck me, please fuck me, please fuck me, please fuck me," as most of his hand assaulted my ass. He kept lubing me until the viscous goo was trickling down the back of my legs.

"What are you saying, Jerry?"

I gave full voice to my desire. "Fuck me, R.J. Please fuck me, sir. Shove your cock up my ass and fuck me hard."

"Are you hot enough?"

"Yes, sir, yes, sir," I panted, rotating my ass in tight circles around his fingers.

He pulled his fingers out in one smooth motion, peeled off the glove, rested his slick cock against my butthole and commanded: "Fuck it yourself."

I took him in one hard pelvic thrust. He gasped at the ferocity of my stroke, grabbed my waist tightly with his strong hands, dug his nails into my flesh. The pattern of pain felt good to my pleasure-starved nerve endings. I rocked forward on my knees, then slammed back onto him, setting up a rhythm that he matched quickly. His hands on my waist were merciless, squeezing and pinching, pulling me back onto him again and again. His cock was fully distended, filling me more, far more, than his four fingers had. My asshole was hot and raw from the condom, but I wanted more.

My cock was throbbing and I longed to touch it, but I needed both hands to steady myself. R.J. had taken over: a part of me was shocked by his sudden animal brutality. He grunted with each thrust—"Gnnuhh, gnnuhh, gnnuhh,"—and the sound was hypnotizing. Then I was grunting with him, pleading for his release, and mine.

"Want my load, boy?"

"Oh, yes, sir." He pounded one last massive thrust into me, and didn't pull out, and I could feel his shaft pulsing as he pumped his orgasm into the condom.

It went on for a glorious forever, and then he began to breathe again, a raspy sated sound as he backed out, his cock kissing my ass goodbye with a soft "pop." The empty feeling was horrible.

R.J. walked back to the drawer, returned with one of the large dildos I keep for those lonely nights. It wasn't my biggest, but it wasn't small.

"Up on your knees." I shifted position. "Face me." I did. He lubed the rubber cock. My own cock ached from not being touched.

R.J. handed me the slick cockthing. "Sit on it, then jack off." I grabbed the dildo and positioned it. He untied the tie looped around his softening cock, and peeled off the sticky condom, tied off its end and dropped it to the floor, all the while watching me drop onto the dildo.

Though I was open, I groaned as my ass cheeks brushed the sheet. "Grab your cock."

There was a little lube on my hand from the dildo, and I smeared it around my cockhead. Then he grabbed my cock and scraped excess lube from the fuck off his hand.

"Play with yourself," he ordered, and I began to stroke my aching cock. It felt great. When he leaned over to stare at me intently, I looked into those piercing gray eyes, more blood pumped into my cock. My orgasm welled up in my balls.

I usually close my eyes when I come, but I wasn't about to let go of the sight of him. The first spurt hit his stomach, a good two feet away. "Yeahhhhh, boy, yeah." Stream after stream of semen poured out of me, onto his abdomen, my balls, my sheets, the floor.

At last I stopped. He stepped forward, pulled my head toward his crotch, made me lick my seed out of his stomach hair, then shoved me down farther until I tongued my self off the sheets. The dildo slid out and dropped to the floor.

We fell back on the bed. He kissed me. His cock stiffened against the muscle of my leg, and my cock hardened in response.

He rolled off of me, lay beside, said: "Do you want to come again, son?"

"If you do."

"I probably can't, but I'll gladly do anything to you that you want if it'll make you come like that again."

I chuckled. "I doubt it. It's been a while, so I guess I had it saved up."

"What do you want to do?"

I hesitated. "Just hold me for a while?"

"Happy to, Jerry." He wrapped his hairy arms around me, and we lay back, snuf, and somehow it was morning.

I sat up with a start as I realized the sun was shining through the window. He awoke at my motion. "What time is it?"

"It's seven-thirty. We slept through the night."

"I was comfortable. You?"

"Yeah." I snuggled back into his arms when they were offered. He held me for a minute, and I kissed him, a kiss he returned with gusto, despite our morning breath.

Eventually we broke—nature called—and he headed for the bathroom, then I took my turn. When I walked back into the room, he was partially dressed. I was disappointed. "Leaving?"

"Actually, I thought I'd buy us breakfast."

"Let's shower first." I led him back to the bathroom, opening the door to the shower. Because of my size, I had installed a party-of-four shower stall—more than spacious for the two of us.

I stripped R.J. and we slipped under the hot, cascading water. He pulled me close, kissed me hard as we soaked under the jets, then turned off the water and gave me the soap. Soon his chest was covered in lather, soap bubbles coating his steel-gray hirsuteness, and I was rock hard. I moved to his genitals. He was stiff. He slid the soap out of my hand, turned me around, soaped my back, lathered my chest from behind, massaging my pecs, gently rubbing my balls and my ready cock. When he was done, our soap-slick bodies slid against each other for a few delicious moments; then he turned the water on again and we rinsed off.

"Kneel," he said. "I really like you, Jerry." His cock was fully hard. "I like what we do to each other. Do you?"

"Yes, sir." I looked up at him.

"Good." He guided my lips to his cock, planted his cockhead between them and slid into my throat. My own cock was still hard and ready.

"Play with yourself. I wanna see you come." I grabbed my cock, stroked it fast and hard. "Slow, son, slow," he said.

We settled into a rhythm of sucking and stroking that soon brought us both to the edge. He pushed me off to finish the job himself, pumping his cock until it exploded over my face. Two more strokes, and I splashed my load against the underside of his balls. Jets of water sprayed over us again when he turned the knob, and the feeling against my tender cock head was almost more than I could bear.

R.J. grabbed me by my armpits and hauled me up. He kissed me again, licking a stray strand of his semen off my cheek. I leaned against the tiles and let him soap me up again, then stepped back into the spray to rinse. Then I soaped him again, and he rinsed. Finally, he turned off the water. We could have rinsed forever.

* * *

He decided to cook for me instead, claiming he didn't want to go to all the trouble of dressing when he knew he was going to be fucking me again before long. I didn't argue: my cock grew hard in my sweat pants as I helped out in the kitchen.

He cooked enough for four, but I noticed that he was no slouch in putting away his half. We didn't talk much, but he reached over twice to squeeze my arm while we ate. I was so happy that I couldn't stop grinning, and I finally said, "I guess you think I'm demented, but I've had a really good time, R.J., and I can't wipe this grin off my face." Then I blushed. He smiled.

After loading the dishwasher we moved into the living room, where he settled in one corner of my large sofa and I sat at his feet, my head in his lap.

He sighed softly, then stroked my head. We didn't speak for a long time; he just ran his hand through my hair, and I wrapped my arms around his knee and sat there, content with him, and with myself.

Soon, though, I felt his cock harden along the back of my neck. I turned and opened my willing mouth to take him in, but he suddenly shoved my head away, grabbed me by the hair and dragged me to the bedroom. His sudden savagery excited me. "Up on the bed, on your knees," he commanded, and I knew he was going to claim me with this fuck.

He rolled a condom down his shaft with one hand, smeared lubricant with the other, wiped what was left onto my asshole. He positioned himself, then paused.

"You're mine, now."

"Yes, sir." Tears welled up in my eyes. He buried himself up my ass in one mighty thrust. His balls slapped mine. I screamed with the pleasure of the pain. And I knew—whether we lived together or separately, whether we were exclusive or open, whether it would last forever or not—today I was his, and tomorrow. It was what we both needed.

Tears flowed down my cheeks. It didn't last long—it couldn't. He exploded inside me and I came without touching myself, my prostate and brain both on sensation overload.

My Daddy collapsed onto me. I took his weight easily, lowering us both to the mattress. I rolled over underneath him until we lay belly to belly, chest to chest, muscle to fur, and he covered my mouth with his. Finally we broke for breath.

"I don't know where or how this is going..."

I cut him off. "It doesn't matter. What will happen, will. I want you, and you want me. That's enough for now. Everything else is just...details."

"I thought you were the shy one," he said, his eyes bright.
I looked straight into those steel grays. "Not any more—not with you."
"Damn right," he said, laying his head on my chest.

The First Branding Journal
Cornelius Conboy

Sunday, May 21

In three weeks I will brand my number one boy. A month ago he asked me if I would mark him permanently, and after much thought and negotiation we arrived at the branding. It will be an "11" on his butt. Eleven is our number; I was born on one, he was born on one, we met on one. On 11/11, that is to say November 11, eleven years ago, we snuck into St. Patrick's Cathedral in New York City and, before they had a chance to throw us out, we married each other.

Since that time we have explored and expanded our limits. His request for a permanent external mark is an outward manifestation of the commitment, love and trust that we have for each other. I can hardly wait.

Wednesday, May 24

In three days I will be attending a workshop on branding being held in a de-commissioned army barracks (God, I love San Francisco). A friend sent an in-depth magazine article that has proved invaluable. On-line, I have discussed a New Yorker's experience being branded six years ago. Others have offered their experiences, good and bad, with the subject. I am not ready to administer the kiss of fire today but I know that I soon will be.

Friday, May 26

The anticipation of the branding is making the boy insatiable. Last night's sex was transcendent, the kind of over-the-top power exchange we fantasize about often and achieve too rarely. I have a new element of play with him. Once his hungry ass has been opened up, after he allows my hands full play inside him, I press my fingers against the inside wall of his butt and trace the brand inside him.

When the moment comes for the red-hot iron on his quivering flesh he will feel it this deep, he will know that my energy will be on him, will go through him to his center and will transform him forever.

He asked that the first thing he feels on his flesh after the iron is my cum.

Saturday, June 2

Last night I realized that, although I am left-handed, the boy has a right-handed butt. While I was inside him tracing out the 11 from within, I got a sudden charge by the thought of having my right hand inside him while applying the iron with my left on the outside. He may end up breaking my wrist, but it is too hot a scene not to pursue.

Saturday, June 10

Tomorrow night we do it. This week has been the most mentally intense period I can remember. One month of foreplay is nearing fruition and it has already exceeded my wildest fantasy. I stopped drinking for the week prior to the branding, he has fasted for the last three days. The sacrament we are about to carry out is not being taken lightly, nor is the potential risk. The branding iron is completed.

I will do the brand in two strikes. The interlude between strikes will fuel his desire and send our endorphins into overdrive. Eleven guests have been invited. At least two are skilled with a whip. The boy's backside will be red hot before a torch ever gets near metal.

Tuesday, June 13

It is done. The night went so far beyond my wildest fantasies that I don't know where to begin. Saturday afternoon the first of our guests from New York arrived. Uzi is an old friend, a filmmaker whose work I have long admired, and I was honored that he could share the ceremony with us. My boy was beyond feeling by this time, he drifted almost in a trance through the day's routine. Finally eleven p.m. came. I look at the assembled guests. Each brings a distinct energy.

At this point my boy needs to be alone, and I take him into a back room and hold him. Our eyes and spirits lock together in anticipation and terror of what is before us. He strips down to his boots and I lock the jewelled collar around his neck, noticing how the large ruby burns with an inner fire, knowing that he will soon burn from an outer one.

I go to see how things are progressing and find the entire party preparing the dungeon. The sling is hung as I instructed, the flogging post is cleared and there is much debate over the height for the stocks. The bottoms are different heights and each has their own preference. I move through the room, picking up the floggers and the cats, laying them out near the whipping post, arranging the candles, double-checking that all restraints are where they need to be and in good condition.

At last I am satisfied that we can begin. I go into the back where my boy is waiting. He shakes as if his spirit is breaking free of the body; he knows that the journey we are embarking on will take us where few have gone, will test us physically and emotionally, will sear through us in ways we have no way of knowing. We lock eyes and souls. We are ready.

Earlier in the day my boy presented me with a wrapped box. I open it to discover a leather hat, its brim as polished as mirror. I put it on and feel a power surge through me. I lead him outside to where the guests are sitting. I thank our friends for coming tonight to help with our ritual, to bear witness to our love, trust and devotion. I look into my boy's eyes and tell him that soon he will be wearing my mark, our mark, that he will have it on him forever just as I am with him forever, just as we have always been and always will be together forever. He speaks softly. He tells me that he is more scared than he has ever been, but with the love and energy and help of our friends he knows that it's going to be great. We laugh and embrace.

I lead him to the flogging post. Slowly, deliberately, I fasten restraints around his wrists and around the pillar. Not too tight, but they will hold him well. I buckle other restraints around his ankles and connect them with chain. I make sure that he has enough room to keep his balance, and know that the pillar will support him no matter what. Finally I bring out the blindfold. Black leather slips smoothly over his head. Softly I whisper in his ear. "Boy, are you ready?" He nods and we begin.

Slowly I lift the flogger over his head, its leather tails cascade down over his shoulders and lower back. I caress his body with my whip, let him get the feel of each pointed strip of leather on his body. Gradually I settle into a rhythm, slowly and gently I increase the force, bringing my arm down over my head and hearing the cadence of each successive strike on his body. The cat dances up and down his back, from shoulders to butt, paying special attention to the right cheek, where our mark will soon be placed. The rhythm increases steadily. The force behind each stroke grows in intensity. I shift speed and my flogger becomes an extension of my arm. With each blow, I transfer energy to the boy. We dance like that and I lose track of the time, I see welts raise up on his body and bring him down slowly, as I had taken him up.

I pick up a new whip, an innocuous-looking instrument to the unknowing, a simple group of a dozen rawhide strips woven together at one end to form a handle. Much lighter than my favorite cat—but this one holds a surprise. At the end of each strip is fastened a sharp metal spike about three-quarters of an inch long that comes to a splendid point. In the wrong hands, this little baby could do serious damage. In mine it takes him to the next level of ecstasy. The boy's backside glows red. He has stopped screaming and now emits only the occasional "Thank you, sir," his voice coming from far away.

Then it is another's turn. Steve is a major Daddy who is well known for his skill with the whip, and I turn the boy over to him. I watch nervously as he uses a leather slapper to supply delirious sensations, and the boy is off again. Though I trust Steve, it is difficult for me to watch as he takes the boy into unknown realms. Their dance together thrills me and I remember that when playing with friends you should always share your toys. With permission, Leather Daddy moves on to my flogger. I am surprised to see it in someone else's arm. His style is different from mine, side strokes prevail compared to my overhead motions. Daddy Steve is exhorting the boy: "Show us how tough you are, show me how much you can take, so that when that red-hot metal comes down on you, you can take it. Show me how strong you are!" To his sublime credit, the boy answers from another plane: "It is not tough, sir, it is want."

I direct Steve away and proceed back into our special communion. The boy has just experienced the flogging of his lifetime and I know it is time to let him down. Pressing my body against his, I slowly undo his wrist restraints and hold him as he collapses against the whipping post. I remove the chains around his ankles and we breathe together. I will not let him come too far down for there is still much to do. I lift him up and lean him against another pillar.

I turn on the torch. The boy is turned around with his back to the pillar, his wrists locked with handcuffs. Again the chains surround his ankles, fastening him securely as I heat the iron. The hissing sound of fire fills the room and a blue light gives out heat freely. The iron takes on a glow of its own, pure heat shines in the darkened room. Slowly I remove the branding iron from the heat and bring it towards my boy, immobile, powerless to resist that which he so wants. I comb his pubic hair with the glowing wand, the smell of burning hair fills the room. Never touching steel to flesh, I stroke his pubes, singeing the curly mass above his dick into a burnt tangle. I hear his breathing coming shorter now; his dick stands rigid out from his body. The hair is gone.

Now he is led to the sling. I watch as he is strapped into place and compose myself for the ultimate focus of the evening. At the table, I handle everything that I will need: the torch has proven its efficacy, the iron is resting. Rubber gloves are in place next to a new jar of Crisco. We are ready. The boy is surrounded by our guests. His butt faces me hungrily and I caress it. I lube up my hands, first pressing one then the other against his waiting hole. Slowly I let him pull me inside, first one finger, then two and three. My hands are alive unto themselves as I work them in and out, back and forth, my thumbs pressing above his balls from the outside as my fingers work the internal muscles they knew so well. He rocks slowly in the sling as with each caress I am pulled further inside him, now four fingers, now six. With parts of both hands inside, I stretch him wide.

Deep inside I see him red and throbbing as I relentlessly stroke his sphincter, urging it to open up and accept me. With four fingers from each hand inside I rotate slowly, rocking the hole back and forth, readying it for the final thrust that takes me totally inside. His sphincter hugs my wrist and I hold it in place, feeling his pulse surround me, feeling the connection of our two bodies. His heartbeat pounds against my arm in a steady rhythm and my wrist responds in kind. I open my fingers and explore the boy's depths. Lightly I brush against the top and bottom of his insides. The left cheek is thoroughly massaged and I move my hand into position on the right.

I can see through his flesh, I can see a straight line from the inked 11 on his outside to where my hand now rests inside. My fingers trace the 11 on him inside and they go through to the surface where it will be marked in fire. I nod to a slave who ignites the torch. He holds the iron over its heat and soon the familiar glow appears. The steel tool stirs from within and comes alive. Our guests gather closer and I remind them to hold down the boy. Eighteen hands are on his body as our eyes meet. "We're going to go there now, boy," I say. I take the iron from our slave. Holding it over the torch, knowing that it is full of its own fire, I move it deliberately to the inked guide.

I didn't hear him scream until later when I watched the video. What I remember is the sudden bucking up, the involuntary reaction when flesh met red-hot metal. The first strike slid for an instant until I exerted more pressure and held it on him, letting my arm and the iron follow the movement of his body. I removed the iron and dropped back, little expecting how drained I would be. I saw the mark, the "1" clearly burnt into his body. There was also a shadow strike, much lighter, but there nonetheless. Our friends had indeed held him but it was a loving laying on of hands—not the immobilizing grip called for.

The iron is repositioned at the torch and I am overcome with the beauty of the brand. This time I make sure he is held securely. I look over at the boy, who is in trance state. His glazed eyes bespeak a bliss unseen before. He now knows what awaits him and desire fills the space. Again the steel glows red, again I take it in my hand and calmly make the second strike. Securely held down, his only movement is a clenching of the teeth, the handle of my flogger held in his mouth for this eventuality. It is done.

I pull myself up, using the chains that hold the harness for support. I walk around to where the boy rocks gently, a drained look of pure ecstasy on his face. I lower myself into his chest and we cling in an embrace of souls. Our bodies have exploded. Like Daedalus and Icarus, we have flown close to the sun. Its energy does not destroy us as we soar through it, rather it caresses us with warmth and light and lets us go, every molecule in our body shattered and drifting back down to the plane of existence we know as reality. I can feel us intermingling on the way down yet somehow we reassemble intact. Physical bodies are altered and psyches are forever changed. At last I am aware of my breath.

The boy is lowered out of the sling. He stands, shakily, his feet connecting with the earth and grounding him. We touch and remain that way as the guests release their energy. Is my boy sucking on Sur's huge black dick? Do I fist one of the boys? It is a blur. I know that when at last I ejaculate it is directly on the brand. Over the next few days I come on it eleven times.

How many of us passed out in my bed later? When I woke there were five. The rest of the weekend blurs: some friends went out, some home. Some returned later, needing to be with others who had shared the experiences. At one point Uzi came by and we watched the video. Eighty minutes of unedited footage, footage I knew had been shot but had been totally unaware of. When we get to the actual branding I lose it. Lying on our bed with my boy's body against me, I know what is coming yet at the first strike I break down and sob uncontrollably. Hearing him scream, seeing him buck, is more than I can handle. I watch as it continues and only regain my composure later, seeing the bliss in his face, matched only by the ecstasy in my own.

The next week in summary
The other boys behaved well, checking in several times a day, stopping by after work. They and I made sure mine spent the next week with his naked butt in the air sipping martinis, eating bon-bons and watching TV. Some boys will do anything to get a week off from work.

Friday, June 22
After ten days, I picked up the flogger again. It was all I could do to remain in control, to only work his upper back and left ass cheek. I had to move around to his front and whip his tits, knowing that the brand is not yet ready for heavy play, as much as both of us want it to be. There will be time for flogging soon enough.

Wednesday, July 12, Final Entry
A month has gone by. My "11" has become a raised mark of pride for the boy. Its flesh responds as sensitively as his nipples and offers all of their possibilities.

motherfuckers
Emanuel Xavier

1989

The fiercest, most notorious graffiti artist in New York City: a puerto-rican banjee boy known to everyone as "Supreme."

A legend in the making with his "FUCK-YOU-ALL-while-sucking-on-a-lollipop" attitude: Mikey X.

They first lowered their sunglasses to clock one another while hustling at the West Side Highway piers.

Supreme: limping up and down Christopher Street with his wooden cane, spitting, crotch-grabbing, smoking big, phat blunts to impress potential clients, the whole time cruising Mikey as he sat trying to sell away his bitter youth.

Mikey: feigning boredom with Supreme's played-out machismo and casting him shade, but lighting candles at night and praying to Oshún, santería goddess of love, for just one night with him—fantasizing the touch of Supreme's milky white skin against his own tanned, olive body; secretly worshipping Supreme while having sex with ugly, old fucks.

Mother's Day

After downing two Crazy Horse forties and smoking a joint, Mikey felt more than pretentious enough to step right up, staring deeply into Supreme's blood-shot green eyes, making out with him right there at the piers—the lampposts hovering, casting carnal images over the Hudson River, sounds of lust drowned out by inane laughter and blaring house music in the background. An overly excited faggot beeps his horn as he drives by, hoping to experience a ménage à trois. LUNCH

BREAK! LUNCH BREAK! Mikey sings out, making it perfectly clear that tonight they belong only to one another.

Without so much as a gesture, they end up back at Supreme's West Side crib. The loft: small, dark, seedy, the smell of piss and Pine-Sol creeping in from the bum-infested hallway. Mikey: captivated by the graffitied walls revealed by the soft white candles Supreme lights.

I'm gonna rape ya, kid! Supreme gleams, ominously, his first spoken words, half joking. Yeah?...well ya' can't rape da willin'! Mikey smirks, bites his lower lip. Supreme lunges before Mikey says another word, thrusting his wet tongue deep inside Mikey's mouth, Mikey's sweet lollipop aftertaste lingering on his saliva, Supreme pushing his stiff cock into Mikey's growing erection.

Mikey: stunned, yet excited by the violent assault, sucking in his breath as Supreme attacks his neck.

Supreme: tossing him viciously onto a bed Mikey hadn't realized lay just behind him, crushing Mikey with unexpected thrilling strength, grinding on top of Mikey, pinning him to the worn, abused mattress, Mikey letting out angry screams as Supreme chews his neck, longing to produce hickeys Mikey will remember him by for days to come.

Mikey: fighting from underneath, desperately trying to push Supreme off, Supreme's teeth tearing through capillaries and sucking until he has left his tag, pulling away to admire it.

Supreme: watching the growing excitement in Mikey's pearl-black eyes.

You bastard, Mikey curses through clenched teeth, the irony in his fiendish smile making him concubine to the quickly reddening hickey.

Supreme: lifting himself off Mikey, reaches down to pull at his over-sized T-shirt, displaying a muscular chest with light, pink nipples.

Mikey: quickly running soft hands down Supreme's definition before peeling off his own tank top, a golden crucifix glistening against his chest.

Supreme: marveling at Mikey's smoothly toned nineteen-year-old body and dark brown nipples, devouring them as if expecting to procure milk, arousing in Mikey a synthesis of pleasure and pain, swelling Mikey's dick.

At that moment Mikey's beeper vibrates with urgent desperation, a trick paging to subdue an insatiable hunger. Supreme snatches it out of Mikey's pocket, tosses it across the room where it smashes against the spray-painted walls.

Supreme: seizing the moment to unzip Mikey's baggy jeans. Underneath, Looney Tunes boxer shorts wrap tightly around Mikey's smooth waist, a thin trail of pubic hair leading seductively from Mikey's belly button towards his bulging crotch, precum stains wet in the image of Marvin the Martian.

Mikey: sighing in ecstasy as Supreme frees his hardening dick from the cotton shorts and feasts on it, closing his eyes to indulge in the warmth of Supreme's mouth engulfing him while gently pulling on his balls, pushing in deeper until Supreme gags, clutching at Supreme's curly brown hair, gently maneuvering himself back towards Supreme's throat and whispering blissful whimpers.

Supreme: caressing the shaft of Mikey's dick with his tongue, pausing to lick his balls, discovering the weak spot between Mikey's legs, resting there, just above Mikey's asshole, then penetrating him with his tongue, saliva streaming down against the hairs surrounding Mikey's entrance, then pulling himself up, edging toward violence, tearing off the rest of Mikey's clothes.

Mikey: lying now completely naked, surrendering on a bed he hasn't yet explored, searching for a pillow while Supreme undresses and introduces his huge uncut dick.

Mikey: tossing the pillow aside, raising himself from the bed and falling to his knees, enchanted by Supreme's altar of a cock.

Now I know why they call ya Supreme! gleams Mikey, gazing up to see his idol smile. It's all yours *papi!* offers Supreme, the words ricocheting in Mikey's mind.

Mikey: skinning back Supreme's foreskin to expose the cock's glistening, purple-red head, licking precum dribbling from the slit, tasting it as it brushes through his lips.

Supreme: beginning to groan, watching as he disappears into Mikey's wet, hungry mouth, his dick getting bigger and fatter, until the foreskin stretches behind the circumference, Mikey relaxing his throat muscles to allow the rock-hard erection in deeper.

Mikey: pushing away to breathe in heavily, fondling his face against Supreme's thick long cock before Supreme digs his fingers into Mikey's hair, pulling Mikey's face back to the awaiting rod, gripping him by the ears, shoving his dick into Mikey's ardent mouth, thrusting until Supreme's cockhead scrapes the back of Mikey's throat, Mikey's crucifix shoved into his mouth along with Supreme's cock.

Yeah, *papi!* That feels good! moans Supreme, while fucking Mikey's face, choking Mikey again and again and again with his shaft, aroused even more by the naked golden Christ ramming in and out of Mikey's throat. Pulling out suddenly, Supreme cries, I don't wanna come yet! picks Mikey off the floor and tongues him down once more, the bitter taste of cock now in their mouths.

Supreme: throwing Mikey back onto the bed, gripping Mikey's arms and pinning him, Mikey struggling underneath him as Supreme spitefully spits into Mikey's open mouth before spreading Mikey's legs apart, ramming his dick against Mikey's butthole, sucking on Mikey's ears, his tongue penetrating deep, as Supreme imagines his cock would, then jumping off the bed and ransacking his drawers for a condom, rolling it down his extended rod, lubricating Mikey's ass, locking eyes with him before jamming deep into Mikey's asshole, feeling the tight bud of skin give way as Mikey shouts in pain, struggling helplessly to pull away from him.

Excited by Mikey's fight, Supreme grabs him by the shoulders, forcing him back down. He is halfway inside before Mikey, using the bedpost, hauls himself away, flipping over. Supreme, lunging on top of him and crushing Mikey with all his weight, mutters Come on *papi!*...ya know ya want me to...ya know ya want me ta fuck you! Sucking Mikey's ear to keep him distracted while he maneuvers his way inside, gradually forcing the resisting muscles to open, Mikey mouthing a silent scream before Supreme inserts his thumb into his mouth.

Mikey: biting the thumb without hesitation as Supreme thrusts harder, pounding in and out, his hollering muffled by Supreme's thumb as Supreme curses under his breath.

Yeah *papi,* yeah, that's it, Supreme screams, that's it. Just bite me harder...yeah...that shit feels good! Thrusting deeper, Supreme feels...hears...Mikey's guts enrapturing him, watches muscled ass cheeks palpitate under his heaving chest. Supreme disappears, reappears repeatedly, in and out of Mikey, searing the sensitive inner linings of Mikey's ass, hints of blood staining the bedsheets, Mikey's asshole burning like crimson as Supreme pierces roughly, the magic pain intensifying, Supreme pounding, lacerating whatever internal walls Mikey's body may have supported, Mikey reaching down to grab his own dick and jerk off, distracting himself from the mounting pain, the bed, knocking knocking knocking against the hollow wall as Supreme shoves his cock in farther and farther, tearing into the core of Mikey's being, his face one endless contortion after another.

Yeah baby!...I want ta see ya come! Supreme pleads, feeling Mikey jerking off beneath him, Mikey beating himself faster, in tune with Supreme's pumping, the stridency of Supreme's thighs slapping against his ass, escalating with the fierce rhythm of their distorted grunts, Supreme plunging further into him, his cum boiling up. Oh yeah *papi!*...you're gonna make me come!...you're gonna make me come! Mikey yells. Yeah baby yeah yeah yeah, Supreme hollers as Mikey convulses beneath him, Mikey's milky white scum shooting out over the bed. Supreme roars, pulls out of Mikey, snatches off the rubber and jerks himself, shooting his own hot, sticky load across and onto Mikey's back, his cum splattering as he screams and screams before toppling on top of Mikey like a corpse.

Both of them, exhausted, struggle for air until the room stops spinning; lying barely conscious, Mikey dimly aware that the golden Jesus crucifix no longer dangles from his neck.

Consciousness returns, and with it a wicked idea to Mikey's mind, causing him to laugh spontaneously. Supreme, turning him over and staring with abandon into Mikey's decadent glistening eyes, plants a kiss on Mikey's lips, falls victim to his contagious laughter.

Mikey pulls himself up off the bed, sits on top of Supreme, and glowers devilishly. A sudden trickle of golden piss floods Supreme's sweaty chest, Supreme's face contracts into bewilderment. Happy Mother's Day, motherfucker! Mikey smiles, ever so wryly.

Blue Hawaii

Robert Goldstein

1.

If any song best expresses the state of Hawaii it would have to be "Tiny Bubbles." For those of you who don't know it, it goes like this: *tiny bubbles/in the wine/make me happy/make me feel fine.* It's this confusion of alcoholism with innocence that causes so much trouble for Hawaii. She doesn't know that she's become a drunken whore: legs spread for all comers. These are my thoughts as I sit in the t-room of a cheap hotel. The music is all-pervasive. Tiny bubbles is replaced by pearly shells. And I've been lucky to get a booth with a glory hole. I'm waiting for some lovely hula hands to grace the stall next to mine. So far, it's been only a couple of nervous nellies and one feisty old fucker who beat off to the strains of "Blue Hawaii": *the night is young/and so are we.*

2.

Now alone for an hour. What do you do when you've been abandoned in the t-room of a cheap hotel? You notice how obnoxious the music is...you cock your head when the door squeals open...you pray that the guy who takes the stall next to you isn't some stupid tourist who mistakes you for an Hawaiian experience: "That Ala Mo-ana Hotel was jus' craw-lin' with Poly-knee-shuns!" *Cum with me/to Blue Hawaii/the night is young/and so are wheeeeeeee!*

3.

Ala Moana Boulevard. Split by metal guard rails. There's a big yellow moon. Drizzle. Splash of neon and chaser lights. Everyone wears a strand of flowers around his neck. The air is rich with scent. Like the perfume counter at Woolworth's: "I'll have a bottle of Blue Hawaii please." Queens stand around in tan and white or tan and lavender or tan and blue. Everyone fresh from the beach, the Kona Gold is in bloom. Buds, buds, boys in the back room smoking buds. John, my yoga instructor, offers me a heart-shaped pill: "Happy Valentine's Day!" he says. I swish the pill around in my mouth. Yup. Tastes like speed. Thanks, John. *The night is heavenly/and you are like heaven to me.*

4.

Moon over yacht harbor. Sailboats lit by torchlight. Boys in bikinis stroll. Brown boys in lava-lavas. Yellow boys in jeans. Some sit on the sidewalk sucking *pakalolo*. Some stand on the corner with dreamy looks in their eyes. Condos blink. Lights set with the precision of stars. Telescopes peer from window to window. One a.m. at the Steamworks. A Chinese queen sucks cock in the sauna. Old guys jerk off in the porn room. Brown shag carpeting thick with grease and dried cum. Tiers of bodies. Sighs and the slap-slap. A boy arches an eyebrow, legs spread. Such smooth skin between his balls and ass-hole. The bounty in the porn room. Some young sarge meets his lieu-tenant. Where smoke drifts in through the peep-holes. Sarge gets a big sloppy kiss. Against a backdrop of hallucinations, touch becomes sight.

5.

That morning I sat in the Burger King on Kalakaua Avenue and watched the latest batch of potatoes stroll by. There was always a cute blonde with his mamma, ready for roasting or mashing. Pretty little potatoes spending in paradise. All those years and all that money saved for just this moment. Saved for the day when I could sip my cof-fee and say, "Aloha! Sweeties! Wouldja like a cuppa coffee? Diamond Head is to yer right and the ocean is miles beyond shore!"

6.

Fort de Russe Beach: where the soldier boys hang out. At noon the sand is strewn with artillery. Sexy tan land mines waiting to explode. Gatling guns aimed at my face. Spread-eagle and loaded. Visions of slaughter, of war waged by the beautiful. I park my towel in the thick of it. A queen in camouflage. The chest of a Marine has been slaved for—and has developed as promised. I flex it mightily as I spread my towel. The lifeguard perched above me. Oily thighs glisten. He stares into the horizon, to his right: Waimano Range. Green reaches for blue. A cloud drifts through the *ko-o-laus.* A 747 drifts by. Gust of wind and the palm trees sway. A pretty boy emerges from the water. How it must relish the run down his belly. He drops to the sand and onto his back—panting from the exertion of his swim. I close my eyes and become that water: evaporating. He grinds his ass into the sand and stops. Moving only to breathe.

7.

That night I meet a Marine at the Wave. He said his name was John. Little white hairs sprouted from his eyelids. Against a starlit wall. Where the skyline of Honolulu had been sketched by a cartoonist. John stood with a knee cocked. Scent of mylie leaves and carnation. Scent of plumeria around the neck of a Marine. He said he "come" from the hills of Virginia. He speaks and those hills come rolling out. Across the bar and into the ears of other queens—who look at John with love. He said his feet ached from an all-day march. On the Big Island from Hilo to Kona. Shards of hardened lava cut through the soles of his boots. His feet stank, he said, and he said he thought he'd never get them clean. I was a drill sergeant with an over-eager recruit. My cock put his ass through its paces. Until four a.m. when I said it was time to get some sleep. We popped our valium like good little boys—and drifted.

Threads

J. EIGO

Santiago in the failing light is weeding through his sparse wardrobe. Everything else he owns he has packed into boxes. Tomorrow he is to move away from the city of his birth. According to plan he has left the clothing for last.

What he tosses to the left he'll retain; what he tosses to the right, discard. The smallest pile is the one at his feet. A scant five garments, each a relic from a former partner, each is stained. What to do with these?

Santiago kneels to arrange the five in a tight circle: a rondo of semi-requitedness, the spots on every one attest to momentary satisfactions. He reaches for a T-shirt, brings it to his face. For the time the room he is in dissolves.

* * *

In this rubble-strewn lot tonight there's a party. This is where the Bronx boys mix, working-class Irish guys from Norwood, Puerto Ricans from further south, Dominicans, Jews, Italians, blacks, Vietnamese, who knows who else? A significant portion sport backward caps and chin fringe. No one is really at home, so everyone is. Here all the boys like boys or else they don't much mind that the others do.

"I see all these faggots now wearin' their flaps outta the back of their heads; how come?"

"That way it's easier to suck a guy off." Queer boys and straight boys and boys unsure of themselves all laugh.

Except Santiago. "And in a glade I came upon a comely lad," he will later write to himself, fledgling English major, half in mockery. This boy who swims the air is coming toward him. Too toothy to be truly cute, in fact he's more. His eyes' immutable soft focus leads you to believe that he looks at the world through a lens of immutably hazy sensuality. His eyes induce you to look at him in this light too, hence sensuous.

Santiago has seen the dude before, but not recently. He wasn't always "Fuzzy," but that's the tag he goes by now. How can anyone who moves so loosely seem so incisive? His knobby hands and stubbled head all bob to incessant inner be-bop bassline—this is a white boy? As they make small talk, Santiago races to keep up with the many messages.

Fuzzy shares an apartment with a man downtown, he says. He doesn't pay a cent toward rent, but nothing in this town comes free. As Fuzzy speaks, both boys' eyes are telling the other boy other things. So that when the sky opens, and everyone scoots for cover but the two of them, neither Fuzzy nor Santiago find it strange to be standing there soaking wet, though they find it funny. They laugh and drip and snort like animals. Fuzzy pulls Santiago in close to him.

"Like a summer storm, he's suddenly upon me," Santiago will later write. The sky goes white and darkens again; it will do this over and over. As if a network of blue lightning had struck the boy and stuck there, this oddly pale stiff cock above him is alive with pulse. Santiago sees it, sees it enter him, feels it.

As unexpectedly as the rumble in the sky, Fuzzy comes. And just as unexpected, like a clean stream of fire, Santiago's bolt of jism hits his chin with a splat. "My love is as deep as a thunderclap; your love, as incisive as lightning." One boy bites the other and he bites back. They roll around so the guy whose back was pressed to the wet ground is now exposed to the drenching sky.

And later this summer night Santiago writes: "The only time I've ever fucked anyone, I don't. How to explain that? The first time is close to zero. On his back, my partner, his knees drawn up to his ears, looks so hot. Having just been fucked, I'm so hot that, before I can enter, I pop all over his cream-colored cheeks. I guess you could say I leave my mark, an illiterate makes an X his signature, white on white, semen even pearlier than his Anglo skin. Of course I'd prefer a lengthier correspondence. He, too, I have to believe. Having botched entry and splotched him, in shame and confusion I wipe him off with the T-shirt I think is mine but is his, blurt an apology, think about running. But Fuzzy takes hold of me before I can. In my head I hear an accusation in a voice that isn't his, until his palpable kiss silences everything but our breathing."

Fuzzy takes his sleeveless black T-shirt and wipes the tears from Santiago, who can smell his own cum, but he (all but overwhelmingly) smells Fuzzy too. Santiago takes the T-shirt, wipes his chest of Fuzzy's spunk and puts the other boy's shirt on; Fuzzy in turn dons Santiago's. Each boy hitches his pants up. Hand in hand in the driving rain they run.

Until a shirt falls away from a face and a bare room reconstitutes.

* * *

Santiago bends to pick up a nylon swimsuit from the floor. The stains are saliva and semen; the faint scent, chlorine. And the voice he hears he hasn't heard in years.

"Save your Bermuda shorts for Bermuda. Here in the naked city, kid, if it's summer we strip." Santiago, at his locker in the college gym, looks up. The redhead with a swimmer's build sports baggy shorts himself. "Hi, I'm Bart. I'm the sophomore who orients freshmen who are trying out for the diving team. I guess that's you, huh?"

"Actually, I was raised in this city. I may need orientation but I don't need a tour guide."

"Ooh! Attitude! I like it! Uptown?"

"The Bronx—"

"Is up and the Battery's down. I wanted to come to New York for so long that I was almost a native before I got here." The fair-skinned redhead turns his back and drops his pants. His butt is even paler than his back.

Unmentionable for the high-school boy except as a joke, this sweaty bodily crevice is more and more on the college freshman's mind of late. The fantasy boy's face may change, the focal detail remains the same. How does it happen that in his soul this foul hole has transfigured to a site of desire?

Before Santiago can even attempt an answer, the sophomore turns back around. "His pubic bush is red as a brushfire. His dick is even paler than he," thinks Santiago. Like many European-American males, Bart has been skinned. Following the lead of his prospective teammate, Santiago drops his walking shorts as well.

"Can I call you Sandy for short?"

"I'm as dark as the earth."

"Once you gain a berth on the team, dude, you'll break the color barrier, that's for sure." Bart drops his eyes and gets more particular: "The skin of your dick is darker than you, and ampler by far than any I've ever seen." Sophomore reaches into gym bag and tosses freshman his regulation Speedo. "These are mine but let's see how you'll look."

Santiago feels hot in the face and flustered, but bends, steps into the swimsuit and pulls it up, hoping to check his treacherous member, distending at all the attention it's received. "You're even trimmer in swim trunks, dude, than you seemed in your street duds: they suit you." Though Santiago is lean, he's hardly meager. Bart's voice is conspiratorial. "And bigger than anyone but a shower-room buddy might expect."

The better to confirm his general impression, Bart sinks to his knees. Like a brush his tongue applies a mouthful of saliva to the nylon-covered cock. The grunt coming from Santiago is more in shock than protest. Through the fabric Bart is nibbling at the foreskin.

With his teeth Bart draws the racing suit down, then like a dog might gnaw at the toe of a sock, nips at the skin of the standing boy and pulls it to its length. Like a bee dips for nectar, Bart's fluted tongue plumbs the funnel of foreskin until, under the pressure of growing erection, flaps unfold to disclose the incomparably ripe animal-fruit of the glans.

Like a man a little drunk, Bart reels when standing up. "Going down is no substitute for lathering up, better hit the showers." Bart leads his new buddy to a shower stall and turns on the spray.

"Our beauty," Santiago will write tonight, "is something even the showerhead weeps to see."

Bart soaps Santiago's cock, then soaps his own butthole out. Upfront Santiago goes to his knees to nuzzle him. "Going down is one of the fruits of coming out. But we can't have sex in the shower in a drought," the older boy whispers as he hooks his hands in the freshman's armpits, lifts him to his feet. "We have to rinse off and move on."

Back at the lockers, Bart reaches into his gym bag and pulls out a small foil packet. "Shower or no, we always wear our rubbers. Stand still, freshman, and stand tall. This wouldn't be much of an orientation to the team if I didn't teach you how to use one of these." Bart unfurls the latex down the length of his future teammate's rigid staff. "There we go: dick in foreskin in latex in orifice."

Can the neophyte negotiate the mechanics of shaft and chute, the pneumatics, the hydraulics? "How do I coordinate the slide?"

"Too much effort can put the brakes on the erotic real quick. After you enter, just make sure that you have it all going in the same direction; then try to relax and let it rip." Bart has hardly finished these directions to Santiago and the freshman feels he's about to come: he's a big guy and the condom's exquisitely tight. Bart reads the signals and helps his partner fight it off. Around the base of the wrapped-up cock, he locks his thumb and forefinger in a tight ring. Santiago shivers and goes still until like a fever it has passed.

On his back on the bench in front of the locker, his knees hooked over his elbows, the limber diver presents the younger man an unambiguous target. Santiago lowers his head to the cleft below his mentor's testicles, tests it first with finger, then nose, lip and tongue: he would first know the territory.

Only then does Santiago plunge with his dick; still he misses. He's simply succeeded in repositioning the other boy's balls in his scrotum. He reaches down, corrects his aim, stabs again and, to his surprise, like a blinded surfer might slambang into clam bed, sinks into Bart. So taken is he with the wonder of it, he shudders uncontrollably.

"When you ejaculate upon entry, Sandy, there's nowhere to go but back from where you came."

"But, Bart, I think I'm still hard."

And Bart, after a moment, in his rectum feels the stiff shaft shift into action. "One of the cool things about sex with another guy is: you can fuck him to a pulp and not have to feel too sorry for him; you know he'll soon be doing someone the same. You'll find there's nothing in nature quite like a bone-jarring fuck."

Santiago, to the extent he can, follows instructions. Soon he's pistoning instinctively, animal and machine, hips set to semi-automatic, a quick stroke he accelerates until he feels he's about to come a second time. Confusedly he pulls out, pulls off the condom, loses grip on his dick, as out of control as a twelve year old's. Like an unattended garden-hose he comes, all over the room.

"Now I want to feel the full weight of your body on top of me." Santiago collapses on Bart, who starts stroking the rump of the boy who's just pumped him.

Santiago raises his head to look down at Bart: is he getting his signals right? "I've only been fucked once and I'm just too tight to take someone your size."

"You're not that tight: you're taking two of my fingers right now."

"Guess it's love," Santiago grins.

"Love is what I save for the guy I live with." Bart playfully smacks Santiago's butt. "But I'd like to see you again and take this further. What's your number?"

Winded, Santiago averts his gaze so he can catch his breath. "I'm trying out for the diving team: you'll see lots of me." He pulls off of Bart and pulls himself to his feet. He picks up the borrowed trunks, pulls them over one leg, dizzily lifts the other as the locker room goes black.

The skimpy swimsuit that flutters from his hand lands on the bare apartment floor.

* * *

No sooner has Santiago lifted the wrestler's singlet to his face, he hears a loud rap.

At Santiago's dorm-room door the boy he's slated to tutor appears, eyes as eager and anxious as a wet puppy's. Fresh from athletic practice, he removes his damp sweatshirt to stand in simple singlet. Santiago's head is aswim with the scent of him; it would verge on stink if he didn't find it invigorating. Santiago shakes his head as if to pull loose from its claim on him; his student follows suit and sprays the room.

Without the boxer's fabled cauliflower ear, neither has this wrestler the delicate vessel that a troubadour would carol. Santiago finds the jug ears that the wrestler in fact presents far nearer his own sexual ideal: easier to steer their owner to greater heights with. Santiago blinks that mental picture away; the wrestler stands before him awaiting direction.

"What's your name?" Santiago wonders, to no avail. The way he smells says more about what he's been up to than *he* does. Santiago stands directly in front of his charge, hooks his own head around him, mouth to ear. "Roll over, boy," he says in slurpy whisper. "Your master's got you a bone." Then he dips in. In Santiago's idiom a tongue in the ear is unparalleled sign of affection: why venture it so soon? The wrestler shivers; his eyes register mild distress. Like in the comics when the ink slips, the lip sync's out of—

"So tell me, has this wrestler aphasia? No, but he's sort of an oral astigmatic," thinks Santiago, "his mouth and his observer's gaze queerly out of phase now." Under Santiago's eyes again, his lower lip sinks dumbly out of frame; then as unexpectedly it snaps back.

"Your name is Santiago, is it not?" is the sentence the wrestler summons at last.

Love blinds, and all this blind love has deafened: Santiago sees at last his partner is hearing impaired. He cranes to whisper his answer into the ear that is nearer his mouth. "Yes, we are Santiago; no more small talk—" Less than halfway through the message, Santiago is simply blowing air. As his lower teeth graze the sturdy lobe (token to him of a virile ear), his tongue trails the auricular spiral, teases the hole.

The second tier of the outer ear is funnel to the inner. Despite its size, Santiago takes the full shell of the wrestler's ear into his mouth; wrestler appears again to shiver, but this time it feels like he's shedding some of the tension. Under intense direct stimulation, tympanic diaphragm registers shifting pressure gradients. Where discomfort is such pleasure as well it nuzzles its way into revelation.

Wrestler, as if goaded thus by the starting gun, tackles tutor and brings him to the floor. This isn't genuine contest but it's convincing travesty. Instinct grips these competitors: now is the time to lead with the dick; hips duel. Soon it's painfully clear to contenders, cocks have distended. Wrestler's dick slips free of his singlet. His trapped balls: rocks in a sling.

"Our eyes flash, his flesh is warm, I feel the flush; before he flips me over he flips it out." Sensations race through Santiago's head as he's spun one last time face down. He knows the scrotum of the boy who pins him is out in the open now only by a musky odor.

Deftly the wrestler sends his hefty hand down the tutor's sweaty cleft. Now where his pioneer hand has been the wrestler sends his member. For the length of the long, hot, sinuous embrace, they are each aware of only the smell and feel of the other's muscle and flesh. Their sweat might mitigate the friction but not eliminate it, the wrestler's against the tutor's butt, the tutor against the slickened hardwood floor.

Each boy halts his moving hips, holds his breath, ears prick; Bowser and Fido communicate, tuning fork to tuning fork attunes. Now each boy howls at uncannily similar frequency until a kind of climactic paralysis fixes each. Eerie presentiment of ultimate rictus? These boys are palpably warm and young and flushed. When Santiago comes he holds his ears for fear the soul flows out. In his head after climax something (like a pocket of pressure) pops: Santiago experiences temporary disruption of hearing.

Now he comprehends: what is dripping from his nose is blood. He lifts his eyes to see the same drips from his partner's. The wrestler takes his discarded singlet, wipes his face then wipes Santiago's:

"Better you leak from your nose than your ears," he grins.

Soon Santiago is looking out the window at his departing pupil. Does being hearing impaired lend him a bearing? Or does the hearer misread it? From a block away it almost seems his big ears send out a signal: keep in touch! One thing is sure: his wide shoulders and barrel chest strain at the shirt the lean Santiago has lent him, while his slender hips hardly keep the trousers up. Santiago turns back to his room.

"This wrestler's language skills will, over the course of the quarter," he vows, "pointedly improve." Santiago picks up the discarded singlet and drops it into a pile of his dirty laundry.

And the singlet falls on Santiago's feet; he stirs and kicks free and sees his apartment.

* * *

Santiago reaches down and brings the jock to his nose. The atmosphere thickens significantly.

Santiago shakes his head to clear it. He blinks the room into focus. This raw space in the meat-packing district is far from the Bronx. Here the boys appear just as rough, but they study to get there.

Stripped to regulation undershorts, Santiago shifts on the floor to restore some circulation to his numb limbs, and looks up at the man standing above him. The freshly cut flattop brutally exaggerates the planes of the face, deeply shadowed and tipped in distant light. "When I dress up I wear a jock; otherwise it's nothing." Having said that the man pulls the pouch aside and aims.

"I think I hear the hiss of rain on asphalt," Santiago will write, "until I crack the parable: drizzle is piss, the pavement me."

"You're a friend of Fuzzy's, huh?" asks the man once the quick shower lets up.

"I am not a pissoir."

"Piss war? I could dig that, if the competition were stiff—I mean, the stiffer the competition, the likelier everyone wins, right?—but tonight I see no one who interests me but you, bud; how 'bout it?"

Santiago doesn't stir, even when the spray resumes; he begins to speak, then freezes, mouth agape. When finally Jake finishes pissing in Santiago's mouth, he pulls the boy to his feet and kisses him fiercely. He tastes too strong for Jake to continue this for long. Across Santiago's face a conflict of electrochemical impulse flickers to a semblance of smile before decaying to neutral. As gently as Jake can manage, he lowers the boy to the provisional urinal he's made this ground and turns to go.

Santiago sits up. He removes and rubs his damp shorts across his chest. "Finish the kiss!" The impossible demand arrests the departing man. Jake turns back and bends to take measure of its maker. Santiago puts the full of his force into the slap he delivers. Even in the dim light he thinks he can see the imprint parts of his hand have left on the face. After the rap his fingers smart from the contact with the hard high ridge of the cheekbone. Their momentary shock is mutual. It chains them.

Santiago is first to break out. But Jake intercepts the slap's sequel before Santiago can land a hand. "This hand is the hand of a girl's; what possible interest could it hold for me?" Santiago with his free hand smacks the man on his bare ass. Jake, when he emerges from his surprise, smiles enigmatically; awkwardly he wriggles out of his jock and tenders it to his momentary partner. Santiago takes and knots the jock around Jake's neck, tighter than an animal collar, tight as a jeweled choker. Jake on hands and knees turns tail, smacks his own ass and, like a brute in rut, proffers it.

Santiago has four fingers up the butt before Jake says: "If you want to fist me let me take you home so I can clean myself out first."

Santiago rather takes his fingers out, takes his cock, pokes through the hole he's presented, and fucks out of control. With the cum he shoots he lubes his hand and fucks Jake with his thumb. He adds a finger at a time. If Jake notices the difference between intruders, nothing about his faithfully humping figure betrays it. To Santiago's surprise, when next he pauses to assess, he finds his fist in a rectum, wrapped in innards. His other hand he wraps around his transitory buddy's prick and pumps.

Upon Jake's climax, Santiago stands, wipes his filthy hands on his shorts and tosses them over Jake's head. "I wipe this pate like Veronica must've wiped the suffering Christ." Picking up Jake's jock he sniffs: "Urine corrodes where semen just plain stains; I'll take it anyway." Better this than wear his own shit-streaked shorts. He puts Jake's jock on, washes up, checks out and goes.

Alone on the final night in his room Santiago drops the jock and stands naked.

* * *

Before the naked window Santiago stands, illuminated briefly in the gloom by a streak of lightning. In the gathering wind he shivers light-ly. Almost by reflex he bends to don a garment lying discarded at his feet. In its style, this is a jacket a varsity athlete might wear, except the letters across the back proclaim the city's premier dance company. Immediately Santiago is enfolded in an old stink his fresh sweat resuscitates. Through the clouds the bare room he's in assumes again an earlier, homier incarnation.

It's the first anniversary of their first fuck. Except for his company jacket, the Leopard sits naked. Santiago presents him a videotape of their last session together. For their every encounter this first year, the Leopard has fucked Santiago wearing this jacket alone. In costume the premier dancer retains his sense of role. Jacket remains focal in this tape that will furnish Santiago a relic, and the Leopard a record, a tool toward improving performance, reviewing a Leopard that not even Santiago has seen, until now. The Leopard pops the tape into the machine.

Tape opens on Leopard in close-up. All the extravagant planes of the face somehow come together to suggest (equally) feline ferocity and calm. A compelling stage presence seems caged by the small screen. The camera pans down, the jacket peeling away from the idealized torso, chest and abdominal muscles ridged deeply in the little light that comes in from outside the room. It comes to a stop at the Leopard's crotch.

"This formidable ivory horn is an organ you ignore at your risk," Santiago thinks. Unexpectedly the camera moves to Santiago's own formidable organ. "My body is no longer remotely my own. This fragmentary fag I call Santiago, if he's not a figment, is fugitive: help me catch him." The camera pans up the young man's body. "High above a familiar set of genitals hangs a stranger's face."

Abruptly the screen shifts to fuck. Onto Santiago the Leopard crawls, his superbly muscular buttocks whiter for the black jacket fanning up over his broad back. When Leopard's body has utterly obliterated Santiago's to the sight, the dancer's oversized thighs and calves power his pistoning butt, his spine's unrivaled flexibility affording his hips enormous orbit. At climax balletic and bestial aspects mesh. The Leopard roars and throws back his head with such force that his jacketed back bends, his cock still embedded in the boy below. Santiago's suddenly uncovered face betrays he is blinded. The tape goes blank.

For the sex that the couple commences post-screening, the tall, dark, normally quiet man knows now how to formulate commands. "Watching myself fucking you has been a lot like fucking myself, understand?" The Leopard stands, removes his jacket, spreads it on the floor, physically persuades Santiago to lie on it, then mounts him. He pulls his jacket around the shoulders of the younger man who, though impaled, manages to wriggle his arms into the appropriate holes. The smell of the sweat of how many shows, how many screws, rises to Santiago's nose; the sweat is somehow his.

The Leopard's low-pitched growl intrudes. "My fucking you in this jacket is a lot like being fucked, isn't it?"

"Why not try it and find out for sure?"

The Leopard dismounts, repositions himself and sits on Santiago's cock. This is narcissism of a second generation; it engenders in Santiago irreparable confusion. As his partner raises and lowers himself, he tries to give it voice.

"You've scratched the lens of desire so that all I've wanted since meeting you might as well be you—and that's not how I want it. Now I feel I am cleansed: I see it's the lens has been soiled."

The rapidly wilting Leopard pulls himself off his partner. "I never understand a word you say: try Spanish."

Santiago reaches for his cock with one hand and the remote with the other; the tape rewinds. "The only language I'm fluid in is the one I use. We've each in a different way made of this jacket a fetish."

With the butt of his hand Santiago can rub a nipple and jacket button at the same time. "Now we see its contents transfigured as well. So let's have an update. When first I saw you I was beside myself, until I saw I was you, as it were, for as long as I wanted." Might ejaculation be a body's defense against the infection a certain attraction represents? Climax, a shaking off of demons, semen the means? The fiend that wracks Santiago's body exits, a jet across our (admittedly diminished) firmament.

The tape rewound, Santiago retrieves it, boxes it, hands it to the Leopard: "Bon voyage, pussy." Leopard opens his mouth, says nothing. Santiago sees him out. A crash of thunder follows hard on the closing door.

Light flashes at the curtainless window; in a simple shrug Santiago sheds jacket like chrysalis and stretches.

* * *

Santiago picks up the jock and puts it on. Then the swimsuit, the singlet, the T-shirt, the jacket. Thus attired, he walks out into a downpour. And he continues.

After some time in the rain, even his most protected parts are wet. "We flow in alternating currents," he conjectures, and wishes for the pen and dry weather he'd need to preserve the thought. "Sweat and spit and piss and semen, let the eye extract from the chaos of skein a system, trace it back, untangle it, take us back to skin."

A dog comes up to sniff him, its owner in tether close behind. "Your dog is soaking wet, sir."

"So are you. I live just upstairs. Come with me and I'll get you some dry clothes."

Does identity register more or less when you're drenching wet? "These clothes are more me than I am, man."

"Call me Izzy. My business? Men's clothing. Retail. I've been in men's clothing all my life. Trust me."

Santiago goes limp in the stranger's arms; still through the layers of soggy fabric Izzy can feel that the boy is hard.

By the time Santiago's eyes flutter open again he's been undressed. The older man asks him: "Stay the night?"

"Bright and early tomorrow I'm moving out of the city."

"Yeah, it's sometimes a pretty grimy place."

"I actually feel pretty clean right now."

Izzy has by now vigorously toweled off all of the boy's body except the crotch. "Is that the glint of intent in its single eye?" Izzy asks himself—only he asks it out loud in the fashion of a man who lives alone. "Does the bead of liquid tell me it's ready for me to go further, or just that it's wet. If only dicks could talk."

Santiago looks down. Through Izzy's thinning hair he reads beads of sweat. He reaches down, curls a strand around a finger and pulls the man close. Upon contact with whiskers, he shivers.

"We'll have to cover you up or you'll catch chill," whispers Izzy. "Come to bed."

A wet tongue on his toes awakens Santiago in the middle of the night. "I usually wear a watch to bed whenever I sleep out; it helps relieve the disorientation I feel when I wake and wonder where I am if I at least know when." But tonight the bed is strange and his wrist as naked as the rest of him.

The face an inch away, however, rings a bell. Izzy despite his bulk lies as lightly upon Santiago as a sheet, or as his shorts would were he wearing any, only Izzy is warmer than shorts would be, and so Santiago feels suddenly very warm.

miserére

MICHAEL PATRICK SPILLERS

They always want to fuck you.

Stretched above you in the dark, breathing hot against your face, they always make that famous, awkward fumble for your ass...begging in hoarse whispers to have a piece before they come.

Never drive more than thirty minutes out of your way for street sex. If you don't find it, you start wasting gas. Take a couple of bucks and follow the night-glow fliers instead, plastered like Band-Aids through the barrio, leading to some smoky techno warehouse where you can order a Corona and smile self-consciously at society's children.

But when the ATM's are down, and you want the mean skin of a boy who frowns at you while you suck his cock—who slips in and out of your arms neatly, like a wet fox—you go to Sixth and Alvarado.

I can see Sixth and Alvarado from my window at night: a splatter of Lite-Brite yellow dots under the ember canopy that smolders above Los Angeles. The wasteland that separates me from that far-off intersection is East Hollywood.

I remember the night I almost didn't bother. I remember watching my clock tick into a.m. while the CD player droned on shuffle, refusing to play track twenty, the only song I wanted to hear: "Miserére." A lazy hardness wrestled out of my boxers, sliding against the blankets, stabbing into the darkness like a headache. Reminding me.

I climbed out of bed and went to the car.

At night the City of Angels is an absurd landscape: a monument valley of asphalt and steel, where forlorn traffic lights blink green-yellow-red for no one. My rusty hatchback is the only thing that moves; a little roach crossing some vast, abandoned kitchen in the night, scurrying to get something done before the lights come on. You get turned around real easy out here. Hop on the wrong freeway ramp and you're screwed, lost, fucked. I remember the night I was ready to give up. I remember making an illegal turn.

That's when I saw him.

He annoyed me at first. Shuffling past the low neon laundromat, untied sneakers flapping, *tatuaje* "EP"—Echo Park—branded on the back of each arm. Pretending he didn't see me. I followed him in the car, my high beams burning against the back of his shaved head. He glanced over his shoulder at each block; scowling, nodding, teasing. He couldn't have even been twenty. His mustache was an eager child's—soft, thin—like scattered eyelashes resting on his lip.

I braked against the curb and watched him saunter up to my window with smug indifference, his corduroys hanging dangerously low. He plopped in beside me with a rush of air that smelled like wet paint and fast food. The door slammed shut and we were off.

* * *

I remember that night. I remember as if it's happening now. I remember my voice against the hum of the engine. *I'm scared. I can't look at him....*

"You live out here?" I'm embarrassed by my own stupid small talk. He just nods; a toss of the head, really. His leg presses against mine. His shoulders are burned brown under the straps of his bleached-white tank top. I want to touch him, but I'm afraid. What if he just needs a ride? What if I've got this all wrong? He could freak out, hit me. My throat tightens. I stop talking and turn on the radio.

"So y'got somewhere to go, Homes?" he mumbles with the halted, rich vowels of a first-generation *emigrante*. I relax a little. It *sounds* right, but I'm not sure. He avoids my eyes. Then I glance at his lap, where his thick, dark hands pull at the clasp of his trousers, tugging at what swells underneath. *I remember....*

* * *

I open my front door. My mind dances wildly between desire and caution as his brawny, warm shape brushes by. I toss the keys on the counter. Silence. I hear him breathing. We stare at each other's silhouettes in the dark.

I lean in to kiss his curled, jailbait lips. He jerks away and says, "I ain't no faggot. I just wanna mess around." He clutches my shirt—literally *clutches* it, the way an angry father herds a disobedient son—leading me to the bedroom, where the cheap stereo still skips my favorite song with each random shuffle. His young fingers struggle with my buttons. I see the tiny scratches and bruises that cover his arms.

I peel off his tank, still almost afraid to touch him, afraid to let my hands rest on the feathery fire that is his skin. I'm afraid it might be against the rules. There are so many rules: don't talk. Just stroke it. Don't touch anything else. Don't hold on. It's not allowed. I'm afraid if he sees my hunger he'll panic, change his mind, disappear.

He leads me to the bed, slouching on top of me, spreading my legs with his iron-strong knees. His homemade tattoos buckle as he squirms with silent, self-assured machismo. He's trying to push his way in.

They always want to fuck you. No matter what you say when they slide into the passenger seat—"I don't do this, I don't do that"—safe across town in your bed they always scrape their wiry hair-down-there against your thighs, *"Come on, let me try it...!"*

I wonder: should I just bottom out some day? Make it all go smoother? God knows I'd be more popular. Because that's what they want. They always want to fuck you. I'm just scared I'll go crazy with need, bringing them—young, wild and angry—inside me. Better to stay on top, so they don't run off with your mind.

"Come on! Come on, *cabrón!*" he whispers. Peppery sweat trickles from under his arms, wetting my body. He wants to shove himself in. I don't know what to say. I want to find words to break his fall, but words never come. I can only lock shut like a vice-grip down there, forcing my legs together, refusing to cooperate, rolling my eyes to the ceiling, waiting for him to catch on.

He gives up with a sudden, bored sigh and straddles me high on his knees, looking like a giant up there with his arms folded. He lets his waistband fall like it's nothing, like what's underneath is no big deal. He doesn't understand that I'm frozen, pierced with desire as his heavy sex tumbles out. It sways, weighted by the thick foreskin. A tiny wet bead leaks out like thin glue, dripping softly onto my bottom lip.

I want to taste him. But he grabs it, pulling it away with a spit-soaked palm. "Only your hands," he mutters. "Just do stuff with your hands."

He doesn't even want a blowjob. If he can't fuck me, he just wants me there, under him, as he strokes it, his hot breath going random. He just wants to feel me down there. Watching.

He tightens like a dark panther. A moan rumbles from deep in his throat...and he squirts hot and wet across my shoulders. I want to enjoy it, but it's so quiet; so soon. He scrambles to pull his briefs up. "Don't get *yours* on me," he says, and I want to pretend he's a clean-freak, but I know what he's afraid of.

I'm covered in his thick blast, but mine never comes. We roll away from each other and I shrivel awkwardly out of arousal; tired, angry, bitter.

I just want to take him back out there, out into the night. I want to get rid of him, but he won't get dressed. He collapses beside me and ignores my prodding.

He starts to snore.

* * *

I remember that night. I remember hating him. I hated the way he sprawled there, taking up half my bed, flopping and sputtering. Stereo music whispered over us as we lay there, sweating under a comforter that started smelling like his skin—ground corn, motor oil.

Then it played. Track twenty: the final song. Bleak and seductive. "Miserére."

He bolted up in bed. "Turn that shit off!"

"What's your problem?" I whined.

"Turn that shit off! Asshole. Stupid fucking *pais...*" He punched my good pillow and muttered at the wall. "That song, eh? Sounds like fuckin' *Himno*. Fuckin' anthem."

"What fucking anthem?" I asked.

I remember his beautiful young body, half-lit by moonlight, sitting up in bed and staring into nothing—groggy, transfixed. An entire world was hidden behind his eyes. He shook his head for a while, almost swallowing it all, almost leaving it inside.

Then he spoke. His sentences were fragments, parcels, broken Spanglish poetry. *"Himno del Salvador!"* he hissed. "Fuckin' stupid, eh? I hate that little boy's voice, y'know? Sounds like me tryin' back then. He was an asshole, makin' me stand there. Fuckin' cold—be slappin' me—'Stand up, motherfucker! Your big brother got it! Big brother got it!' I ain't no fuckin' big brother! *Solo mi, pendejo. Solo soy yo!"*

My head ached. It sputtered too fast. I tried to ignore the words, but they bled through me. I watched him lie back against the headboard.

"Hands be black from the fields 'n shit," he muttered. "Then they take the fields away. Fourteen families. Fourteen families own that country—*la gente* don't mean shit. Fuckin' anthem playing on the radios, on the speakers, in the streets. Like that'd shut us up."

Track twenty twisted around his voice.

"Fucker hit me till I felt crazy. 'You a *maricon* or you a man? You gonna own your country? Or you gonna suck cock!' *I was eight fuckin' years old,* man! Shit!"

I couldn't move. I was stunned. The rules were broken; the words tripped from his handsome mouth so quickly. I wasn't supposed to listen. *It's not allowed.* Best to slip in and out without a scratch. He spoke from somewhere deep down and I wanted to be bored—but the words cut like a scythe.

" 'No food till you sing it, eh?' Ain't singin' no *Himno!* I ain't your soldier, motherfucker! Ain't my goddamn war, asshole!"

Ripped-up images danced in the room, almost touchable: automatic rifle strapped against father's heavy blue trousers. Older brother being a good little boy, older brother serving the Revolution like a man—and the little boy in my bed must have refused. Father scolding him, punishing him, beating him into a forced military salute—beating him into singing that anthem all alone on that hill until he got it right.

"I show you a fuckin' war! This is my war, *papi!* I'm a soldier now!" His tears left streaks of salt across his temples as he lay there, refusing to blink, clawing at the gangbanger tattoos on his chest. "I'm a soldier now, *papi!* I'm a soldier now..."

I remember....

I remember him under me.

I remember him hiding his eyes against my cheek; locking his broad chest beneath mine. Clamping his legs around me. Holding me—pink and hard—deep between his thighs.

"Do it!" he hissed.

His powerful body curled beneath me like a gateway. Like a magnet. My hands reached around him for the first time; traveling around and down the small of his bronze back...down into the cleft, gently spreading him apart...shocked at his permission, drunk with the touch of the coarse hairs protecting it...hidden, moist, pulsing against my fingertips.

I wanted to plunge in. I wanted to hear him growl. But it wasn't safe.

He found me with his hand and pushed it closer. His sweat was the lube. He kept spitting into his palm and bringing it down there. I wanted to stop, but I couldn't. I kissed his tears, his thick hands pushing me deeper, grumbling against my flesh.

I felt myself disappearing inside him. He tightened, crying out. I wanted to back off, but he held me. *"Do it! Do it!"* His hands clamped against my backside and pushed. I couldn't stop. The hilt of my cock pressed against his flesh as I sank all the way in. I was blind with feeling. I clutched the back of his head, where the homeboy stubble bristled against my palms—my lips pressed around the muscles of his mouth—tasting his spit—falling....

I couldn't stop. I didn't know how. The sheets were soaked, the rules were deliriously broken, and I remember the feeling—the drunk feeling. A boy's hard, wet walls around me, inviting me, embracing me.

It's the only feeling that makes things go away. It's all we both knew.

I shot—loud and deep—into his body.

His cock exploded against my stomach, dousing me with a thick, gray stream. He whispered over and over, to the rhythm of his climax.

"I'm a soldier now, papi. I'm a soldier now..."

* * *

At sunrise I watched his tangled-up shape hiding under the covers. Daylight rendered him smaller; a little boy. I fixed him some cereal and tied my tie while he rubbed his eyes and stared at the bowl. He stayed silent, poking raisins with a sleepy finger. Neither of us spoke.

I dropped him off where I found him.

I was sweating under my collar that day. It's always hotter downtown. Even in early morning there's this haze of anger that rests over McArthur Park.

He hopped out of the car without a word. I watched him in my rearview mirror, his baggy corduroys flapping, like a postmodern Charlie Chaplin wandering into the chaos.

Part of me wandered off with him. We had a lot in common, him and me. I wanted to hold on to him. I wanted to build a house around both of us and lock out the world, but you can't do that. If they come to you, like little gods, with all that's beautiful throbbing in their greased palms—you have to just watch them sail by. You can't grab on for too long. You have to stay casual. Don't talk. Don't touch. It's not allowed.

I think I loved him.

In one night I loved him. But I can't tell anybody because they'll laugh at me, and I can't ever find him again. So wherever he is right now—I just hope he's safe. And I hope he's warm. Because I'm not. And I want to hold him again. But it's not allowed. There's no way to find him again. I'll never find him again.

He never told me his name.

Griffith park elegy

AL LUJAN

If this story were a pile of bones, I would fracture them, pulverize them and scatter them across beautiful landscapes like the ashes of so many beautiful lovers. So intense and horrific was that afternoon that all I could really do is romanticize it, when all I should really do is let it go and not repeat what took place. Or what I believe took place. It disorients me.

I was in Griffith Park, in the heart of the City of Angels. Hanging out in a section referred to as the "meat market" where men young and old, rich and poor, gay and not gay, follow their instincts and their hard dicks like divining rods, through a series of dirt paths that wind, in and out, through the heavy brush. Most paths twist back onto each other or branch out into small clearings where men pose, pout and hold up the trees till coaxed into the moaning bushes. They circle through the maze in search of the Minotaur, sometimes finding him in the rustling plants. Other times what they find instead is an under-cover cop busting them for obviousness.

That afternoon I marched to the topmost clearing with intent. Without distraction. It's the second highest lookout in the park. It faces west across a field of dense, brown haze that blankets the basin, except for the shaggy heads of the sixty-foot palm trees that poke through here and there. That area ain't too popular with the guys, although the bushes to the left and the bushes to the right are par-ticularly squirrely. Wide open areas make these guys uncomfortable. Some would probably go into an agoraphobic coma were they caught without a bush to scurry about in.

The vista is accessible by a dirt road that connects from the east side. Park police off-road vehicles frequently tour the area, shooting pebbles into the foliage with those knobby tires they use to hug the hillsides. Scares the hell out of those bush queens with sex-offender histories. But not enough for them to actually leave. The vista is visible from the observatory on an adjacent peak. If you put a quarter into the binoculars and aim in the right direction...welcome to Los Angeles.

Me? Well, I'm an exhibitionist. I love the great wide, white sky, the fires of dusk and the risk of getting caught, as much as I love my fond memories of blood, mean teachers and the fist fights I've won.

I planted myself on one of the C-curved benches put here some forty or fifty years ago when this area was some hetero lover's lane or tourist lookout before the observatory was built. Benches of wood and concrete, unpainted since the seventies, carved with symbols and initials. (T.D.+S.G.'63, EL HUERO CON LA PEE WEE CON SAFOS Y QUE, and I SUCK DICK *4 p.m. to 6 p.m. M thru F*).

I sat at the foremost bench facing out. A bench where winos died drunk and lovers fell together entangled in arms, scarves and hair. A bench with a personality like mine. Quiet. Private. With a secret history in this part of town. There I sat with my legs spread and a look that said, "I've got less important things to do, only the serious need apply."

My olive and black Pendleton was folded across the knee of my pants, pressed with origami-tight creases. Just like my T-shirt. Just like my boxers. I resisted dressing this way growing up in East L.A. Dressing like my brother, Flaco, and his *pachuco* homeboys from our block. They hung out in our garage since I can remember. Pants slung low, lowrider posters, *Calle Diesiocho* along with every members' *placa* on the walls. A weight bench, beer cans and KRLA on a radio connected to a car battery. The smell of weed, sweat and anarchy in the barrio.

Now, my *cholo*-without-a-gang look worked me an angle on that hill. Unapproachable, rough trade, mean-dicked, risky challenge. The bold motherfuckers who cruised me knew they'd either be getting to blow a sadistic, gang-bangin', drive-by Richard Ramirez *maniaco* or just be getting punked. Only the biggest freaks would conjure the nerve. The kind I could do anything to and who'd do anything I said. Like a Dockers-wearing CPA type who gave my shoes a real spit shine. A nervous, fey princess with fluffy hair whose hairbrush I broke smacking it across his bare butt. Or a tweak freak who tells me that I don't need to use a rubber with him. Yeah, right.

Every once in a while I hook up with a man who turns the tables. But that Sunday afternoon was particularly quiet. I could hear birds and winged bugs nearby. The sounds of slurping and grunting, down the hill, were more than audible, they seemed amplified and exaggerated, like porno. I felt horny and impatient. I'd been up there for over two hours and no one made it up. Not even an obscured "pssssst" beckoned me for a blowjob in the bushes.

The sun was sinking into the grimy distance and I felt February on my face and hands. The salmon-colored streetlights that pacify the barrios and the ghettos were coming on in sheets across the horizon. I hit my flask to pacify the chills that were making my body jerk. I reconciled a fruitless afternoon of meditation. I stood and put my Pendleton on. Buttoned only the top button like a true *vato loco*. I turned to the path behind me to head for home. Home to call fuck buddies who would come to me, although that was not exactly what I was in the mood for when I planned that afternoon.

I looked back once more. Goose bumps covered my arms. The blood in my body felt cold and thin. A man was seated at the opposite end of the bench I'd just left. My heart was racing, for a couple of reasons. I thought about my options and said, "What the fuck?" I sat back down. The warmth that my body had left on the bench had dissipated. It was cold on the backs of my legs. In fact, the temperature had fallen considerably in the last couple of minutes.

We sat under the elongated shadow of an olive tree some twenty-five feet away. The fronds of the palm trees, just ahead, swayed and rustled in gusts of wind that I could not feel. The winds picked up clouds of dust from the paths leading down, obscuring them.

The impending dusk gave the stranger a dark, menacing feel. He sat quietly, staring ahead at the swirling, cherry-vanilla clouds that were changing shapes as fast as they were changing color. His profile was still and sharp like stone carving. His dark hair was pulled back into a tight braid down his back. He wore charcoal-colored Dickies with knife-like creases and a white T-shirt that was luminescent against his brown Aztec skin. A stray *cholo* on the hill. My lucky day.

He sat next to me, staring ahead; I dared him with my eyes. He had tattoos on his forearms, hands and neck. Blue-black letters and symbols. A portrait of some ruca and a spider web on his left elbow that, in prison, signifies that he killed a man while doing time. At the edge of his eye, a black indelible teardrop. This man was trouble and he was unraveling my upholstery. He was the number thirteen, black cats, burning crosses, bad luck personified. He had the quiet disposition of a seductive cult leader. He oozed: run and don't look back. But I couldn't. I wanted him.

My mother would sometimes tell me, *"Mijo,* el diablo is exactly who you want him to be. If you recognize him you must be in trouble with *Diosito."* Then and there I finally understood what she was talking about. That evil ain't just some white dude with a goatee and a tail. One could see that and run. Evil is in every nationality, in every religion, and every sexuality.

It was too late. This seduced fair Catholic wanted to capture that tattooed dirt-under-the-nails hard-drinking boyfriend-smacking welfare-check-stealing lying cheating *demonio.* I pressed my thigh against his. He didn't move his away. Well, that's all the encouragement I needed. His smell drove my hand. I reached over to feel his thigh. Without turning, he intercepted it and held it in his fist. I tried to pull back but he held tight. For the first time he turned to look at me and that's when I freaked out. His eyes were black and shiny. I don't just mean that he had dark eyes, I mean they were solid black and cold. His face showed no emotion. He was silent. My heart was absent in my chest. He pulled at my hand still in his grip. I resisted and then yielded. He leaned into me, I imagined, to tell me never to go where I'm not invited. He led my hand to his face and released it onto his smooth cheek. He pressed his hand onto mine and guided it across his cold lips. Now, I've made some fucked-up choices in my life. Gone against my better judgment plenty of times. But the fact that I resisted withdrawing my hand scared the hell out of me. He led my trembling hand to the back of his neck. With his free hand he did the same to me and pulled me into him as if to kiss me. That surprised me because prison trade never, never kiss on the mouth.

I tried to look away from those crazy eyes, at the darkening sky, but his strength had us face to face. He held my head and put his mouth on mine. His, our mouths suddenly warmed to fire-like temperatures. I was drunk with lust and horror. Euphoria tinged with a residue of uneasiness. The kind of uneasiness that makes most men impotent.

My ears were suddenly filled with high-volume moaning, sighing and gulps for air. The sounds our bodies make when excesses of pleasure and pain push language past mere words. Terrible, beautiful, animalistic music.

That's what my ears heard. Within his violent kisses I felt his voice. Smooth and deep like silk boxers that give me erections as I walk. And that's exactly what his voice was doing to me. He wasn't necessarily saying anything. I can't recall specific words. But events in my life were being narrated by our twisting tongues. He knew things about me. Things I've never told anyone.

He knew that I sat at my father's bedside for three days as he rotted with cancer, and that just before he started that gasp for air that signaled the end, my father's last words to me were: "You disappointed me."

He knew that it was me who burned a swastika on the side of an old dead tree by my house with a butane torch I stole from school when I was ten. (I wasn't being anti-Semitic. I didn't understand what it meant. I had a crush on the only white guy at my school, and he had it on his pee chee folder. I wanted him to notice me.)

He knew the terror I felt later that night as the sky exploded in amber when the tree that smoldered quietly all day ignited.

He knew the shame I felt as a child when we would have to sleep on the floor during certain holidays so we wouldn't be struck by random bullets coming from intoxicated, hot guns and how I prayed for God to make me an angel before dawn so that I could fly myself out of that barrio for good.

He knew that I reached around and felt my sharp shoulder blades protruding and that that's all that they were. That I was simply a child testing the existence of God.

He knew that my lover, reeling with AIDS dementia, forgot that he was gay, that I was his lover, or even who I was, which allowed his family, with their high-priced lawyers, to lock me out of our home. And that after a while I just couldn't fight them anymore. He died without me.

He knew these things about me. These profane ordeals in my life. And I still wanted him. My shirt was drenched with sweat that turned icy in that night that turned black while my eyes were closed. I pulled away unable to catch my breath. I tried to stand, to flee. I felt lightheaded. The blood that supplies my brain with oxygen was pulsing in my lips and groin. He steadied me and pulled me back onto his lap. Before I could scream, I heard the ripping of the seam of my pants. He impaled me onto what felt like a knife, cold and hard like his lips started out, but soon it seared me inside. He sat there, motionless, with me on top kicking and flailing. No thrusting, no sounds, no more words.

With his mouth he punctured and gnawed on the back of my neck. I felt my spinal cord being sucked out of my neck and out of my ass. I prayed that the wetness that soaked my pants was my piss and not my blood mixed with his cum. He squeezed my torso to the point where things went black. Then a bright electric jolt shot through me with such force that my fingernails and nose shot blood into the dirt.

"Goddamn...that felt good." Did I say that or did he?

I awoke sitting erect on that bench, my head thrown skyward. The sounds of sirens all around me. Intense hot breath enveloped my aching body. The violent suns that illuminated the black fog were in reality a series of palm trees engulfed in balls of flames. They surrounded me on all sides. Black ash snowed upon me and all I could do was sit there and cry.

All that I have left are burn scars, bad dreams and three cranberry-colored, crescent-shaped hickeys on the back of my neck that won't go away no matter how hard I scrub. If you'd like me to show them to you, put on your hiking boots, bring your faith, and meet me at the park some sacred Sunday afternoon.

scenes from a sex life (striving for intimacy)

DOUG MIRK

1. Phone sex #74

I knew this would be one of those times I would get fucked & there would be no touch—just dicks, just two dicks together in the same room doing whatever it is dicks do. I knew this from the minute you entered my room & we took off all our clothes, no questions asked. My room, even in its current messed-up state, is a web & I know that. I could see you eyeballing all my things but no, there would be none of the usual questions asked about all my books & religious icons & kitschy knickknacks. No, no personal connection, no touch, just dicks.

You took off your shirt & I saw your beautiful Latin chest just as you described it over the phone. I wanted to suck on your nipples for a few minutes, but the message was clear: no touch. I wanted to suck on your nipples & then I wanted to wrap my arms around you & hold you, feel your skin against my skin. I wanted you to give me some strength, some comfort, but that is not what you came here to do: no touch. Even when I leaned down & sucked your cock for a few minutes, that was out of line; it wasn't what you came here to do. You didn't say anything, but I knew. I took it out of my mouth & looked up at you with my puppy-dog eyes. I looked up at you & I wanted to touch you, grab onto your legs & lick up, up, up & down, the whole time holding onto you with both arms, rubbing all over you, all over those big sad muscle-boy muscles. I wanted to hold you, let the passion go, feel feel feel you up & down, but the message was clear: no touch.

There is something to say for cutting to the chase, knocking down all the preliminaries & getting to the business at h&. I knew nothing would come of this, really. All the touch in the world would be just a big fake phony illusion, so I didn't mind it when I was looking up at you, wanting to hold you, looking up at you with my puppy eyes & all that you said was, "You want this big dick up your ass?" The message was clear. I just rolled over, stuck my butt up in the air, reached for the condom by my pillow, & held it up with my h& behind my back....

For the first time in a long time it hurt & I don't know why really. Your dick wasn't especially big, *nice* but not especially big. I groaned when it went in & I had that fleeting feeling I used to have back when I was much younger: "I don't know if I can take this—this may be too much for me to bear—maybe I should tell him to take it out." But that feeling is only fleeting, & after just a few seconds, your dick felt right at home there inside me—filling me.

This is bullshit. Your dick hardly filled me. It was just there, an object inside me making my heart pound hard, & I groaned & bucked up against you, wanting, wanting, wanting to turn this into *something*....

In our phone conversation, you asked me how I liked to get fucked & I told you on my back with my legs up in the air, but that's not true really: I really don't care how I get fucked, I just like to get fucked. No, that's not true either—you know the best way I like to get fucked? It's when someone's really close to me leaning down on top of me, my body at a ninety-degree angle & I can see his dick pounding up & down inside me if I angle my head up the right way—& his arms are around me the whole time, & he's looking in my face & sometimes kissing me & if you open your eyes up that's all you can see is his face, his eyes looking down into you, almost ready to explode out of his head from the force he's exerting. There is nothing comfortable-looking about this position, but really, to me, it's about the most comfortable position in the world.

Anyway, on the phone I told you I liked it while on my back. At that moment, it sounded appealing, but really, if sex is going to be impersonal, it may as well be from behind with my head buried in the pillow & my eyes closed. That way I can think of someone else.

But you turned out to be a really nice guy. I could tell you were remembering our phone conversation, & you asked me if I'd like it while on my back. "Sure," I said, hoping that you would twist me around while you were still inside me. There's something romantic about that, something connected, something that says, "I don't want to waste a second of this hard-on outside of you." But instead you pulled out & told me to turn over, & then, back inside, you leaned up against me, a rocking fuck—back lunge back lunge back lunge. It felt good. I noticed your dick is rather thick, thicker than K—'s. Maybe that's why it hurt at first.

I couldn't really look at your eyes while you did it. To tell you the truth, there was something about your face that I didn't especially like, too many pimples when you were a teenager or something. I also knew that looking at you would be awkward, awkward, awkward. Like, "Of course we're not in love or anything, & what am I supposed to be thinking about as I gaze into this guy's eyes?"—that's what I'd be thinking. So instead, I focused on your chest while you slid me back & forth across your dick. I looked at your nice buff Latin gymboy chest & I thought, "Yeah, this is hot, this is nice. I like the power & strength this all represents & your dick in my ass feels good—& your chest really looks hot."

I could see you, I could see you getting off inside your head as you pounded into me & you started jerking me off. "I want to see you come. I want to see you come all over your chest," you said & you ran your h& up & down my cock & I knew that you were getting off on the fact that I was getting off on your hot buff chest. I uttered my little precum groan, & you said, "Yeah baby, come, come, come," & I did & you pulled out & you put your pants on & you never came yourself.

"Maybe I could call you later tonight & we could finish where we left off," you said, but you never did.

2. Sex club (from a journal entry)

I wind up in a sex club where, upon entrance, I am practically mauled by a tall, h&some stranger who takes me into a back cubicle & fucks me silly. I didn't even get a chance to figure out my way around the place—just one innocent step into the glory-hole booth & he's upon me. Before I know it (after some dick sucking & ass licking & a nice wet kiss), he's whispering in my ear asking, "Do you want to find a private room?"—of course I agree. Within minutes I'm bent over, breathing poppers & getting a good old-fashioned fucking like I haven't received in months. This goes on far too long & eventually we have to "take a break" (i.e., part company).

We both go to the bathroom to clean up & on my way out, this shirtless black wonder is st&ing by the drinking fountain, eyeing me. He rubs his cock with one h& & grazes my thigh with the other. Really, I am tired. I do want to take a break. (I don't really know the last time I was fucked so much I felt like I needed a break—has it ever happened before?) But this is too good an opportunity to pass up. I'm still in disbelief that a guy as hot as this is approaching me this assertively. "How'd you like to have my big dick up your ass?"—& we go right away to the nearest cubicle. His dick is big, huge, like in some kind of a fantasy or porn movie. He unbuttons my pants & touches my ass & I bend over & put his dick in my mouth, but I don't even really have to appease him with this. I can tell that the main thing he wants is exactly what I have come here for, & I turn around & he slips it in me, & it feels good, good, good, major pounding, & I keep thinking, "This is just too much like exactly what I wanted—it's uncanny." That's exactly what I'm thinking as I'm getting fucked.

Eventually he says he wants to fuck me in the sling & we go to another room behind a curtain of chains & I pull off my shoes & my pants & my socks & hop right in, put my feet right up in the stirrups like that's where they've always belonged. This time he enters me with no preliminaries whatsoever, no gentle get-used-to-this—just several quick blam, blam, blams. He leans forward & tells me to open my mouth. I comply & he lets loose a long stream of spit.

"What do you say, boy?"

"Thank you. Thank you, Sir."

"That's what I like to hear. Thank me for what, boy?"

"Thank you for spitting in my mouth, Sir."

"Tell me you like it, boy."

"I like your spit, Sir," I say & he leans forward again to give me some more, the whole time pounding me with his beer-can cock.

"Thank you, Sir. Thank you, Sir. Fuck me, Sir."

Guy number one comes back & asks for a turn, so they trade off with me in the sling, my feet in the air on a row of chains. "Fuck him," they encourage each other, & whenever guy number one fucks me, I see guy number two's face above mine, telling me to open my mouth wide & spitting inside me.

"What do you say, boy?"

"Thank you, Sir."

"That's a good boy. Now let me see you swallow."

They think about double fucking me, but the logistics are too difficult. Instead, guy number two says he wants to fist me. He makes a valiant attempt—several fingers go in, the whole sling crashes into the wall behind us, but I am too tight. I scream inhuman screams & eventually he stops. Guy number one has left & guy number two says it's time for me to get up. He asks me my name & I ask his. "My name's David," he says. "Dave for you."

We go to the bathroom to clean up, & then I go to the couches where they play porno movies—three different movies at once suspended in the air above the black leather couches. Dave sits down at the couch adjacent to mine. We are the only two people left. He whips out his dick again. I'm not feeling so confident. I'm not so sure he wants me again, but he motions me over (I think) & that dick looks so nice & I would like to suck on it for just a while. So I crawl on my knees to him, his long legs sprawled out across the floor. I put his dick in my mouth, & he says, "If you want to suck my dick, you have to show me your pretty little ass." I undo my pants & wiggle my ass around for him while I try to deep-throat his dick. It's hard to do, though, because it's so big & fat. After awhile he says, "Let's go to the glory holes," & we go there.

I start to suck & he says, "Did you forget that you have to show me your ass?" So I drop my jeans to the floor. As I suck him, I can still taste below the layers of soap & latex, the faint flavor of the shit juices from the inside of my own ass. He moves to a stairway where he can see me better. I show my ass off good for him, writhe it back & forth while I suck. Finally I feel his dick flop all the way down to the back of my throat, & he says, "Yeah, that's what I like," but I can't help gagging just a little bit. I take it out of my mouth & lick his balls, slobbering all over them as he jerks himself off. He pushes my head back & comes all over my face. There's an impulse inside me that finds it unpleasant, unnecessarily gross, but I decide instead to really like, to really enjoy, the feel of his hot manly cum dripping on me, & I do.

Later, after my third wash-up in the john, I go back to the leather couch to watch porno & jerk myself off, & unexpectedly, he comes up behind me, puts his arms around me & talks sexy into my right ear. I come with him holding me, talking about how he'd like to fuck me while I'm sucking someone else off—just like the guy in the movie on the left that we're watching—& I say I'd like the opportunity to eat his ass just like the guy in the movie on the right.

I'm feeling a little more ballsy now, & I ask if I can give him my phone number: "I'd like to play with that big dick of yours again sometime." I give my number to him & then leave, rubbing my h& across his reclining chest & saying, "Take care"—such a macho little tough boy I am.

I wonder if he'll still like me in the daylight when it's more obvious I'm in my thirties. I wonder if I'll still like him in the daylight—maybe he'll be just another sleazy dude that doesn't really attract me. As I'm leaving, though, I decide to keep the fantasy alive, & I erase these doubts from my mind.

The surrogate
JAMESON CURRIER

My first year in California I had come to believe my body separated me from other gay men, a body I could hardly understand or seldom seem to keep healthy, a body I could neither shape nor sculpt to the perfection many of my peers so easily achieved themselves. Much of this may have had to do with my self-consciousness and often low self-esteem when I walked into the gym on Santa Monica, though it may also have resulted from a lack of motivation and an absence of discipline in wanting to achieve what I also perceived as an often frivolous and irrational goal for my age. Whenever I went to the gym with Vince or Jeff, I was so vividly aware of how imperfect I physically had become: the lumpiness around my waist, the thighs that wobbled a bit too much, the skinny forearms that ended in large calloused fingers. Around me, of course, the tanned, hairless West Hollywood boys stretched and pumped in their bright spandex shorts and tank tops, wiping the sweat carefully away with their short white towels, their biceps cresting into peaks with a casual but calculated flex of their arm. That was the year an aerobics boom had happened, the same year the sex bathhouses had become food bars and trendy clothing stores selling skimpy clothes for exorbitant prices, the same year that perfect bodies of young gay men seemed as easily manufactured as a skimpy clingy Calvin Klein T-shirt.

And that was the year, too, I first noticed my body beginning to pull away from me, the color of its youth fading into a series of lines around the eyes and the steely string of muscles from my thighs to calves aching at the end of the day from a combination of weariness and supporting what I believed was too much weight for my frame. I suppose I wanted to mistrust my body—imagine that its heartburns and charley horses were the result of something more serious, something which could move me into that other category of gay men, those who struggled with infections and the onslaught of exotic diseases—the rumor had it, after all, that that year fifty percent of the men in West Hollywood were HIV-positive.

But the truth was, of course, I was undeniably healthy myself, increasingly so, rebounding steadily from the abuse of cigarettes and booze, having cast those addictions aside with my continental shift. When Nathan died I was at the apex of those addictions, yet at that point in my life I ironically looked and felt fitter than I had ever been before. Now, I could not stop eating nor retaining water, in spite of the fact that I sweated uncomfortably in the California heat. What energy I had once found from booze and cigarettes I had been unable to replace. In its wake a growing depression, lethargy and apathy had rooted itself.

Often at the gym I would stand with my head folded into a book or a magazine, not really reading, of course, but frozen nonetheless into an antisocial stance. Vince would find me, as he had done so for years, eager to make a campy comment or a joke about someone he had seen or something he had witnessed, hoping to draw out an equally catty response from me, something like remarking, over the coiffure of some young Adonis, "Did you see her? She looks like she waxed those locks into that position." Now, however, his comments usually failed to provoke a retort; seldom, either, could I grin or even offer the slightest reaction. Instead, I would only lift my eyes up to meet his, trying to shade their fear and confusion by directing their attention to the object of his remark. "You're not even gay anymore," he said angrily to me one day when I had once again failed him.

Not gay anymore? I thought as I watched him stomp away from me. Had I separated myself from everyone? Did I no longer belong? Blend in? It was true I was not having sex anymore with other men, but I was also not eagerly pursuing that goal. But didn't the fact that I had slept with men for years count for something? Didn't I still socialize with gay men, albeit rather dully? Didn't I live with a lesbian couple, after all? Didn't that count? Wasn't I here, at that moment, reading a *gay* newspaper? In a *gay* gym?

Or was Vince, instead, referring to my loss of humor? My lack of merriment, the withering of my spirit? It was a fact that I had become more dour than merely pouty. I was, that year, just thirty-four but possessed, at times, the cranky demeanor of a bitter old man of seventy whose life had not turned out the way he had imagined. Or was I resentful, instead, of the cluster of Peter Pans around me who refused to grow up, resenting in its place my own willingness to let my life be determined beyond the physicality of my body and face? Had I come, therefore, to hate gay life or to hate its sometime shallowness? Was I misjudging others or had I come to despise myself?

Vince stood before me that day waiting for his hateful remark to elicit an uneasiness in me. It worked, of course; I looked frantically away from him, out into the room of gay clones biking, running, lifting, sweating, trying to find something—anything, really—to say that could prove him wrong. I walked over to him and nodded my head toward a blond guy on the chest machine and asked, "Do you think it's bottled?" Vince arched his eyebrows and looked out into the room where my gaze had landed. It was then that he turned back to me and took the paper I was reading, an issue of *Frontiers,* and briskly thumbed through the pages till he landed on an ad in the yellow pages toward the center. He tore the corner of the page out and handed it to me. "Do me a favor," he said. "Call him. He's a friend of a friend who owes me a favor. He's not cheap. So I'll arrange to have the first four visits on me."

* * *

"You seem tense," Mitch said.

I nodded in response, unable to say anything, conscious of the faint smell of his aftershave and his moist breath against the flesh of my neck, creating a wave of goosebumps. We were lying on Mitch's bed, fully clothed, his body wrapped around mine spoon-like, enveloping it, really; he was a good six inches taller than myself and at least thirty pounds heavier.

"This is all we have to do," he said. I nodded again, or, rather, I imagined that I nodded. Here I was, with another person believing I was tense, strung out, not able to function. I realized, though, that I had lost control of my body, tightening it as if afraid of enjoying Mitch's presence even though an erection strained against the waist of my jeans like I hadn't felt since I was in high school.

Wasn't this the purpose of a surrogate? I thought, trying to relax myself by opening my mouth and taking slow, quiet breaths. To make me get hard? To make me feel sexy? To make me want to have sex? To make sex comfortable, enjoyable? I smiled at the paradox of the situation that I knew only I understood at that moment, the logical illogic of it all—Mitch had thought that I was impotent, or at least that's what Vince had led him to believe when he had arranged the appointment after I had finally acquiesced to his badgering. Mitch's mission was to make me want to have sex, to be able to express myself sexually, doubtlessly, when the truth was, of course, I had always thought I had too much sexual feeling, too many thoughts of sex. I masturbated every morning in bed before I got up and again in the evening after I had shut my bedroom door and was pretending to read, my head full of the images of men I had seen throughout the day—on TV, at the gym or the store, the UPS delivery man, the guy in the car next to me at the gas station. Sometimes, in the afternoon, if I was bored, I would jerk off in the bathroom while Amy was taking her nap. The unfortunate thing, some people thought, was that I was doing this all by myself. And the truth was, I would sometimes agree with them; but the expression of it, now, with Mitch, another man, left me feeling oddly iniquitous and cheap.

Not that he was cheap, of course. As Vince explained, Mitch was well compensated for his services. When I had spoken to Mitch on the phone two days before to schedule an appointment, he made a concerted effort to stress the legitimacy of his practice.

"I have a degree in psychology from UCLA," he said, as if academics and its textual wisdom could better solve any sort of sexual dysfunction. "I'll make it very comfortable for you," he added in a softer whisper, as if he suddenly realized he needed to balance the erotic nature of his services as well. "I have an hour free on Thursday between seven and eight."

Nothing will happen, I told myself on the way over to Mitch's apartment. I had jerked off an hour before I was to arrive, to *prevent* anything from happening. So I was disappointed, *really* disappointed, to find Mitch so attractively sexy. I had convinced myself that Vince had set me up with one of his young West Hollywood buffed-muscle-boy activists, someone who probably doubled as a hustler or a porn star or both. So I was startled when Mitch opened the door and I discovered a much older man than I had expected, someone whom I imagined to be closer to fifty than forty.

But there was, nonetheless, something highly appealing to him. At first I thought it was the short style of his hair, one which revealed the silver in his scalp like fibers of wool. Then I thought, perhaps, it had something to do with the running slope of his nose juxtaposed against the squareness of his jaw. But I knew, of course, it was more the aggregate of him than anything else—the way he looked, moved me into the room, guided me toward the sofa. He was casually dressed, more so than I had counted upon even if he had been a younger man—a maroon sweatshirt without sleeves that showed both his defined arms and the damp strands of hair in his pits, and a pair of old khakis, threadbare at the knees with paint splattered about the thighs. He had the demeanor of someone assertive—part father, part coach, part drill sergeant. As he waved me inside the room, I caught myself forcing my eyes away from him—glancing instead at one then another of the furnishings of his Art Deco bungalow, the Hurrell portrait of Vivien Leigh that hung above the sofa, the glass coffee table cluttered with Erté statuettes of semi-but-elaborately clad dancing chorus girls.

I'd forgotten, truly forgotten, what it was like to be so drawn to someone. Knew it dangerously so at that moment, however; knew, too, that if Mitch possessed any smidgen of the psychological acumen that he professed to have, he could have easily taken advantage of me. It wasn't until he scratched his jaw that I realized he reminded me of Will—a bulkier, more well-fed pumped up version of him. *Will,* I thought, realizing the waters beneath my bridge, wanting to know what had become of him. It was as if Will had suddenly returned to my life after an absence of decades, and what I wanted most of him was to be able to explain to him what had happened to Nathan.

Mitch mentioned that we would begin our session with breathing and desensitization exercises. *Desensitization exercises?* I thought. From a sex surrogate? Shouldn't we be doing *sensitization* exercises? Already I was confused. Already my hard-on was creeping painfully against the fabric of my pants, sore because of my previous hour's attention to it.

And so Mitch had me stand in front of him taking deep breaths—him staring at me straight on, me, still averting my eyes. I stood there trying to remind myself of the clinical nature of my appointment. Trying to deflect my emotions. There was nothing romantic to it, after all, nothing remotely intimate with having a man, a stranger, breathe as you did two inches away from you. Intimacy is what I wanted, of course; romance was exactly what I needed. But what I *truly* needed was a surrogate for Nathan. Under no circumstances could I afford to expect that from Mitch after the end of our four sessions. And the realization of it trapped me in a spiraling misery. Mitch countered my degenerating mood by placing his hands on my shoulders and telling me to do the same to him, which I did. Something I didn't understand about myself was making me stay.

The odd thing, of course, was he asked me so little about myself. All he wanted from me was physical response. "Touch me here," he said, placing my hand against his chest, then moving it up to his neck and his cheek. "Put it here," he said, taking my other hand and bringing it against his waist, as if we were dancing.

We hugged each other in various permutations and then he took me into his bedroom and had me sit on the edge of his bed. He had me massage his shoulders—we were still fully clothed—then he massaged mine. Towards the end of the hour we had assumed our spoon-like positions and he asked me if I wanted to come by again tomorrow.

"I can't," I answered.

"The more we see each other the easier this will be," he said.

"Next week," I said. "I don't want to use this up so quickly."

I felt him nod against my shoulder, and I wondered if he expected this to continue beyond the four-time commitment. A few minutes later, I sheepishly said good-bye, awkwardly offering my hand outstretched for a handshake.

He took it and smiled back at me, the first genuine response I felt that I had attained. On the sidewalk to my car, however, I was already planning ways to cancel the next week's appointment.

* * *

My second appointment with Mitch was spent in his bedroom watching porn movies, or, rather, lying once again on his bed, fully clothed and with Mitch entwined around me, the two of us watching a tape of highlights of porn movies, bits of guys sucking and fucking each other, and then a compilation of cum shots. "I want you to get so worked up that you could come in your pants," he had announced to me at the beginning of our session, and we did not speak to one another again once the tape began. That's exactly what happened toward the end of the hour. I had gotten so worked up from watching the tape, fantasizing about *Mitch,* his hand on my crotch, groping and kneading and massaging it, that I easily came. Back on the sidewalk on the way to my car, I cursed myself again for showing up for the appointment, feeling both needy and sleazy, determined that this was exactly what I *didn't* need.

The clothes came off early during my third appointment with Mitch, however. When I arrived at his bungalow, he led me directly into the bedroom and we undressed each other, then lay together on the bed, naked, facing one another. Oddly, he didn't seem surprised that I had an erection before we finished undressing; he ignored it, really, concentrating more on us achieving our reclined positions in front of one another on the bed.

"You need to trust me," he said, his eyes connecting to mine. "Nothing I will do is unsafe or risky."

I nodded back to him as shyly as I had done the first time I had seen him.

"Tell me what you find sexy," he said.

You, you, you, I thought, *you fool.* Did he not perceive that I found him attractive? With an erection sticking boldly out at him? Or did he expect that from all of his clients? Still, I was tongue-tied. He must have known that it's hard for some people to express verbally what they find so visually attractive about someone. "I'm not too particular," I said, shrugging my shoulder, and as the words came out I felt they sounded wrong, as if I were cheap or didn't care who I slept with as long as I slept with *someone.*

He nodded. "I'm drawn to younger men," he said, adding a high little laugh. "That's natural when you reach my age. But I also like guys who are different than myself—more ethnic or exotic—Hispanics, Asians, blacks. A sexy man is a sexy man, though. However the package works."

He rolled over on the bed, away from me, and stretched his arm out and reached and opened the drawer of a nightstand beside the bed. It was the first, unrestricted glance I could take of his unclothed body without him noticing my perusal. He had a lighter complexion than I had imagined, two spongy-looking scars visible at the back of his left ribs, a birthmark at the right side of his back. The shape of him was bulkier than I had imagined, too, as if a young man's physique had been covered with a layer of pale, padded rubber. His ass, however, possessed a beautiful shape, rising in the air as if it belonged to a younger man.

He withdrew a notebook from the top drawer, rolled over, and assumed his position parallel to me, the book placed evenly between us. Before opening it, he reached over and touched my cock, his fingers playing with the head. "Does this bother you?" he asked.

I shook my head no.

"I don't want you to come till I tell you. Hold it back if necessary," he said in the tone of a doctor, then withdrew his hand.

"Touch me here," he said, and he took my hand and placed it against his own cock. It was semi-erect and warm as I lightly clutched my palm around the shaft.

He twisted his body so that he could flip open the notebook and I felt the movement make him grow stiffer in my hand. He flipped through a few pages, both of us looking at photographs of male nudes clipped from porn magazines, video jackets, brochures and advertisements that were pasted or taped in a random assortment to black, scrapbook-like pages.

"Too young?" he asked me when he stopped at a photograph of an Italian-looking boy with wild curly black hair and full lips so beautiful it was breathtaking.

I smiled and nodded and said, "Much."

"Show me who you find hot," he said, tilting the book in my direction.

I reached up and flipped through the pages, realizing as I did so that Mitch's hand was at my cock. I stopped on a page with a photo of a blond guy posed in white briefs, his hands positioned at his pelvic bones like a champion swimmer. Mitch smiled. "He is sexy," he said as if to confirm my choice. "What do you like about him?" he asked.

I was surprised that I had to verbalize it; I had never done so before, so, instead, I pointed to the parts of him that I admired, the V-shaped slope from shoulders to waist, the long blond hair and blue eyes, the tip of my index finger finally resting along the chest of the model. "Here," I said, my finger at the point of his heart, as if I had chosen a good, honest man.

"Close your eyes and keep him in your mind," he instructed. I did as Mitch said and he began lightly stroking my cock, twirling the tips of fingers against the sack of my balls.

"What's his name?" Mitch asked.

"Nathan," I answered immediately, before I had a chance to think about my answer or could change my mind.

I heard him flipping through the pages of the notebook. "Look here," Mitch said and I opened my eyes. "Like him?" he asked, pointing to another model with a similar physique, but a darker complexion and a rougher look because of dark hair, dark eyes and day-old stubble of beard on his face.

I nodded, though not as particularly taken with this guy as the previous one.

"Now imagine him with Nathan," Mitch said.

I shifted uncomfortably. Mitch must have sensed my uneasiness.

"Imagine this is Nathan's hand," he said, giving my cock a squeeze.

This is not working at all, I thought, feeling whatever sexual mood I possessed immediately evaporate from my body. I wanted Nathan out of my mind. I wanted to have sex with other men. I wanted a relationship. I wanted a relationship with Mitch. Something in me had snapped off and I thought about just jumping up off the bed and leaving the room. It was then that Mitch leaned down and kissed my forehead, a gesture that felt so sincere my eyes popped open and I heard him whisper, "Was he your lover?"

I nodded, squeezing my eyes shut and all at once I felt myself gasping for breath. Mitch didn't ask me any more questions. He pulled himself closer to me, the heat of his body now intruding against my own, and he stroked my skin at the shoulder as if I were a pet who needed affection.

After a few minutes he rolled away and we were back looking at the notebook. "What did your first boyfriend look like?" he asked. I wanted to respond, *You, you, you, you fool,* again, but held it inside me. "He was a teacher," I said.

"Older?"

I nodded.

"Was it just a crush?"

"More," I answered, consciously aware that I was holding my details close to me. "We lived together."

"You must have broken his heart," Mitch said.

Hardly, I thought.

"Did you love him?"

"Yes."

"And you got over it. You found space for someone else."

Space for someone else, I repeated in my mind, in just the same way—the same intonation, the same flat accent, as Mitch had used. Space for someone else.

"I used to have a boyfriend who looked like that," he said, pointing to a young, pouty teenager with brown hair and irises so dark they looked black. "He could make me do anything for him. I used to cook for him, do his laundry. I was about twenty-three, right out of the Army. He was eighteen. I even drove him to San Francisco so he could see one of his old boyfriends." Mitch tilted his neck back and grinned in recollection. "He had one of those heads that just rotate. If they weren't looking at him, he was looking at them," he said, with a laugh arising out of his stomach. "It was frustrating to walk down the street next to him. He was so busy cruising and being cruised I would just go nuts. He was trouble right from the day I met him. He didn't last more than four months. But I learned a lot about what to expect from a guy if you want him to stick around. And how to feel when it was over. How to move on. I didn't know it at the time, but it was the best thing that could have happened to me.

"Lie back," he said, and he returned his attention to me, jerking my cock till I came. When I left I was eager enough to want to see Mitch the next day, but I cautiously reminded myself I *needed* to wait another week.

* * *

On my fourth appointment with Mitch I was decidedly more aggressive. When he suggested we begin with a shower, I began undressing him in the bedroom. But it was in the bathroom, under the warm, flowing spray of water, that his body became so fully real within my hands, the body that I had imagined for weeks touching and pleasing. I lathered him up with soap, racing my hands about his chest and stomach and then lifting his arms toward the ceiling to feel and scrub underneath them, twisting him to soap up and rinse off his back and buttocks, twisting him again for the groin and legs. He grunted and groaned, braced himself against the pressure of my hands, cleared his throat as if to catch his balance. I felt myself smiling, really smiling, thrilled by the capacity of pleasure to astonish the body. I wondered as I felt his skin, silky and sleek beneath my touch, if I was capable of making him feel as good as the way he made me feel as I held him. He stopped me, though, not long after he cleared his throat, and moved me back into the water and began to soap up my body.

I did not, however, give up my attention on him. As he washed me I reached for his cock, keeping it lubricated with soap as I rubbed my hand back and forth around it. But I was surprised, nevertheless, when I felt him tense his body and reach down to stop my hand. When I looked down, I noticed his cum beading off the hairs of my wrist and washing down into the bottom of the tub. I came, myself, a few minutes later, and as we dried and dressed again, I realized the hour was almost up. I had made up my mind in the shower that I wanted to see Mitch again, would keep seeing him for a while or as long as I could afford these sessions.

"If you want, I can arrange a three-way for next time," Mitch said. I was sitting on the edge of the bed, pulling on my socks.

"A *three-way?*" I answered, startled.

"I could get my lover to join us."

"Your *lover?*" I responded, dumbfounded. I stood up, moving quickly to the door. *Lover?* I thought, deflated both by the concept of the word and the realization that I would not be able to attach its meaning myself to Mitch. I couldn't say anything else, and I stopped by the doorway. I was wounded, really wounded again. How had I let this happen? Let myself feel something for Mitch in such a short space of time? Feel this *deeply,* too? Was I this insecure? Or just this stupid? He was a *surrogate,* after all, a *professional* surrogate.

"I'll call you if I can work it out," I managed to say, and left him while he was putting on his jeans. I shook my head back and forth, back and forth on the whole drive home, pretending I had to brush my hair away from my eyes in case another driver caught sight of my misery. It was only when I was back in my own bedroom that I found a calmer space in my head. I knew I would never see Mitch again. But as I lay on my bed—my eyes alighting on the few possessions I had dragged across the continent to reaffirm my identity—the paintings, the crystals, the small shelf of books—I knew I already had what I wanted from him: the recognition that I could still find that space within myself.

εxhibitionist мemoir: An εxcerpt

Roberto Friedman

"Have a hard-on and make others have one, too. The heat which shoots out from you and spreads is your desire for yourself, or for your image always unfulfilled."
— Jean Genet, *le Funambule*

Hi there. I'm a young man, twenty-three years old, five foot ten, one hundred fifty pounds, brown/brown, hard gymed body, eight-inch cut cock, who really likes showing it off for appreciative gentlemen. I have curly brown hair, a hairy chest, bubble butt, and a big mushroom head on my thick, veiny cock. I'm packed. For two years now I've been showing hard in the parks and the beaches, and lately in gentlemen's houses for private, undisturbed viewing. I really get off knowing that men are watching me stroke my dick, milk it for them like their personal cow. I never considered writing down my adventures until I met a gentleman who is a publisher, and he thinks people will want to read about me. I don't know if he's right, but I'm writing it all down for him in case he's right, and I become a star.

My adventures as an exhibitionist began in the cruisy parks and beaches of San Francisco, show-off and voyeur capital of the universe. First I noticed that gentlemen were looking me up and down when I stripped down to a Speedo and basked in the ever-loving sun. One day I found myself out at Land's End beach, playing with the drawstring of my shiny blue bikini. I'd untie the ends and let them fall over my crotch, then rub my hands up my flat stomach and across my chest to my nipples. In doing so, I noticed I'd attracted the attention of gentlemen all around me.

The attention I got made me more bold. I rolled over onto my stomach and let them admire my small, round ass packed tight into my Speedo. I began to make small thrusting motions with my pelvis into my beach towel. By now all eyes in a circle were on me. I hooked my thumbs in the sides of my bathing suit and slowly, teasingly, peeled it down over my cheeks, down to a rolled-up strap over my thighs. My bare ass gleamed white. I'm proud of my tan line. The onlookers arranged themselves closer for a better look. To reward their attention, I pushed my butt up in the air, thrust it up and down.

Then I flipped over on my back. The front of the Speedo was still up, and all the kind interest I was getting had made me hard, so my cock was swelling sideways but was still trapped in the bathing suit. The patient gentlemen could make out the outline of the head of my dick, could see its long shaft strain against the sheer nylon, could see the soft pouch of my balls filling out the bottom. I lifted up the tight-wrapped package, bent my knees and pushed down on my feet so my strong legs were flexing, spread open, framing my cock and balls. I closed my eyes, opened my mouth and played with my nips, because by this time I was real excited by the show I was giving. I felt the focus of all those eyes on my body, all those older gentlemen eager to watch me peel down the front of my Speedo, free my dick and sack. No way could I let them down. Gently I lifted the top of the suit, and instantly the big round head of my dick popped out. The tight swimsuit held it straight up, hot and beginning to ooze precum against my stomach, where it inched towards my chest. I touched it lightly with the inside of my right palm, spread the natural lube around the head, making it gleam. This really drove the gentlemen crazy. One of them encouraged me in a hoarse whisper: "Yeah, stroke it for us."

O.K.: those are the initials I go by. I chose them because that's what I say to invitations like that. Show hard! Give us a look at you stroking off that tool! OK, man, I'm at your service.

So I did: I pulled down that rubber-band bathing suit, down to my ankles, and the full length of my prick swung out. My balls, filled up with spunk, rolled free. The open air felt good on my sex parts, my first time working them outside, in public, with an appreciative audience. I knew right then, as I pulled my rock-hard dick out with my thumb and let it spring back with a thud against my hard belly, that this was a pursuit I wanted to devote the rest of my young life to. The rewards are so instant and obvious: I could see them in the thirsty eyes of the gentlemen drinking me all in.

They watched every inch of my prick as I stroked it up and down with my thumb and forefinger, as I poured suntan lotion on the length of it like squeezing mustard on a hot dog, then slicked it up. They appreciated the subtle rubs I did on the tip of my penis, in a spiral with first my finger round the slit. And when I began pumping it hard, first with one hand so I could work my nips with the other, then two-fisted, stroking that sex muscle for all I was worth, I knew I was playing out in flesh and blood the fantasies that swirled round these gentlemen's daydreams: the captain of the swim team wanking off after the meet, or the lifeguard relaxing on his bed after the all-clear. I was letting them watch me pleasure myself the best way I knew how, so I was spreading the pleasure around.

When I knew I was right on the edge of spurting, of letting my juice fly, I stopped stroking and let them see my cock throb with its own pulse. The knob was purplish, the vein along the shaft standing up. I squeezed my balls, left then right, and a small white bubble opened at the slit.

The gentlemen around me were salivating, no doubt picturing them-selves licking the length of it, their lips cleaning off the tip, swallow-ing the mouthful of plush head. But when one of them put out a hand to help move on the show, I brushed it off. They can watch all they want, ask to see everything, but I'm not here to be pawed over. That was true back then, and it's true to this day: look, don't touch, that's my motto.

So here's the climax of my act, nature has no bigger finale. OK: I got up on my knees in a squat, I like pounding my meat this way. Pulled at my tender nips, standing straight out in total arousal. And slowly, exquisitely, I pulled on my tube, standing straight up, examined on all sides by my gentlemen, and when I felt the delicious tidal wave start to well up in my balls I stroked harder and faster until I was whipping that thing in a fever, they could hear the slap and stroke of my oil-slick dick in my palm. And when I felt my spurt coming I gave out a soft groan and reared back on my haunches, threw my head back and squirted, shot streams of hot white juice, gushed streamers of jism up to my chest, all over my belly, cum drenched my fist, a hot lick hit my cheek, and my dick itself was creamed with the sticky stuff. Whew.

I dropped back onto the towel, let them look over the tracks of cum shot all over my wracked body, my prong still red and swollen, my bush of pubic hair matted down with oil, sweat and cum. I was spent, happy knowing that every drop I squeezed from my cock was watched, accounted for.

Then came the reviews. "Good show, kid." "You shoot real good." "You're covered in cum." "Yeah, best spurt I seen in years." Even though I was exhausted, these words of praise aroused me, let me know it was all worth it, my audience was pleased, I had not shot in vain. And when I felt my strength back, I got up, ran nude into the frigid waves of the Pacific Ocean, washed off and swam, knowing the men were still watching me. Some watched long enough to see me return to my spot and perform an encore. This was my first big show, but it was to become my life, and my gentleman friend the publisher wants me to tell it all. I will, and I hope I please him.

The Lady in the Hatbox
R. L. KITZMAN

So you're hot and tired and bored and alone and you climb out your bedroom window onto the iron fire escape in the alley and you can see into your neighbor's buffet apartment. Red neon from the street blinks *Terminal Bar* and bathes the two occupants colors of pink and the shadows maroon and the blue lava-lamp purple.

Despite the heat the one named Bear wears unbuttoned dress pants, a trench coat—its belt hanging on the sides of his waist like two dead snakes—no shirt no socks no shoes. You can see his furry chest and his left nipple winks like a little pink Christmas light because it's pierced with a gold ring. His feet are large with long toes and clean clipped nails. Bear's head, capped with lustrous wavy blue-black hair, tops a thick neck, and little wire-framed glasses have slid halfway down his flat sweaty nose perched over lips thin as two lines. His unshaven cheeks look like he's smeared coffee grinds, espresso, on his face.

The other occupant, Hubert, wears sweat pants and baggy white socks and a tank tee that displays *Jesus is coming, look busy.* A tiny cross dangles from his right ear. He is slight of build with pale unblemished skin. His straight long and light brown hair—even in this heat—wafts when he moves and you see finer hair yet hang from his armpits when his lithe limbs reach for things. He's a bit nelly but pretty as a Botticelli and you ache not a little at such a sight of beauty.

Hubert irons a cowboy shirt by the light of a yellow pole lamp. It illumines a poster of a death child dressed all in black with a studded face who looks over Hubert's shoulder and proclaims: *No-Time! After*

Generation X, Generation Why? The death child stares at Bear, who slouches at a small table, works a crossword puzzle—and coughs. A hatbox sits in front of him. Hubert can look down on it and frequently does. It's frilly and lacy and light blue, then lavender, then light blue again, over and over and over, except for the bottom, which seems to be stained. That part...well, that part...when the outside red neon flashes, it turns redder.

You can see the two men as clear as the living day. But it's the dead of night and they can't see you. The alley is quiet and with their window open you can hear them too. It's an acoustic and visual miracle. Thank God something is. You know it would have to be a miracle if you can see clean clipped toenails.

Bear coughs again—hard, dry, raw. Hubert tells him he's sick. Bear chuckles and comments how he, Hubert, doesn't know how sick, but he, Bear, doesn't call him Hubert. He calls him Hubbie. And Hubert, or Hubbie, corrects him and says his name is Hubert, not Hubbie.

"For the love of Mike, shut up" says Bear.

"No you shut up" says Hubert/Hubbie.

"No you shut up."

"No you shut up" yells Hubert, and then he exclaims "infinity!" in triumph—short-lived—because Bear barks back "No you shut up, infinity plus one!" He adds a ha! And that's that.

Bear sucks on a pencil, green, and without looking up asks Hubert for an eight-letter word meaning "sudden grasp of reality, simple and striking."

Hubert looks up slowly from the cowboy shirt he irons, stares long and hard at Bear, scrunches his face...and replies with a sigh *"epiphany."*

"E-p-i-f-u-n-n-y" spells Bear. "Just fits." To which Hubert, again staring long and hard at Bear, asks "how did a guy like you get to be a guy like you?" to which Bear replies "just the luck of the DNA draw I guess."

Hubert shuts off the iron, hangs up the cowboy shirt. He turns toward the sink—strands of his hair brushed by the breeze—and he picks up a long and silvery knife and slices open a pomegranate and folds back its flesh and sucks out the hard red seeds. He puts the long and silvery knife back in the sink. You see him do this. And you can see red drops dribble down his chin and then you remember this is an acoustic and visual miracle, thank God.

Hubert points to the pale blue/lavender hatbox and says "it's leaking" to which Bear grumbles "oh for the love of Mike." Hubert says how beef-brained Bear is and that he should have used more plastic so the blood wouldn't leak. At least that's what you think he said and it would explain why the bottom of the light-blue hatbox turns redder when the outside red neon flashes.

Hubert walks over to the table where Bear is concentrating on his crossword puzzle and asks Bear "who's Mike?" Bear responds with "Mike who?" "The Mike you always want the love of" says Hubert. Bear tosses his pencil, green, and looks up at Hubert and calls him "a pip, pal, you're a real pip, you know that?" But what Hubert still wants to know is "who's Mike" and Bear claims that "it's nobody, just an expression." Hubert tears the flesh and sucks out some more hard red seeds and asks "wasn't that your daddy's name?" at which Bear stands up fast, sending the crossword flying, and again he throws down the pencil, green, and he leans forward and points at Hubert and growls through clenched teeth—you know, like he's practicing ventriloquism—"don't push it."

Hubert smiles and goes back to the sink. He washes his hands and dries them on pale-pink paper towel. He walks back to the table—Bear still stands—and lifts off the lid of the pale blue/lavender hatbox and pulls out a tiara that seems to be stuck in some hair because he's disentangling it. In the weird light the tiara sparkles and turns from dazzling diamonds to radiant rubies, diamonds to rubies, diamonds to rubies. Hubert puts the tiara on top of his straight long and light brown hair and tells Bear to "look at me, I'm a Gabor sister." And with his clear complexion and full lips he wouldn't need much rouge or lipstick to look like someone's sister.

Bear yells at Hubert "don't do that" but Hubert yells back at Bear for him to relax, "she doesn't need it anymore." Bear says "you look like she did" and Hubert comes back with "yes, it does take balls to be a drag queen."

Bear furrows his face and says "Dr. Godit is waiting for both pieces of merchandise, delivered on time and in prime condition, and if not, we're lion's meat, not to mention we don't get paid, and I for one want to get paid so I can get out of this rat hole"—which you take slight offense to because you live here too and choose not to think of your hole as a rat hole, a mouse hole maybe—"so put the damn thing back in the box"—and then Bear screams—*and put the lid on!*

Hubert doesn't flinch. Hubert doesn't blink. Hubert merely sighs "put *on* the lid" emphasizing *on.* And Bear shakes his head and says "what?" Hubert replies that "you should never end a sentence in a preposition; say put *on* the lid, not put the lid *on.*" Well, Bear is clearly looking at Hubert like he's speaking Portuguese and spits out "what are you talking about Hubbie?" to which Hubert/Hubbie spits right back "my name is Hubert, not Hubbie." But Bear only grins and sings "Riiiiiiiiiiiiiiiiiight." Hubert says it's guys like Bear who give thugs a bad name with his ungrammatical sentence structure and trigger happy temper.

"Like this?" asks Bear, grinning, and he whips out a gun from his trench coat.

Hubert flinches this time. Hubert blinks too. "Yeah, something like that."

Bear's gun is big, thick, a dull metal gray with a rounded and grooved blunt-nosed barrel. His hand that holds it trembles.

"You should lay off the latte, Sugar Bear" says Hubert.

"Don't call me that" says Bear, motioning with the gun. "I've gone over to decaf, what more do you want—Hubbie?"

"To see you put that gun down" answers Hubert.

Bear continues grinning—he really does have the most extraordinarily white and beautiful teeth, teeth that blink pink—and asks "don't you mean put *down* that gun?" Hubert replies "right, lost my head" and Bear says "you and Missy here on the table."

So Hubert repeats the request for Bear to put *down* the gun but Bear, through his Cheshire catlike smile, whispers something, which is the first time during this acoustic and visual miracle that you have not been able to hear what was said. But you're not the only one because Hubert asks "what" in a tone of incredulity so maybe he did hear Bear but couldn't believe what he heard. Bear repeats himself for Hubert. And this time you hear it too.

"Strip."

This situation is rollercoasting to an out-of-hand land but you can't get off the fire escape, can't move because you'd be discovered and Bear has a gun and he probably knows how to use it and you prefer your life, such as it is, even in your meager mouse hole. And also you can't move because—because you don't want to move.

"Strip" repeats Bear.

Hubert asks him if he's crazy and Bear replies that he is "crazy, yeah man, crazy" then "strip" comes zipping out of Bear's mouth again like he's blowing a poison dart through a tiny pole of bamboo. Then he adds "as in" and then he sings "Seventy-seven" and then he snaps his fingers twice and sings "Sunset *Strip.*" Hubert asks him if this is his imitation of Kookie, and Bear hisses "yessss, yes it is, wanna borrow my comb?" Hubert says that "if I have to strip that would be an effort in futility because my hair will muss." Bear humphs a laugh and says "riiiight, but it won't matter, nothing will matter in the end." And as a clever afterthought he adds "except your sweet end, soooooooooooo sssstrip."

"No" says Hubert quietly, calmly, blandly. "And stop waving that gun like some John Wayne, what will the neighbors think?" But you—being a neighbor—think Bear's waving that gun more like some Travis Bickle than some John Wayne. Bear shouts "stop telling me what to do and *strip!* or so help me I'll hold real still and shoot you between your eyes!" And you stiffen with the hope that Bear doesn't fire and lodge a Hindu blood spot between those lovely blue eyes—yes, you can see Hubert has lovely blue eyes—and Bear holds out his arm straight and real still, he's so close to Hubert's forehead.

Hubert's hands rise slowly and grasp the diamond/ruby tiara and he removes it as though he's passing on the crown, which he is because he sets it on the lady in the hatbox. A few stones on the top of the tiara peek out of the pale blue/lavender hatbox. And you can see Hubert's hands carefully take the bottom of his tank tee—*Jesus is coming, look busy*—and slowly bring it up over his screw-head navel and his flat satiny stomach, and then up a little further exposing his rosy puce nipple buds—the left one pierced with a gold ring—and then finally lifting it up over his head revealing the light brown soft down of his armpits. He completes pulling the tank tee over his head and his straight long and light brown hair is mussed for a second but Hubert shakes his head and it all falls back into place.

And then you sneeze—and freeze.

In the same second Bear wheels round and whispers "what was that?" You can see the sweat beaded on his forehead and glittering his hairy heaving chest but you hope to God he doesn't see you.

Hubert takes his chance. He knocks away Bear's hand and he flies away—but the gun doesn't—away to the tiny kitchenette (it's not far) to reach the sink. Bear curses at Hubert and his flailing arms lunge after him, his glasses fall from his face. Trying to get round the table, he knocks it and rocks the pale blue/lavender hatbox with the red/redder stain and the crossword and the ironing table, and the iron it props up drops with a thud and the lamp cord rips from its socket and all is plunged into blinking shades of red shadow. Like watching a slow old silent film, you see just before Hubert reaches the sink Bear grab him by his straight long and light brown hair and pull him back from the sink and Hubert cries out and his head snaps back and Bear wheels him round and like some crazy Charleston, they dance a *danse macabre.*

The red neon light stops flashing. It must be very, very late.

In the tumble the refrigerator door swings open and slams and its bright and white light electrifies the scrambling scene full of grunts and groans and trench-coat shadows and flashes of flesh. And you wish you had a spotlight to see better (the acoustic and visual miracle does have its limitations). But you don't, so you unfreeze and climb in through the window and kneel close to a wall; you're so close you could be another layer of paint. You can see the back of Bear's trench coat and his thick neck and blue/black locks and the dull glint of gunmetal gray pressed to Hubert's temple. Hubert's face is terrified and his blue eyes strain from trying to see the gun and from gazing into the face of Bear only an inch away. You can feel the cool air of the open fridge float your way and as it hits the hot air a steamy mist blurs the bright electric light.

"Now what?" asks Bear.

"You—had pizza for lunch" says Hubert.

But Bear is not amused and yanks on the straight long and light brown hair he squeezes and Hubert yelps as his head snaps back again. Bear binds Hubert with one arm and leans him hard against the kitchen counter. "Sweet Baby Bear don't" pleads Hubert. "Stop calling me that" says Bear and Bear is a raging bear and calls Hubert names and says how he's going to teach "Hubbie" and they slide to the kitchen floor with Hubert asking "what are you going to do" and Bear replying "you should know what I'm going to do." "I don't know, Bear, I don't know, I've...I've got an idea"—Hubert winces—"it's just an idea mind you but still, you'd have to be crazy." Bear says "crazy, you think I'm crazy" and he jerks and Hubert cries out and Bear starts chanting "crazy crazy crazy" and making soft weird noises, ape noises and grunts but he's so soft and yet so menacing as he rubs the gun in Hubert's face, on Hubert's temple, in Hubert's ear. Then Bear whispers for Hubert to "be very quiet, be vewy, vewy quiet, it's wabbit season." He snorts a laugh and then rips down Hubert's sweat pants which makes Hubert let out a scared "ah!" and then "baby don't, you're hurting Hubbie." But again Bear tugs hard and again Hubert lets out a scared "ah!" and Bear sneers "I thought your name was

Hubert." Hubert agrees saying he lost his head and Bear agrees but adds "that's not all you're going to lose." And Bear tells Hubert to turn around but he can't because Bear has his arms pinned. And so Hubert can turn around Bear releases his arms and Hubert turns, sighs relief and drops them in the sink—the sink, where an opportunity awaits—and after Hubbie has sighed his sigh of relief Bear says "ain't it amazing how everything is so...so relative" and asks "is Hubbie comfortable?"

Hubert begs Bear not to do it like this, that why don't they go lay *down*. Bear snaps "lay down?" and Hubert tries to grab back this grammatical faux pas and says "or is it lie down, never can remember." Bear tells him to "watch your prepositions buster." *"God!"* shouts Hubert "get it over with get it over *with"* and Bear pauses and chuckles and sings "ooooohhhhkkaaaaaaaaayyy."

With the gun in one hand Bear's other hand gropes the mid-section of his body and all you can hear is the crackling rustle of his trench coat and all you can see is the maneuvering of his arm and Hubert's sweatpants disappear ever further down his smooth and hairless hips and thighs. Hubert cries out again because Bear has found something of his own with his free hand and has thrust his pelvis forward.

"Wait" stops Hubert. Bear wonders out loud "what now" and Hubert implores him to use some lubricant and Bear rephrases "lubri*cunt?"* Again he jabs Hubert who again beseeches Bear for "anything anything!" Bear says "for the love of—" and breaks off, adding "such a delicate thing." And Hubert agrees "yes yes delicate, delicate." Bear threatens Hubert not to think about going anywhere, not to think period and Hubert agrees with "no thinking no thinking, do, just do." And he droops his head.

Bear turns and leans back and rummages through the refrigerator—the gun still dents Hubert's cheek. And while Bear rummages, Hubert fumbles in the sink and holds up the long and silvery knife and grasps it tight and lowers it and his hands back into the sink.

Bear pulls out a banana and declares "don't need that" and he pulls out a sausage and says "don't need that" and declares "I have got to go to the grocery store. Aha!" discovers Bear. He pulls out a glob of something and puts it up to Hubert's mouth and whispers in Hubert's ear to "taste it...go on...llllick it." Hubert does. He says "raspberry." "Razz for your azz baby" says Bear, who hoots a couple of *ha-ha's* and echoes "razz for your azz, pretty funny huh pretty baby." Hubert agrees with the "hysterically humorous quality" of Bear's pun and urges Bear to "just get on with it." Bear pulls up and yells "don't tell me what to do, don't you ever tell me what to do!" And while he repeats this so very loudly in Hubert's ear Hubert is crying "sorry sorry so sorry" but Bear misses the eye-wateringly soft sobbing apology. He thrusts his hips forward and reminds Hubert to "remember it's cocked" and nudges Hubert's cheek with the gun, adding "ready to go off any minute." Bear reaches into the refrigerator again and scoops out another glob of razz for Hubert's azz and applies it under his trench coat.

And then Bear moves to mount his Hubbie. And with one splitting plunge he rams into Hubert and Hubert screams *"gaaaaawwwd* oh god oh shit fuck damn, stop Bear *stop* you're killing me!" and he bucks and he tries to get away but Bear shouts louder "shut up shut up SHUT UP, you'll wake the neighbors and we wouldn't like that now would we?" (And of course being a neighbor, you are awake. You are very awake.) Hubert pants "no no we wouldn't like that" and Bear says "but you like this Hubbie huh, you like this" and he pokes his hips forward and then back and forth, back and forth, back and forth and asks again "huh Hubbie?" but all Hubert says is—and this in rhythmic stutters through gritted teeth—all Hubert says is "my—name—is—Hu—bert." Bear goes on "riiiiiiiight, but you like this huh, you like your Sweet Baby Bear like this, huh?" (pound) "huh?" (pound) *"huh?"* (pound).

And with his free hand he grasps the straight long and light brown hair of Hubert and turns his head and Bear plants his lips hard on those full and rosy lips of Hubert's and sticks in his wet tongue far and you can see his cheeks making chewing motions, swallowing whatever he can suck from thirst. Hubert breaks away from the lip-lock and cries out and you see some silvery strands of hair stay within Bear's paw.

Bear says "okay, we'll see about that." And his paw disappears under the trench coat and you can see his arm move forward and around Hubert's waist and he bends a little further over Hubert and once again he puts his mouth close to Hubert's ear and coos "ooooooooooo baby, I think what I have in my hand answers my question." And he pulls out his hand and puts it up to Hubert's mouth and says "lick it." Again. "Lick it." Again. *"Lick it."* Hubert's tongue comes out slowly. He licks it. "Salty, huh" says Bear. Back goes his hand round Hubert's waist and as he moves his hips, so he moves that arm. Hubert prays "no god no" and calls Bear a sick bastard and Bear twists his statement to "yes god yes" and calls Hubert a sick liar and they go back and forth "bastard!" "liar!" "bastard!" "liar!" bastardliarbastardliarbastard until *"liar infinity!"* roars Bear and a low-pitched bellow builds from his gut and he slams and he slams and he slams into Hubert one last deep thrust, one final assaulting inner caress (ha!), freezes, shivers, and his wet and slick, sticky and saline gruel flushes out, gushes out deep into his Hubbie, deep, deep, so deep within his Hubbie who with every hammer bangs the sink and bucks back to escape (hmm?) the searing internal skewer and Hubert gulps and gasps "no god no don't make—don't make me stop don't make me *nooooo!*" but the inferno burning below his belly boils over and a flame of white fire erupts and shoots and spills and pukes into the pistoning hand.

And then the two-backed beast collapses. Hell, you collapse.

And the Bear's long exhalation is like one long aspiration. Only you hear Hubert whisper "infinity plus one" because this is an acoustic and visual miracle and because Bear is quietly recuperating from his little death. And you hear Hubert begin to chant "I'll kill you I'll kill you I'llkillyou I'llkillyou I'llkillyou" each with a deep pant.

And then Bear starts coughing. Bear coughs again and then again and the Cough grows, it's dry and deep, raw. And Hubert sees his chance. With a bawl he throws off Bear and Bear goes flying back and he whacks his head on the fridge and lies there on the kitchen floor moaning but not moving.

The gun takes winged flight—and lands by your hand.

Hubert slumps forward and hangs on the counter, heaving, trying to catch his breath, his senses. Starting with his back you see it blotched red and button dented from the force of Bear's press and you see sore-looking red stripes between the shoulder blades and taut muscles. Some of his straight long and light brown hair is matted. The dark shadow of the concave curve of his waist draws you down to the rose tattoo and to the red smears that shade the two moonlike globes of his ass and you're lost in the black crevice of his quivering crack. He rocks from sobs.

Hubert looks down and reaches down and with one hand feels himself. It comes back glistening in the white and bright light. He reaches down again to pull up and over the dark side of his moons what remains of his sweatpants. He reaches into the sink and in both hands comes out the long and silvery knife. He holds it up like a holy icon and moves it so it catches the glint of the white and bright light.

He turns and you see bruises already forming on his chest from the door handles underneath the sink, on his face from the edge of the counter top, on his neck from the teeth of his Sweet Baby Bear. He crawls over to where Bear sprawls and he straddles his chest (*Mike* surrounded by a heart is scripted on his breast) and the knife in Hubert's hand comes to point and rest, shakily, under the neck of his Bear.

Hubert slaps Bear. "Oh Beeeeeeeeeeeaaaaarrrrrrrr" he sings. He slaps Bear again. "Bear. Wake up. Come on, wake UP." And Hubert mumbles something about prepositions but even though this is an acoustic and visual miracle you don't hear that. (It's very selective, you notice, this miracle.)

Bear stirs. "What...what...what the—"

"Don't move" says Hubert tightly. "Be vewy, vewy quiet. It's wabbit season." But on second thought adds "but wait. It's not a wabbit in my twap. It's a beaw in my twap. A Sweet" (jab with knife) "Baby" (jab) "Beaw twap" (JAB).

"Ow!" Bear focuses. "Hubbie...Hubbie, put that knife down."

"Hubert!" screams Hubert, looking up to the heavens—in this case blocked by a grimy ceiling—and he shakes his head and looks down at Bear and asks "don't you mean put *down* that knife?"

"Ah for the love of Mike. I...uh...lost my head, right right, put down that—"

"I'm going to cut it off" interrupts Hubert.

"What?" asks Bear.

"It. I'm going to cut" and he reaches back and rustles into the trench coat and grasps what he seeks and continues "it. I'm going to cut IT off."

"What are you crazy?" says Bear. And Hubert agrees "yeah, crazy man crazy" and now it's Bear's turn to swear "no man no I swear" and Hubert butts in with "yes man yes I swear" and then they both go "no, yes, noyesno*yes!*" And Hubert adds with his last *yes!* triumphantly *"yessss,* infinity" and with a concluding cackle tosses in "plus one."

He continues patiently. "Now. I'm going to cut it off, stick it in Miss Veronica's mouth, and so we don't have to wait for Dr. Godit, I'll send the whole box to him. He's an art collector—among so many other things. He'll get a little extra for his money. Call it *Fellatio, Still Life Number Thirty-seven."*

Bear begs "no, nononofortheloveofMike *nooooo!"* and Hubert over-yells "yessssssss!" and Bear's head tosses with fright—is he sobbing now?—and after a spell, so softly you barely hear, Hubert says "unless..."

"What" whines Bear. And when he gets no answer whines again "unless what?" His voice cracks and Hubert tells him to "shush, I'm contemplating." Bear begs again "what what what, I'll do anything, *what?*"

And after a teasing time lapses Hubert answers "I'll make you manless unless..." (another teasing time with Bear whispering "yes yes?" and you straining ever so bravely closer) Hubert continues with a grin "I'll make you manless...unless you do it again." "Again?" asks Bear. "Again" answers Hubert. "And this time put some oomph into it." Hubert pokes his Bear who jerks and cries "ow! You cut me, you cut me you son of a—" but Hubert stifles this tirade with another poke and a "shush, it's just a scratch you big...Sweet...Baby Bear. Now get it on—bang-a-gong! Now!"

Bear can tell Hubert means business but insists that he can't. Hubert says "think, think that you can." With mucus on his nose and lip, Bear's voice, high and cracking again, emits a saliva-filled choke of "but I can't, not with that—that thing pointing at me."

Hubert's face belies no reaction. He looks Bear in the eye. He reaches back, grasps his object, turns slightly and with the knife pointing at the object he grasps, pointedly says "tryyyyy."

"Okay" says Bear "okay okay I think I can I think I can IthinkIcan" and Hubert nestles close to Bear's ear and sings "choochoo baby, choochoooooooooo Sweet Baby Bear."

They shift their weight, adjustments are made, Hubert sits up straight, throws back his head and emits a long "ahhhhhhhhhhhhh-hhhh." They pause for an eternal moment.

"Hubert" says Bear.

"What" says Hubert.

"Do you think we could shut this door?"

"Why?"

"The light is blinding me."

"Sure Bear sure" says Hubert. And he shuts the refrigerator door that illumined the scene in bright and white light. Once again, all is shadow.

Bear coughs.

Hubert puts down the knife. He spits on a finger and dabs the cut on Bear's thick neck, sticks the finger in his mouth and sucks on it, pulling it out with a pop.

"Bear?"

"Yes."

"Do you have it?"

"Yes."

"Do I have it now?"

"Yes."

"Kiss me?"

"Yes."

And in the time of No-Time, in the shadow of this acoustic and visual miracle—is that moon glow...or the lava lamp?—you can see Hubert bend forward, see their mouths part, lips press, teeth and tongues devour and slurp and smack as Bear grasps Hubert's hips and pumps his own.

You will leave before they finish any more of this scene because this scene you can leave and you do leave, as quietly as you came, like a ghost mouse back to its ghost hole. You take the gun with you.

Lance as a Redneck spiritual adept

Ferd Eggan

Oh, beautiful one, do not withhold from me that which makes you: blood, worms, germs, flesh, phlegm, foul-smelling excretions, urine, sperm, feces and bone and everything that makes you what you are and will eventually turn to dust.[1]

It's just a tool, an instrument, an outfit, and I'm just a raving fool. He says: let's slam this crystal at the same time and plunge our hands up each other's butts, make hand puppets, dance on each other's arms. I say: I see there's no self to protect and maintain, my pal, when we're writhing and grunting pigs on the greasy sheets.[2] He says: stick your fingers in your butt and feed them to me; and he could say: let's bump up a little higher and I might say: I see God—glowing with power from my first chakra (it's the asshole, stupid) all the way out through the top of my head. Aim me, I'm a flashlight, quivering and shaking beams of power, a sizzling isotope of ordinary light. And he says: I just want to be accepted; and I should say: well, I want somebody to be special to and be specially bad with. But all we've got is just an instrument for ecstasy (Robin says: it's Greek for "out of self"[3]). So we say: leave intersubjectivity alone—let's get stupid.[4]

He didn't say: ichor is thicker than water. Watch out, the god descends too close, he scorches. I won't say: wrestling with the fucking angel again, (Genesis only says: "a man...until dawn broke."[5]) and this one dazzles and ultimately disappoints. They're limited in near-divinity; he almost says: "aw shucks," and gives glamour from a jaded superficiality that's a little inept, that shows its hand, that slyly reveals the emotional vulnerabilities and spiritual depths: underneath the phony tinsel is real tinsel. Can one say[6]: "Theophany[7]"? The beauty of the three men outside Abraham's tent, the beauty of this man breathing very heavily over me. Ecstasy is different from love. Only a fool would mistake them.

And realizing all the above, I say with delight but no desire: come now chaos, slime me with greasy transcendence, let my eyes roll back in my head one more time; hurry entropy, obliteration. Let me stretch around your big psychic and spiritual gifts, let me chew that long scar off your belly. Come chaos, noisy and nasty, rinse me away from this stinking world with your heavy waters stored deep, near the throbbing core, cooled quickly on our slippery surfaces. I want the raw/the cooked, the sacred/the profane,[8] I'll be a front/back door man/woman/child,[9] yeah, smite me there near the socket. Call me pig and bless me as dawn breaks.[10]

All this says: real, subhumans, not sentient, vessels for sensation, electrical charges in blood and a bag of skin, wallowing in perverted filth for amusement, excitement, radioactivity, love, sainthood.[11]

Notes

1. From the Sutras, tattooed in Sanskrit on the arm of Cory Roberts-Auli (deceased).

2. Jacques Lacan, *The Language of the Self* (Baltimore: Johns Hopkins University Press, 1968).

3. Robin Podolsky, personal communication. Like this noted lesbian writer, the OED translates "ecstasy" as deriving from (Ἑκοτασισ) "out of place," alluding to the late Greek use of the word to mean "the withdrawal of the soul from the body." The first definition listed is: "The state of being 'beside oneself,' thrown into a frenzy or a stupor, with anxiety, astonishment, fear, or passion."

4. cf. Madonna and also Leo Steinberg, *The Sexuality of Christ in Renaissance Painting and Modern Oblivion* (New York: Pantheon, 1984).

5. Rachel Adler, noted Jewish feminist theologian, translated from Hebrew in a personal (telephone) communication.

6. Mr. Rogers.

7. A Greek word meaning "the descent to earth of a god": antonym of "apotheosis." Vanderbilt University Divinity Library, personal communication with the author.

8. Claude Levi-Strauss, *The Raw and the Cooked* (New York: Harper & Row, 1969), and Mircea Eliade, *The Sacred and the Profane* (New York: Hartcourt, Brace).

9. Willie Dixon, "Back Door Man," RCA Records, 1974.

10. R. Adler, ibid.: This passage is considered a primary textual moment in naming and hence the initiation of a special human-divine relationship.

11. See Bernini's Baroque sculpture *Saint Teresa in Ecstasy* for a particularly dramatic visual/tactile realization of this central goal of Western Christian spiritual practice.

Je T'Aime, Batman, Je T'Adore

Kelly McQuain

To Bob Kane and Donald Barthelme

>:Rob00062

I can't hide the truth anymore. I love Batman—his furrowed brow, his chiseled jaw, his Bat emblem emblazoned atop pectorals hard as marble. I love his sculpted stomach, his running-back thighs and gymnast calves, the impressive bump of the safety cup sewn into his shorts.

These feelings grow as wild as I do—in the past year I've shot up a good six inches, the *Gotham Gazette* now dubbing me the "Teen Wonder" instead of "Boy Wonder." Why is life so confusing? I long for simpler days, when fighting the Joker, Penguin, and Riddler was enough, when each fisted blow produced an explosive *BAM!* or *POW!* I could almost see.

Yesterday, Alfred caught me preening in the mirror, trying to master a hustler's roguish come-on. He pretended to be dusting, but I could feel his eyes undressing me. Alfred's old, has only five hairs on his head, but still I got a chubber simply from being desired by a man. But I have standards. I want a super hero.

>:Rob00063

Last night in the Bat Cave, as I sat typing this computer journal, Bruce crept up so quietly I was nearly discovered. Damn his Bela Lugosi moves! I hit the exit key just as his gloved hand clamped down on my shoulder.

Whirling around, I experienced familiar breathlessness upon seeing the width of his shoulders, his tapered waist. "Just finishing my French homework!" I lied, glad my mask was on so he couldn't see my eyes.

"Good," Bruce said, adjusting his cowl. "Let's patrol before it gets late. Tomorrow's a school day."

"Sure." (I wished he hadn't reminded me. At school, everyone teases me for being his ward, calling me "pretty boy" and "millionaire jailbait." I can't fight back, can't flaunt my Bat-training. Even my French teacher arches an eyebrow, his slimy mind imagining naughty scenarios Bruce puts me through each night. If only it were true!)

As Bruce revved the Batmobile, I flung my yellow cape around my shoulders. Over the past months the hem line has crept up my calves, reminding me of the frilly shoulder piece the ringmaster wore back in my circus days. My red tunic feels snug as well, and my green shorts never more skimpy. But I like how these old clothes show off the muscles thickening my boyish limbs. Only drawback is the difficulty in concealing the Bat-boners that pop up with increasing frequency, so I've taken to wearing my utility belt lower on my hips, like a gunslinger's holster, like I'm ready to shoot.

Hidden hydraulics rumbled as the faux cave wall raised before us. I leapt over the Batmobile's fin, sliding into shotgun. Bruce shot me a look that said "ever hear of a door?" He pressed the turbos, and in a roar of flame we rocketed toward Gotham City.

Dark woods flashed by. I tried not to stare as Bruce's powerful hand gripped the gearshift. We turned off the old logging road onto the Gotham Expressway, and the familiar peaks and spires of the city loomed before us.

"Stay alert, chum," Bruce said, patting my knee.

I bit my lip. Suddenly the Batsignal cut a golden swath across the sky. Skidding through a maze of streets, Bruce pulled up beside Police Headquarters—completely disregarding a conspicuous fire hydrant. It thrilled me how easily he took the law into his hands.

Commissioner Gordon greeted us in his office. "Working out a bit?" he asked, seizing me in a neck hold and rubbing my head.

"You'll wreck my mousse!" I cried.

The Commissioner laughed and let go, his fingers tweaking the nape of my neck. He directed Bruce's gaze toward what appeared, to the untrained eye, to be an ordinary piece of mail. "From the Joker," Gordon announced. "That madcap menace broke out of Arkham Asylum again. Sent me this birthday card."

"Your birthday?" asked Bruce. "I didn't know. Robin usually keeps better track of such things." He shot me a wicked glance.

"That's just it," said the Commissioner, lighting his pipe. "My birthday was months ago."

Bruce picked up the card with a pair of Bat-tweezers. "Obviously that crazed sociopath is taunting us with clues to whatever crime he's hatching."

"Well, duh," I said.

"Don't give me any lip," Bruce glared. He studied the card. I slunk up beside him, breathing deep his intoxicating perspiration, resting my head against his hard shoulder.

"Robin. Do you mind?"

"Sorry," I said, lifting my head. I concentrated on the card. In the Joker's messy handwriting an inscription read, *Sorry—no present! But you'll soon have a GRAND time OPENING your front page to discover what I have in STORE!* As Bruce read aloud, the madman's usual trademark—a Joker from a deck of playing cards—fell onto the desktop.

Bruce rubbed his chin. "A card within a card. Anything else?"

"Well," said Gordon. "I had the lab boys look it over. It's a Hallmark."

I cracked my knuckles, imagining the Joker's jaw. "At least he cares to send the best."

Bruce frowned. "A Hallmark," he continued. "That, combined with the Joker's peculiar emphasis on the words *grand* and *opening,* can only mean one thing. He's going to rob the Hallmark card store at the brand new Gotham Shopping Plaza."

"A brilliant deduction!" cried the Commissioner. "Should I send a patrol to check it out?"

"No," said Bruce. "The Joker's slippery—he's already struck once today; he'll let us stew awhile before hitting again."

"Your insight astounds me," croaked Gordon. Bruce's chest swelled at the compliment. He shook hands with the Commissioner and ordered me to gather the evidence. From my utility belt I extracted a Bat-baggy. It pained me to recall the countless hours I had spent stenciling bats onto endless, ordinary Zip-loc bags.

Outside in the Batmobile I asked, "Why do villains insist on sending us clues? Don't they know we'll figure them out?"

"Ah," said Bruce. "You have much to learn. Criminal minds are compelled to throw such crumbs. Sometimes I think they want to be found out, to be punished, to feel the rock-hard fist of the law pounding their flesh."

"Holy Freud," I muttered.

Bruce pushed the pedal to the floor; the Bat-speedometer shot up several notches as we ricocheted through Crime Alley. My partner's enthusiasm fired my own, hot tremors emanating from the epicenter of my crotch. I fanned myself with my cape.

The Batmobile skidded to a halt as Bruce spotted a purse snatcher. In one savage motion he pitched himself onto the hoodlums. He was hard on crime. I loved it.

I began to rise, but froze when I noticed my Bat-chubber had created an embarrassing pup tent in my shorts. While Bruce delivered the old one-two, I pulled my aching python free. He whirled to kick the lawbreaker in the abdomen. My prick thrashed with a life of its own! As the dark knight delivered the final blow, I shot a huge wad beneath the dashboard.

Maybe Bruce would think it was gum.

I watched my partner loom over the criminals, cast in a light I had never before noticed. Always a still-waters type, he seldom showed emotion—not even Catwoman wagging her tail could get a rise out of him. This pent-up fury spent on a common hoodlum, this primal release—what did it mean? Was it a crumb he threw my way, a desperate clue I was meant to decipher? I stuffed my limp pee-pee back in my shorts.

Bruce glanced my way. "Don't just sit there," he panted. "Throw me your Bat-cuffs."

>:Rob00064

I can't believe what I'm reduced to.

Yesterday, coming from the shower, I saw Alfred gathering our uniforms to throw in the Bat-washer, so I filched Bruce's cape and took it to my room. Shutting the door, I dropped my towel and admired myself in the armoire's mirror. I ran my hands over my nipples, down my chest, toward my crotch. How could someone not want this virgin skin, these limbs plump with young muscle? Pretty boy. Pretty bird. If Bruce had any sense, he'd lock me in a cage so only he could ravish me. Doesn't he notice the Riddler salivating as he takes me hostage, the Joker catching his breath as I bend to retrieve my Batarang? No. He's as blind as the proverbial bat.

Naked on my bed, I whipped the blue cape in the air. As it parachuted over me, I imagined Bruce's dark eyes and muscled torso swooping down—a vampire mad with bloodlust. His finned gloves gouged me, his belt buckle ground my pelvis. My costume ripped as his fingers gripped my ass and his Bat-cock pierced my butthole. I wanted him to need me like he needed Gotham's criminals—locked in a battle not of good or evil, but of desires rampant in us both. I wanted to be more than just the boy behind the mask.

Pulling out, Bruce whacked my face with his billy club of flesh until I cried, "Excessive force!"

"Eat my fat worm, little bird!" he grunted. "Chew that Bat-boner!"

I did, and I liked it.

Suddenly Bruce's seed pelted the back of my throat like a hail of bullets. I gripped my own cock, a thousand Batsignals exploding as I came. Tears eddied in the eyes of my mask as Bruce nuzzled my cheek, grateful....

"Excuse me, Master Dick," said Alfred, barging in and cutting short my reverie. I bolted up, covered my crotch. "Have you seen—excuse me, but why is Master Bruce's cape in here?" He averted his eyes from my compromising position.

"It's not what you think! I was cold! I needed a blanket!"

" 'The lady doth protest too much,' " replied Alfred, shutting the door.

0>:Rob00065

I paused outside of Bruce's study. Desire warmed me at the sight of my partner relaxing in his favorite chair, reading the newspaper—handsome in his smoking jacket, a silk cravat knotted at his throat. From a vial in my pocket I poured several colorless, odorless drops of liquid into the snifter of brandy I had brought for him—a concoction derived from the Batcomputer's catalog of Poison Ivy's Spanish-fly recipes. Bruce looked up as I entered the room. "Alfred thought you might enjoy a drink," I lied.

He folded his paper in half. Our fingertips brushed as he took the glass. "Thank you," he said grimly.

My pulse quickened as the brandy wetted his lips. Before he could take a full sip, the Batphone rang. Bruce rose, crossed to his desk, switched on the speakerphone. Commissioner Gordon's voice rattled the air: "The Joker's swiped a wrecking crane from the site of the new convention center!"

"Holy demolition," I said unenthusiastically.

Bruce's voice sank to the dramatic register of the Batman. "That's lowbrow even for him; there must be a greater scheme!" I stared at the glass in his hand, willing Bruce to take that first swallow. "Robin and

I will head to the Plaza to see if that madman strikes there as expected."

Hanging up, Bruce flashed the crisp stretch of pearly whites that passed for his smile. He dumped his drink in a houseplant then flung the empty snifter into the fireplace. I wanted to scream!

"Ready for a little action, old chum?" he asked.

Anytime, anyplace, I nearly confessed.

Bruce pressed a secret button and a bookcase slid aside to reveal the entrance to the Bat Cave. He leapt through the gloomy portal. Sliding down the Batpole after him made me yearn all the more. It felt bittersweet having my legs wrapped around something long and hard, but cold, just like Bruce.

On the way to Gotham Plaza I broached a delicate subject.

"I think it's time I received an allowance." I wanted to update my costume with a new mask or a rakish scarf—anything to get Bruce to notice me.

His eyes narrowed, becoming more angular than usual. "You don't need an allowance," he said coldly.

"Everybody else —"

" 'Everybody else' hasn't devoted their lives to battling crime," he intoned.

"It's not fair!" My voice broke like the waves in Gotham Harbor. "I know crime doesn't pay, but crime fighting should be worth something!"

Bruce's arm shot out, seizing my collar. "Look, mister," he growled, "we've got a job to do! Financial compensation is not our motivation." He shook me like a rag doll, producing a strange stirring in my utility belt.

"At least give me a cut of the Bat-merchandising," I pleaded.

"I will not tolerate insubordination!" His spittle stung my cheeks with each word. "If you're going to behave like a child, you should wait in the car." He shoved me against my seat.

Pulling into the Plaza parking lot, Bruce cut the engine and we coasted to a stop. A van, marked Clown Catering, was parked near the employee entrance. Bruce leapt out and raced toward the mall. I pressed the button for the Bat Wet Bar and snuck a cocktail as Bruce launched a Batrope to the roof, then scaled the building. His cape caught the wind, lifting from his shoulders. I sighed at the movement of his back, the tremor of muscle and tendon as he pulled himself over the rooftop and disappeared.

Sipping my drink, I scanned the deserted parking lot. Banners announcing grand-opening sales fluttered in the breeze. Suddenly a terrific crash came from the back of the mall near the card store. Cinder blocks crumbled as a section of the wall gave way. The Joker's heinous laughter pierced the air. Through the dust came a menacing wrecking crane, driven by none other than the Clown Prince of Crime!

"Holy wanton destruction of private property!" I cried as Bruce leapt from the ruined facade. The Joker whirled the crane's iron ball through the air, shattering the wall above Bruce's head. With inhuman agility the caped crusader dodged the debris. The wrecking crane turned, thundering toward the Batmobile, the iron ball swinging back as the Joker aimed my way. I dropped my cocktail and launched a Batrope to the mall roof, leaping clear as the Joker smashed the Batmobile to smithereens. He whirled toward Bruce once more. "You might have a lot of balls, Batman," he taunted, "but mine's bigger!"

Bruce double-flipped into the air as the ball crashed toward him. Avoiding the blow, he grabbed onto the cable as it swung back around.

"Curses!" screamed the Joker, locking the crane controls in a head-on collision with the crumbling plaza wall. He leapt toward his get-away van.

Bruce glanced up. "Quick, Robin, throw me your Batrope!" The wrecking crane volleyed toward destruction.

"Maybe this is a good time to reconsider that allowance," I said woozily. Being cruel turned me on.

"The rope, Robin! The rope!"

"Is that in my job description? Do I even have a job description?"

"I'M NOT KIDDING!"

"All right, all right." I threw him my rope, and he began climbing up. "But you're probably violating child-labor laws."

Bruce vaulted the building's cornice, grabbed me and shoved me down. Blood surged toward my groin at such manhandling. "Punish me if you must," I said, hoping he'd beat my ass with his utility belt.

From below, the Joker's laughter echoed in our ears as he escaped.

"You rotten whelp!" screamed Bruce.

He shook me by the scruff of my neck. I loved it.

A terrific shock jolted us apart as the crane plowed into the plaza. The roof crumbled like cardboard; I plummeted toward doom like a wounded bird. Would Bruce clutch my lifeless body to his? Would he shed a tear? At the last second, his gloved hand seized my wrist. I dangled for life—the closest to climax I got all night.

Bruce pulled me up, held me close. Sniffing, he asked, "Have you been drinking?"

>:Rob00066
Bruce punishes me by patrolling alone—still mad that we had to bus it home. No sign of the Joker, so Bruce busies himself poring over the birthday card, searching for more clues. I go mad from neglect, frittering away hours on the Solo-flex, using the Batcomputer to hack in and change my French grade. This evening I shaved my legs, deciding that if I'm going to wear those damn shorts I have to do something about this embarrassing bikini line. Dark curly hairs have begun to trickle down my inner thighs. If I'm to win Bruce over, I have to look hot.

In desperation, I sought Alfred's advice. "You've known Bruce longer than I have," I said as we cleared the dinner table. "What's the bug up his Bat-butt?"

The butler fixed me with a knowing wink. "His idiosyncrasies are getting to you, are they?" He smiled. "It's true, he's always been rather complex. Take him at any level of social intercourse: he's a man possessed of fearful strengths and endearing weaknesses; a careful strategist but impetuous risk-taker; a gregarious host yet reticent with his feelings; a bon-vivant but a street brawler; a non-conformist yet a supporter of moral absolutes; an appreciator of both abstract and realistic art—"

"You're saying he's schizoid?"

"Not exactly—what were Walt Whitman's words of wisdom?" Alfred's British accent cut through the tongue twister with laser precision. "Ah, yes. 'I am vast, I contain multitudes.' "

>:Rob00067
Today while Bruce was at the Wayne Foundation, I peeked in his desk and came across an application for Andover. He's planning to ship me to boarding school! A small notebook was filled with forgeries of my signature. I cried over an ad addressed to the *Gotham Gazette*: *SWM seeks subordinate younger WM partner for nite-time activities...*

I mustn't lose him! I used to spend nights worrying—what if he were shot or crippled? Or sprayed with acid and disfigured like Two-Face? What if he got testicular cancer—a real possibility the way he keeps his balls knotted up. Would I still love him? Of course.

I've seen other boys develop crushes on mentor figures—coaches, teachers, Catholic priests—but our relationship penetrates deeper. If Bruce has taught me anything, it's the courage to face our darkest parts. But ever since his parents died, Bruce has locked everything up! There was no comforting stranger for him like there was for me. I must show him the way out. Now, before he sends me away.

>:Rob00068

The Bat Cave is very quiet. I study Bruce's shoulders as he hunches over his crime-analysis equipment. His head does not turn, but he knows I am here. There's still a chance.

Unfastening my cape, I throw it on the Bat-trampoline. The prospect of our joined flesh sends shivers through my body. What will happen after we touch? Will Bruce still send me away? Will he be jealous and obsessed, tortured by the memory of our union—an empty shell, drifting from one sidekick to the next, looking for the silky texture of my skin in their inadequate flesh? I pull off my gloves and kick off my shoes.

"Fascinating," Bruce says, still not turning. "The Bat-spectrograph has isolated seven different monofilaments on the card sent to the Commissioner."

I remove my tunic and drop it on the floor, catching a glimpse of myself in the polished instruments above Bruce's shoulder. Will you be regretful, maudlin—nights spent in endless self-flagellation, days spent reciting countless Hail Marys?

"Five of them are used in textile production around Gotham City."

I remove my shorts and stand naked, growing hard, waiting. I must confess my love. Say it fast, blurt it out so we can pretend we didn't hear it if the words are too painful.

"Another matches the Commissioner's wool sweater."

Finally, I remove my mask. "I love you," I whisper.

Bruce freezes. He does not turn, he does not speak.

I am doomed.

>:Rob00069

Bruce, unable to fathom the Joker's next move, has given me the cold shoulder for days. He was studying plans for a new Batmobile when I tried to engage in small talk.

"So, the Joker knocked over a card store—"

"Quiet, Robin—wait! That's it! The Joker knocked over a store of cards. And tomorrow, the Gotham Museum will display a rare collection of playing cards by Aubrey Beardsley. The other night's crime was a metaphor of his real scheme. Good work, chum."

Redeemed, I accompanied Bruce into town on the Batcycle. Unfortunately, I had to ride in the little sidecar. "Holy humiliation!" I fumed, but after a while, the hypnotic vibrations of the motor lulled me into the usual sexual thoughts. My thighs tensed as yet another Bat-boner popped up, my shorts stretched so tight I could make out each engorged vein.

At the Museum, Bruce leapt off the Batcycle, whisked a Batrope into the air and scaled the building. In my condition, I could barely scale fish. Still, I drew my cape around to disguise my chubber then clambered up. Looking down, I noticed my green slipper tarnished by feces from an uncurbed dog. Faint brown footprints trailed up the side of the museum. "Holy shit!" I yelled.

Bruce flashed an icy glare. "Don't swear, Robin. It reflects poorly on our image." He made his way across the rooftop, dropping through a skylight in the east wing. I lingered, scraping my shoe.

Suddenly, a dark figure pounced from the shadows, knocking me against the wall of an access stair. Dazed, I looked up to find the Joker grinning more hideously than usual. "Ah! The Boy Wonder—oops!—Teen Blunder. Say, is that a Batarang in your pocket or are you happy to see me?"

My face blushed as red as my tunic.

The Joker grabbed my throat in an iron grip. "Your partner may stop my henchmen below, but you're my ticket out of here! One move and I'll break your neck!" Being insane gave him the strength of ten.

He pulled me to him, slipped his hand down the back of my shorts. "I know your desires," he whispered, "the fierce longing to tangle with Batman." He pressed a chalky finger against my ass. "But you'll never occupy his attention like I do." He ground his fist into me. "You're just not bad enough." I strained against him, thinking of Bruce. There was a wildness in the madman's probing that curled my toes.

"Ahh, my little finger puppet," cooed the Joker, slipping a digit inside me. "It's a shame I must destroy you." Any protest stuck in my throat as my Bat-boner tore at my shorts.

Suddenly Bruce burst through the access door, unconscious hoodlums slung over each arm. "Holy full house!" I cried as he threw them in a heap on the rooftop.

"Let the boy go," he scowled. Maybe Bruce did care, after all.

"One step closer and I snap his neck," warned the Joker.

"All right, take it easy," replied Bruce. He lowered his arms and his cape slid down his shoulders. Our foppish foe dragged me toward the roof's edge. "Let me get rid of Robin," the Joker prissed. "He's just baggage! It's you and I who are meant for each other." He plunged another finger in me, nearly driving me mad.

"Whoa, nelly!" I cried. I could tell the Joker was trying to distract Bruce so he could hurl a lethal round of razor-edged playing cards, but I wasn't about to free his hand. I clamped my ass cheeks harder.

His fingers floundered inside of me like a trout caught in a net. "Face it," he leered at my partner, "you don't give a damn about the kid's plight." He squeezed my throat tighter with his other arm. Oxygen deprivation intensified my rush. "So pathetic, it reminds me of a poem," chortled the Joker, clearing his throat.

> "There once was a boy who was sobbin'
> Cause his dick was so hard it was throbbin'
> He felt sad to be slighted
> For his Love, unrequited,
> Wouldn't bugger the hell out of Robin!"

Suddenly Bruce's hand flashed in a streak of midnight blue. Light glinted off whirling metal as his Batarang coursed through the air, cracking hard against the Joker's elbow.

"Ack!" the clown cried, "My funny bone!" With his other hand still tangled in my shorts, I easily walloped the Joker's face until there was nothing left but bruises and battered flesh. Bruce watched but said nothing. Perhaps it was just the sight of my ridiculous, mangled shorts, but his scowl softened, seemed to give in.

While Bruce secured the criminals for the police, I headed back to the Batcycle, happy to find a rusty nail had punctured the sidecar's front tire.

Fate had finally dealt a hand in my favor. We left the sidecar behind when we rode home. I sat behind Bruce, my arms circling his waist, my weary head resting between his shoulder blades. With my ear pressed against his back, I heard the tumble of his inner workings unlocking like a safe. His cape whipped the air, surrounding me like a dark flower. I inhaled his sturdy scent, reached down and released my straining boner, resting it against the soft cloth of Bruce's shorts. As Gotham fell behind us, I worked my shaft snugly beneath his utility belt and rocked against him like a baby. If he noticed, he did not say anything. Once or twice a light sound escaped his lips—a murmur of pleasure? We turned onto the logging road, each bump offering new levels of sensation. The friction built to a fever pitch. The woods whizzed by. The cave entrance loomed before us.

And like all good heroes, I came just in the nick of time.

sex with god

Tommi Avicolli Mecca

I'm thirteen, standing in an alley with Ant'ny. We're paging through a copy of *Playboy* we just stole from the neighborhood drugstore. Ant'ny's getting all hot and bothered and I'm getting hot and bothered watching him getting hot and bothered.

So Ant'ny starts touching himself—down there. He unzips his pants and pulls it out. "Hey, get down on your knees," he says in a hoarse whisper, like Marlon Brando in *The Godfather.* Well, good bottom-in-training that I am, I immediately obey.

"Suck it, you know you wanna." What would any normal boy of thirteen do, down on his knees in front of this *siciliano* hunk-in-training? Devour the damn thing like there's no tomorrow, right? Slurp, slurp. "Ahhh." Slurp. Slurp. "That's it, suck it, eat me, oh, oooh, oooh..."

No, he doesn't come. There's suddenly this problem. Standing over Ant'ny's right shoulder, exactly where the nuns planted him—is God.

Just what are you doing, young man? (Think booming italics.)

Who me? Oh, hi, God, I wasn't doing nothing, just sort of—uh—admiring your creation. What an amazing job you've done here, I couldn't have done better. Now, why don't I just get up and go back home and help Mama with the dishes? Or say a novena?

Shit, what am I doing? I can't fool the creator of all creation, the maker of all things, the omnipresent, omnipotent, eyes, ears, nose and throat of the universe. I mean we're talking serious Big Cheese here.

But does Ant'ny care? Nah, he's beating off, oblivious to God in all His splendor standing no more than three feet behind him. I'm expecting lightning bolts any second.

Then I notice something. God has one hand under his toga and he's...pushing my head down on Ant'ny's cock with the other and I'm pulling out my own cock and now everything's happening in unison, my head bobbing up and down on that delicious cock, my hand on my own cock and God's hand on his....

There's an unbelievable crash: it's the sound of three beings coming, one of them the supreme being of all supreme beings, the head honcho of all time and space. Bad aim though: well, maybe not. His cum squirts all over my face, dripping down my chin onto my shirt. I don't think Mama's gonna appreciate having God's cum stains on my T-shirt. But imagine the notoriety. Pilgrimages to my house, guest spots on the radio, books, a TV movie, my shirt hanging in a church in Roma, my picture everywhere. I'll be more famous than Our Lady of Fátima. With the money I'll make I can even get a nose job and have my hair straightened—permanently. Then I won't look so Italian. I can look like those cute kids on TV or in the movies. I'll have it made. Perfect complexion, new clothes, dates with Sal Mineo! Wow!

Sure wish I could tell Mama I was creamed on by the supreme creamer. Speaking of which, He's gone now. Just like that. Poof. Would you believe Ant'ny never notices? "Yo, same time tomorrow," he says, walking away.

You know, I think I'm gonna like puberty....

* * *

Bless me, Father, for I have sinned. It has been one week since my last confession. I talked in class three times, swore five times, had seventeen impure thoughts and touched myself ten times.

"Did you derive pleasure from it?" Yes, Father. "How many times?" All ten times.

If I could see Him, if I could climb to the top of the highest mountain and stare into His ancient face, I'd ask: Why do you let my people die?

But there is no mountain, no face, no reason.

At sixteen, I told the priest I did not believe. He had me stay after school to scrape gum from the bottom of desk tops and sweep floors. There were no answers, only retributions for wrong questions.

Father, it has been decades since my last confession. I touched myself and many other men; I tasted cum, tongue, dick, ass more times than anyone can imagine.

But I have committed no sins.

about the authors

GARY BOWEN has published nearly two hundred works, mostly short fiction, in such places as *Best of Drummer: Fiction; SM Visions: The Best of Circlet Press; Bending the Landscape: Horror; Dark Angels: Lesbian Vampire Stories;* and *Hot Blood: Strangers After Dark.* His first novel, *Diary of a Vampire,* was a finalist for the Stoker Award. His most recent book, *Man Hungry* is a collection of short erotic gay fiction. His Western anthology, *Western Trails,* will be available in 1997 from Masquerade Books.

PANSY BRADSHAW is the co-author of *Betty & Pansy's Severe Queer Review of San Francisco* and was a contributing editor to *Steam (A Literary Queer's Guide to Sex and Controversy).* Born to poor white trash (almost half a century ago), he was wrapped in swaddling clothes and laid in a manger...the rest is history. Currently Pansy lives in rural Montana, where he is writing about love among the cowboys and the sheepherders.

KEN BUTLER grew up in the Bible Belt but managed never to feel guilty about being queer, perhaps because he figured out early that many of those farmers and miners liked getting their cocks sucked by another guy. He has a degree in music but somehow ended up in theater administration. He's happily ensconced in an intergenerational relationship of very long standing.

JUSTIN CHIN is a writer and performance artist. His performances have been presented nationally. His writing has appeared in *Men on*

Men 5: New Gay Writing, Eros in Boystown, and *Premonitions: The Kaya Anthology of Asian American Poetry,* among others. *Bite Hard,* a collection of poetry and spoken word, will be published by Manic D Press in Spring 1997. A short portion of "Queen" was shown on the HBO documentary *Sex Bytes.*

CORNELIUS CONBOY, San Francisco Leather Daddy XIII, is a natural-born Sadist. He writes a monthly leather column for *Oblivion* magazine (http://www.OblivionSf.com) and has also been published in *Drummer.* He was chosen to speak on "family values" at San Francisco's 1996 Pride celebration, and is a sought-after emcee and activist within the leather community. He celebrates change, growth, and the spiritually transformative nature of radical sexplay whenever he can.

JAMESON CURRIER is the author of a collection of short stories, *Dancing on the Moon,* published by Penguin. His short fiction has been anthologized in *Certain Voices; Ex-Lover Weird Shit; Men on Men 5; Our Mothers, Our Selves; Man of My Dreams; All the Ways Home* and *Best Gay Erotica 1996.*

ROB GOLDSTEIN was born in Charleston, S.C. in 1952. He decided to become a writer at the age of seven and now makes computers for a living. His writing has appeared in such anthologies as *Sundays at Seven* and *Queer View Mirror 2.* His computers can be seen in the homes of many frustrated users in San Francisco.

FERD EGGAN is a writer who lives in and loves L.A. He has two published books, *Your LIFE Story by someone else* and *Pornography,* and his written and photographic work has appeared in many magazines and at NAME and Randolph Street Galleries in Chicago, The Gay & Lesbian Community Center in NYC, A Different Light Bookstore in SF, and Highways in LA. He was one of the founders of the National ACT-UP network, and is now AIDS Coordinator for the City of Los Angeles. As such, he reminds readers that all narrative writing is fundamentally fiction. He is, however, single and often available.

J. EIGO'S AIDS work has been chronicled in the books *Good Intentions* and *Against the Odds.* His theater work has been staged in such cities as Los Angeles, Philadelphia, Baltimore, and Squaw

Valley. His writings have appeared in publications as diverse as *Chicago Review, Fruit, Steam, Dance Ink,* and the *Food Drug Cosmetic Law Journal;* and in the anthologies *Likely Stories, Stallions, Theatrical Gamut,* and *Butch Boys.*

ROBERTO FRIEDMAN is published in the *Washington Post,* the *Lambda Book Report, Evergreen Chronicles,* and the *Bay Area Reporter,* where he is assistant editor. His short fiction has appeared in *Certain Voices,* and *Revelations,* and chapters from his novel, *Bad Reputation,* appear in *modern words* 2 and 4.

JACK FRITSCHER, with nearly three thousand pages in print, covers the genres. The founding San Francisco editor of *Drummer,* he is the author of two novels, *Some Dance to Remember* and *Leather Blues,* and two collections of erotic stories, *Corporal in Charge of Taking Care of Captain O'Malley* and *Stand By Your Man.* His non-fiction books are *Television Today, Popular Witchcraft: Straight from the Witch's Mouth,* and his memoir of his bi-coastal lover, *Mapplethorpe: Assault with a Deadly Camera.* His coffee-table photography book is *Jack Fritscher's American Men.* He has directed more than one hundred Palm Drive videos, and lives north of the Golden Gate Bridge with his spouse of eighteen years, Mark Hemry. Visit them at http://www.jackfritscher.com

KEVIN KILLIAN, poet, novelist, playwright, critic, lives in San Francisco. He is the author of a novel, *Shy,* a book of memoirs, *Bedrooms Have Windows,* and a book of stories, *Little Men.* Masquerade/Hard Candy will publish his second novel, *Arctic Summer,* in 1997, and in 1998, Wesleyan University Press will publish *Poet, Be Like God: The Life of Jack Spicer,* which Killian is writing with Lewis Ellingham. His work has appeared in *Poetics Journal, Artforum,* and *The Field Reporter*—the official journal of the Sally Field Fan Club.

R.L. KITZMAN was the winner of the 1995 John Preston Erotic Writing Prize for the story included in this collection. He won another short-story contest thirteen years ago sponsored by The Saint in New York City, for a story entitled "Mr. X." He knows he won't have to wait that long again for his future efforts to be recognized. He is a good son and a Colorado native who lives in Denver and follows the Science of Mind principles. He would make an excellent lover.

AL LUJAN is a San Francisco-based writer, visual artist, and performer. He was raised in East Los Angeles and served a tour of duty in the U.S. Navy before moving to the Bay Area. His writing has appeared in *Beyond Definition: New Queer Writers of San Francisco; Best American Gay Erotica 1995; Ripples;* and *A La Brava.* His artwork has shown at Galeria De La Raza, Folsom Street Interchange and Artist's Television Access, and has been featured in *Q/San Francisco.* He is working on a one-man show to premiere Spring of 1997, and works as a caregiver at Coming Home Hospice.

KELLY MCQUAIN works in Philadelphia as an educator and freelance artist and writer. His fiction has appeared in *The James White Review, The Philadelphia Inquirer Sunday Magazine, Kansas Quarterly/ Arkansas Review* and in the anthologies *Certain Voices* and *Generation Q.* In 1994 he was named a Fiction Discipline Winner by the Pew Fellowships in the Arts. McQuain is currently completing a first novel in which the only masks his characters wear are psychological ones.

TOMMI AVICOLLI MECCA is a writer, performer, and activist living in San Francisco and working at A Different Light Bookstore. He is co-editor of the upcoming *Mary Loves Angie; Vinny Loves Sal,* a collection of Italian/American and Canadian queer writing. His book *Between Little Rock and a Hard Place,* analyzing President Bill Clinton's connection to the queer community, was published a few months after the 1992 election, and predicted not much good would happen. Among his recent publishing credits are *Fuori* and *Queer View Mirror.* The pieces published in this volume are from his performance work, *Il Disgraziato,* which he will gladly perform upon request (he's easy, in more ways than one, he's been told).

DOUG MIRK is a Los Angeles-area grade school teacher by day and a sex writer some of the rest of the time. His work has appeared in *The Ecstatic Scene Zine, Diabolic Clits, Steam, American Dane* and *Boy's Life.* He is currently busy having new experiences about which he may or may not write in the future.

SCOTT O'HARA is rentable at your local video store in about twenty-six different skinflicks; he also founded, and for three years edited, *Steam (A Literary Queer's Guide to Sex and Controversy).* His first two books are *Do-It-Yourself Piston Polishing (For Non-Mechanics)* from

Masquerade/Badboy, and the memoir *Autopornography: A Life in the Lust Lane* forthcoming from Haworth/Harrington Park.

LAWRENCE SCHIMEL is the editor of *Switch Hitters: Lesbians Write Gay Male Erotica and Gay Men Write Lesbian Erotica; Food for Life and Other Dish; Two Hearts Desire: Gay Couples on Their Love;* and *Tarot Fantastic*, among others. Under the byline David Laurents, he is editor of *The Badboy Book of Erotic Poetry; Wanderlust: Homoerotic Tales of Travel; Southern Comfort;* and *Hard at Work.* His stories and poems appear in numerous periodicals and anthologies, including *Drummer, Torso, Mandate, Honcho Overload, First Hand, Lambda Book Report, The Saturday Evening Post, Physics Today, The Writer,* and *Modern Short Stories.* He lives in Manhattan.

D. TRAVERS SCOTT is a frequent contributor to *International Drummer* and appears in such magazines as *Harper's, Pucker Up, X-X-X-Fruit,* and *High Performance,* and the anthologies *Reclaiming the Heartland; Best Gay Erotica 1996; Switch Hitters; Memory, Practice, Pleasure: Gay Male Performance (forthcoming from University of Minnesota Press);* and *Forbidden: New Defiant Lesbian Writing* (forthcoming from Alyson Publications). He is the editor of *Strategic Sex,* an anthology of writings on public sex. He occasionally embarrasses himself on stage as well. He lives and works in Seattle.

SIMON SHEPPARD is a fairly kinky San Franciscan whose work has appeared in anthologies including *Best Gay Erotica 1996, The Badboy Book of Erotic Poetry, Bending the Landscape: Fantasy, Strategic Sex, Switch Hitters, Grave Passions,* and *Happily Ever After: Erotic Fairy Tales for Men,* and in magazines including *Drummer, Powerplay,* and *Steam.* "Devil in Disguise," a story he co-authored with Kevin Killian, will appear in *Noirotica 2.* Special thanks go to Fakir Musafar and to Ludwig, King of Bavaria.

MICHAEL PATRICK SPILLERS was born and raised on six acres of weeds in the Ozarks. He rang in the '90s by moving to Los Angeles, where he wrote, produced and performed in the hit stage play *White Boy* at Highways. Michael left his heart in Missouri, but his libido rests somewhere in East L.A., and his dreams go only as far as an imaginary Baja *pueblo*—where a big dog and a beautiful boy are out there just waiting to be found....

EMANUEL XAVIER, the real Mikey X, cruises dark and decadent paths with unbridled and distinctly Latin passion in his publishing debut, "Motherfuckers," and in his short story/poetry collection *Pier Queen Radio Blues* (forthcoming) as well. Of Ecuadorian/Puerto Rican descent, Emanuel grew up on the streets of Brooklyn and has recently completed his first novel, *Sanctuary*.

about the editors

RICHARD LABONTÉ is general manager of A Different Light Bookstores in San Francisco, West Hollywood, and New York City. He has been a gay book reader for thirty years, a gay bookseller for eighteen years, a gay book editor for a few months, and a gay book reviewer, over the years, for *Lambda Book Report, Bay Guardian, The Body Politic, LA Weekly, In Touch, Blueboy, Torso, San Francisco Review of Books, The Advocate, Q San Francisco, The Ottawa Citizen, Tribe* magazine and, his favorite, the *Feminist Bookstore News*. When not traveling among his bookstores, he lives a sedate life in San Francisco with Percy, a dog, and Asa, a man, and too many books to read.

DOUGLAS SADOWNICK is the author of two books, *Sex Between Men: An Intimate History of the Sex Lives of Gay Men, Postwar to Present*, published in 1996 by HarperCollins, and *Sacred Lips of the Bronx*, which was nominated for a Lambda Literary Award and was published by St. Martin's in 1994. He has written articles on sexuality, AIDS and gay culture for the *L.A. Weekly, L.A. Times, The Advocate, Genre, Out* and *Frontiers*. He attended Columbia College and is currently pursuing a graduate degree in clinical psychology at Antioch University. He works as a psychotherapy intern at the Los Angeles Gay and Lesbian Center, and he teaches gay male writing workshops at the 18th Street Arts Complex/Highways where he served as co-chair.

ʙooks from cleis press

SEXUAL POLITICS

Forbidden Passages:
Writings Banned in Canada,
introductions by Pat Califia
and Janine Fuller.
ISBN: 1-57344-019-1
14.95 paper.

Public Sex: The
Culture of Radical Sex
by Pat Califia.
ISBN: 0-939416-89-1
12.95 paper.

Sex Work: Writings by
Women in the Sex Industry,
edited by Frédérique
Delacoste and Priscilla
Alexander.
ISBN: 0-939416-11-5
16.95 paper.

Susie Bright's Sexual
Reality: A Virtual Sex
World Reader
by Susie Bright.
ISBN: 0-939416-59-X
9.95 paper.

Susie Bright's Sexwise
by Susie Bright.
ISBN: 1-57344-002-7
10.95 paper.

Susie Sexpert's Lesbian
Sex World
by Susie Bright.
ISBN: 0-939416-35-2
9.95 paper.

EROTIC LITERATURE

Best Gay Erotica 1997,
selected by Douglas Sadownick,
edited by Richard Labonté.
ISBN: 1-57344-067-1
14.95 paper.

Best Gay Erotica 1996,
selected by Scott Heim,
edited by Michael Ford.
ISBN: 1-57344-052-3
12.95 paper.

Best Lesbian Erotica 1997,
selected by Jewelle Gomez,
edited by Tristan Taormino.
ISBN: 1-57344-065-5
14.95 paper.

Best Lesbian Erotica 1996,
selected by Heather Lewis,
edited by Tristan Taormino.
ISBN: 1-57344-054-X
12.95 paper.

Serious Pleasure: Lesbian
Erotic Stories and Poetry,
edited by the Sheba
Collective.
ISBN: 0-939416-45-X
9.95 paper.

Switch Hitters: Lesbians
Write Gay Male Erotica
and Gay Men Write
Lesbian Erotica,
edited by Carol Queen
and Lawrence Schimel.
ISBN: 1-57344-021-3
12.95 paper.

GENDER TRANSGRESSION

Body Alchemy:
Transsexual Portraits
by Loren Cameron.
ISBN: 1-57344-062-0
24.95 paper.

Dagger: On Butch Women,
edited by Roxxie,
Lily Burana, Linnea Due.
ISBN: 0-939416-82-4
14.95 paper.

I Am My Own Woman:
The Outlaw Life of
Charlotte von Mahlsdorf,
translated by Jean Hollander.
ISBN: 1-57344-010-8
12.95 paper.

LESBIAN AND GAY STUDIES

The Case of the Good-For-Nothing Girlfriend
by Mabel Maney.
ISBN: 0-939416-91-3
10.95 paper.

The Case of the Not-So-Nice Nurse
by Mabel Maney.
ISBN: 0-939416-76-X
9.95 paper.

Nancy Clue and the Hardly Boys in A Ghost in the Closet
by Mabel Maney.
ISBN: 1-57344-012-4
10.95 paper.

A Lesbian Love Advisor
by Celeste West.
ISBN: 0-939416-26-3
9.95 paper.

On the Rails: A Woman's Journey, second edition,
by Linda Niemann.
Introduction
by Leslie Marmon Silko.
ISBN: 1-57344-064-7.
14.95 paper.

THRILLERS & DYSTOPIAS

Another Love
by Erzsébet Galgóczi.
ISBN: 0-939416-51-4
8.95 paper.

Dirty Weekend: A Novel of Revenge by Helen Zahavi.
ISBN: 0-939416-85-9
10.95 paper.

Only Lawyers Dancing
by Jan McKemmish.
ISBN: 0-939416-69-7
9.95 paper.

The Wall
by Marlen Haushofer.
ISBN: 0-939416-54-9
9.95 paper.

VAMPIRES & HORROR

Dark Angels: Lesbian Vampire Stories,
edited by Pam Keesey.
ISBN 1-7344-014-0
10.95 paper.

Daughters of Darkness: Lesbian Vampire Stories,
edited by Pam Keesey.
ISBN: 0-939416-78-6
9.95 paper.

Women Who Run with the Werewolves: Tales of Blood, Lust and Metamorphosis,
edited by Pam Keesey.
ISBN: 1-57344-057-4
12.95 paper.

Sons of Darkness: Tales of Men, Blood and Immortality,
edited by Michael Rowe and Thomas S. Roche.
ISBN: 1-57344-059-0
12.95 paper.

DEBUT NOVELS

Memory Mambo
by Achy Obejas.
ISBN: 1-57344-017-5
12.95 paper.

We Came All The Way from Cuba So You Could Dress Like This?: Stories
by Achy Obejas.
ISBN: 0-939416-93-X
10.95 paper.

Seeing Dell
by Carol Guess
ISBN: 1-57344-023-X
12.95 paper.

SEX GUIDES

The Good Vibrations Guide to Sex: How to Have Safe, Fun Sex in the '90s
by Cathy Winks and Anne Semans.
ISBN: 0-939416-84-0
16.95 paper.

Good Sex: Real Stories from Real People,
second edition,
by Julia Hutton.
ISBN: 1-57344-000-0
14.95 paper.

COMIX

Dyke Strippers: Lesbian Cartoonists A to Z,
edited by Roz Warren.
ISBN: 1-57344-008-6
16.95 paper.

The Night Audrey's Vibrator Spoke: A Stonewall Riots Collection
by Andrea Natalie.
ISBN: 0-939416-64-6
8.95 paper.

Revenge of Hothead Paisan: Homicidal Lesbian Terrorist
by Diane DiMassa.
ISBN: 1-57344-016-7
16.95 paper.

TRAVEL & COOKING

Betty and Pansy's Severe Queer Review of San Francisco
by Betty Pearl and Pansy.
ISBN: 1-57344-056-6
10.95 paper.

Food for Life & Other Dish,
edited by Lawrence Schimel.
ISBN: 1-57344-061-2
14.95 paper.

WRITER'S REFERENCE

Putting Out: The Essential
Publishing Resource Guide
For Gay and Lesbian
Writers,
third edition,
by Edisol W. Dotson.
ISBN: 0-939416-87-5
12.95 paper.

Women & Honor: Some
Notes on Lying
by Adrienne Rich.
ISBN: 0-939416-44-1
3.95 paper.

Since 1980, Cleis Press publishes provocative books by women (and a few men) in the United States and Canada. We welcome your order and will ship your books as quickly as possible. Individual orders must be prepaid (U.S. dollars only). Please add 15% shipping. PA residents add 6% sales tax. Mail orders: Cleis Press, PO Box 8933, Pittsburgh PA 15221. MasterCard and Visa orders: include account number, exp. date, and signature. FAX your credit card order: (412) 937-1567. Or, phone us Mon-Fri, 9 am - 5 pm EST: (412) 937-1555 or (800) 780-2279.